# The Moonstone Marquess

### Moonstone Landing Series
### Book 2

## by
## Meara Platt

DRAGONBLADE PUBLISHING, INC.

## ARE YOU SIGNED UP FOR DRAGONBLADE'S BLOG?

You'll get the latest news and information on exclusive giveaways, exclusive excerpts, coming releases, sales, free books, cover reveals and more.

Check out our complete list of authors, too!

No spam, no junk. That's a promise!

### Sign Up Here

www.dragonbladepublishing.com

*Dearest Reader;*

*Thank you for your support of a small press. At Dragonblade Publishing, we strive to bring you the highest quality Historical Romance from some of the best authors in the business. Without your support, there is no 'us', so we sincerely hope you adore these stories and find some new favorite authors along the way.*

*Happy Reading!*

CEO, Dragonblade Publishing

Additional Dragonblade books by
Author Meara Platt

## The Moonstone Landing Series
Moonstone Landing (novella)
Moonstone Angel (novella)
The Moonstone Duke
The Moonstone Marquess
The Moonstone Major

## The Book of Love Series
The Look of Love
The Touch of Love
The Taste of Love
The Song of Love
The Scent of Love
The Kiss of Love
The Chance of Love
The Gift of Love
The Heart of Love
The Hope of Love (novella)
The Promise of Love
The Wonder of Love
The Journey of Love
The Dream of Love (novella)
The Treasure of Love
The Dance of Love
The Miracle of Love
The Remembrance of Love (novella)

## Dark Gardens Series
Garden of Shadows
Garden of Light
Garden of Dragons

Garden of Destiny
Garden of Angels

**The Farthingale Series**
If You Wished For Me (A Novella)

**The Lyon's Den Series**
Kiss of the Lyon
The Lyon's Surprise
Lyon in the Rough

**Pirates of Britannia Series**
Pearls of Fire

**De Wolfe Pack: The Series**
Nobody's Angel
Kiss an Angel
Bhrodi's Angel

**Also from Meara Platt**
Aislin
All I Want for Christmas

# Chapter One

*Moonstone Landing*
*Cornwall, England*
*July 1818*

C ORMAC STOCKWELL, MARQUESS of Burness, stumbled out of
his newly acquired seaside home in Moonstone Landing, his
throat parched and his shirt unbuttoned. He groaned as his gaze
met blinding sunlight and pain seared through his brandy-soaked
head. "Blast it, Melrose. Why did you summon me out here at
the break of day?"

"My lord," his head butler said in a tone that revealed his
disapproval of the orgy that took place last night—and was still
going on, if one considered the naked bodies littering his parlor,
"it is noon."

"Have you no shame?" A young woman with a melodic voice
dismounted her horse and strode across the courtyard toward
him. Without so much as a greeting, she launched into a diatribe.
"You are a disgrace. How could you be so depraved...*wonk, wonk,
wonk*...debauched...*wonk, wonk, wonk*...vile..."

He blinked and tried to focus on the little harpy with an angel's voice, but it was hard to do while she was talking so fast and
his head was splitting. He could hardly keep up with her words. It
was all a buzzing blur. "Never, in all my days...*wonk, wonk,*

*wonk*…amazed you still have a functioning organ left in your body…*wonk, wonk, wonk*…"

He glanced down at his trousers.

Well, that organ was working perfectly fine.

Not that he intended to advise her of that fact.

Indeed, not. It was a wonder he had managed to properly button his falls, something not easily done when drunk and functioning only with one arm. As for his shirt, a formal one for evening wear, he'd merely tossed it on and left it open and untucked to flap in the wind.

It was the best he could do on short notice.

If she did not like it, she could leave.

He blinked again, intending to move his gaze upward to focus on her face as they stood in the brilliant sunshine, a soft sea breeze whirling around them while she continued to excoriate him for his bad behavior. But it took too much effort to move his gaze off her breasts when they were swelling magnificently as she continued her scathing rebuke. "Reprehensible…*wonk, wonk, wonk*…vile…"

She was repeating herself now. He was certain she had already referred to him as vile.

So what if he was? What business was it of hers how he chose to destroy himself?

Who was she, anyway?

Miss Temple of Virtue?

Well, she did have the body of a goddess.

Finally, as the sun disappeared behind a passing cloud, he managed a good look at her face.

*Blessed saints.*

Not only the body of a goddess, but the face of one as well.

Softest pink lips.

Eyes a glistening bluish green…or were they greenish blue? Well, it did not matter. They sparkled and were the color of aquamarines, exquisite eyes to steal any man's breath away.

Her hair was dark, and several curls had blown loose in the

wind to flick upon her sweetly blushing cheeks.

No, she wasn't sweetly blushing.

She was mad as hell and looked like she wanted to punch him.

She took another deep breath into her magnificent lungs. "And I will never...mark my words...ever...*wonk, wonk, wonk...*"

Gad, would she never stop railing at him?

"...your nieces...and—"

He immediately jerked to attention. "What about my nieces?"

"Oh, so the mindless marquess does have a voice after all."

"Who are you? Chairwoman of some society for the prevention of lechery and general moral perversion? Why did you mention my nieces?"

"Because they are here, you dolt." Her hands were clenched into fists and her eyes were still blazing.

"Here?"

"Yes, they arrived in Moonstone Landing this morning. Did you not read your brother's letter? The one that was waiting for you when you moved in last week? Or have your satanic rituals taken up so much of your time, you never bothered to open it and read what he wrote? Now, the little girls are here, thinking they are to stay with you for the summer."

He wanted to shake his head, but it was pounding too hard and hurt too much to move. "No, there must be some mistake."

"Obviously a lapse in judgment on your brother's part. But you cannot send them back. They are too overset and already in tears. They seem convinced you want them. I will have you know, they will not set foot in your home until your lascivious friends are gone and the house is scrubbed from attic to cellar to rid it of the vermin no doubt brought in by them. They'll be impossible to remove once they infest the woodwork."

Did this gorgeous creature never stop talking?

"Nor will I allow you to set foot in Moonstone Cottage. It is my home, and—"

He drew her up against him.

Lord, her breasts felt good against his chest. "You live next door? At Moonstone Cottage?"

"Yes, if you were ever sober enough to find out and pay a proper call on your neighbors."

"Who are you?"

"Let go of me and I shall tell you. Did you bathe in a barrel of brandy? You reek of it." She pushed against him.

He released his grasp, but not before he had nuzzled her neck to take in her scent. Of course, she smelled wonderful. A hint of lavender and meadow breezes.

"Ugh! I rue the day Squire Westgate sold this beautiful place to you. Had I known you would turn his manor house into a brothel, I would have bought it out from under you. How in heaven's name does Cain consider you a friend?"

"You know the Duke of Malvern?"

She nodded. "He is married to my sister, Henley."

"You are one of the Killigrew sisters?" His heartbeat quickened. "Are you Chloe or Phoebe?"

She tipped her chin up in defiance. "Phoebe. That's Lady Phoebe to you, although I would much prefer you never address me at all."

"Phoebe," he repeated softly, a smile spreading on his lips. "So you are the little lioness."

She obviously had no idea what he was talking about. "Stop staring at me so stupidly. Can you do something other than gape? Good grief, now you are smiling. I forbid you to smile at me. And I am a woman, not a jungle animal. Speaking of which, I've seen jungle animals cleaner than you. If you wish to see your nieces, you had better wash up. And sober up. Dress like a gentleman and try acting like one. Can you do this for an afternoon? Let us say four o'clock this afternoon? Against my better judgment, I am inviting you to join us for tea."

"I'll be there."

Her beautiful eyes narrowed. "Sober?"

He nodded.

4

"And groomed?"

He sighed. "I shall be presentable."

He cast her another rakish smile that worked on most women, but only made her roll her eyes. "You are hopeless," she muttered. "So help me, if you dare take a step out of line while at Moonstone Cottage, I will shoot you so full of holes you will look like a shredded pincushion."

She turned and strode to her horse, but he followed and stopped her before she could climb back up. He drew her up against him once more. "Phoebe—"

"That's Lady Phoebe to you."

Did her eyes always blaze so magnificently?

She opened her mouth to lambaste him again.

"Enough," he said, and kissed her with all his heart.

For this, he was rewarded with a punch in the nose.

Her hand was little and his hide was thick, so he barely felt a thing. She probably did more damage to herself than him.

He kissed her again, crushing his lips to hers and knowing he was utterly lost to this girl with aquamarine eyes and a honey-sweet mouth.

She punched him again. "What is wrong with you? Have you no shame? How could you... Why did you... Well, what do you have to say for yourself, you unmitigated clot?"

"Two words."

She looked up at him, utterly befuddled. "Two words?"

"Yes." The clouds had passed and the sun shone down on her once more. By heaven, she was an angel, and he was not letting her go.

"Pray tell. What might those two words be?"

He wanted to kiss her again, was not nearly done exploring that soft mouth of hers. But she was impatient for his answer, and he did not want her launching into another diatribe about his failings.

He knew what he was and what he needed...her. "Marry me."

# Chapter Two

"MARRY YOU?" LADY Phoebe Killigrew was certain the Marquess of Burness had completely taken leave of his senses. "Marry *you*?"

"That's what I said."

Of all the nonsense!

She had expected something stupid to spill from his lips, but never anything like this.

She wanted to hit him again, but refrained, since she was not a violent person and had never hit anyone in her life until just now, when she had struck him twice. Twice! And they had only just met. "I would sooner marry my horse."

He must have thought her response amusing, for he cast her yet another surprisingly appealing smile. "Seems I have a bit of work to do to change your mind."

Was he serious?

Were he not so dissolute, she might have considered allowing a courtship. He was quite handsome, of this there was no doubt. Dark hair, striking blue eyes that were a bit bloodshot at the moment. He was big and muscled, and although he did reek of brandy, she had exaggerated the truth when accusing him of smelling foul. Beneath that odor of brandy was an appealingly clean scent of musk and maleness.

She was never going to admit such a thing to him. "Lord

Burness, I do not appreciate your jest."

"It is no jest."

How long was he going to continue this farce? "If that is so, then do not waste your time hoping to gain my favor. I am never going to marry you. The sun is more likely to disappear from the sky than I would ever exchange vows with you. My only concern at the moment is your nieces. Do you think you can pull yourself together long enough not to frighten them?"

"They are not afraid of me," he said with a light frown. "They know I love them."

She shook her head and sighed. "You have an odd way of showing it."

"You have not seen me around them. I'll be at your home at four o'clock and prove it to you."

"Well, this is not only about your nieces. You and the Duke of Malvern are best friends. He speaks of you in glowing terms. Yet here you come to Moonstone Landing, and the first thing you do is shame him with your inexcusable behavior. Why?"

He appeared hurt by the remark. "It is not that way at all."

"Then kindly explain to me what you are doing, because I do not see a trace of valor in any of your actions."

"No, I don't suppose you would," he admitted, the pain evident in his every word. "How much has Cain told you about me?"

"Mostly it is my sister, Henley, who spoke of the friendship between you and her husband. She told me of the difficulties you have had in adjusting to...to the loss of your arm. I am truly sorry for all you've had to endure. But it has been three years now, and it seems as though you are still angry and rebellious."

"I did not ask for your opinion."

"Now you are just getting defensive. Frankly, I do not care whether you want my opinion or not. I am speaking to you because I need to be certain your nieces will be safe with you. This assumes I will turn them over to you, which I won't do while those friends of yours are in your home. Get rid of them first, or there will be nothing to discuss."

"They are not friends."

She put her hands on her hips to await an explanation, but he said nothing more, so she pressed on. "Then why did you invite them here?"

"It is none of your business. Cain will understand."

"Well, he and Henley are in Bath at the moment. Apparently, Cain's sister and her husband are joining them there, so they have taken the twins with them for the family reunion. I doubt they will be back before the end of the month. Something you would know if you opened any of your letters. I'm sure he left word for you, especially knowing you bought Squire Westgate's home. We were all here when your furniture arrived earlier in the month."

"So, not only are you a bossy bit of goods and opinionated, but you are a spy, too," he said, sounding almost genial.

Did he really not mind that she had berated him?

She arched an eyebrow and cast him a wry grin. "Yes, indeed I am. Now aren't you glad I turned you down?"

"Actually, Phoebe, not in the least." He cast her a look that would have had her swooning if she ever dared lower her defenses around this man. "I—"

The sound of high-pitched giggles distracted them both.

"Oh, hell," he muttered, his gaze fixed on the parlor windows of his home. Two of his female guests—two scantily clad female guests with their bosoms spilling out and leaving nothing to the imagination—were now peering out and calling to him suggestively.

Phoebe did not think of herself as one easily shocked, but this blatant display *did* shock her. "You are too much."

She mounted her horse and rode off without looking back.

Tears filled her eyes, and she blamed it on the wind rather than dare admit this man had overset her. She had never met him before, but received such glowing accounts of him from Henley and Cain. Now that she had finally met him, he was nothing like the man she had expected.

How could he and Cain possibly be friends?

Cain was an excellent duke, a faithful husband and doting father to his twins, a son and a daughter. He was kind, compassionate, attentive to all who depended on him. The Marquess of Burness was a drunken, carousing wastrel.

Thoughtless and depraved.

Utterly lacking in morals.

She wiped the tears from her eyes with a rough brush of her arm across her cheeks.

The arm.

Yes, that was it.

Whatever good qualities this marquess once had were lost along with his arm. The man was now a shell of himself. Valor, duty, and sacrifice were replaced by anger, resentfulness, and bitter defiance.

Did he not understand he was hurting his loved ones as well as himself?

The ride back to Moonstone Cottage did not take her long, and she used the little time she had to restore her composure. She did not want his nieces to be further alarmed, which they would be if they saw her in tears.

In any event, she did not know why she was crying. The marquess was not worth her shedding a single tear.

Upon returning home, she found her sister, Chloe, seated in their garden under a shade tree, reading a story to the man's young nieces, Ella and Imogen. The girls scampered to their feet when they saw her approaching. "Did you see Uncle Cormac?" Ella, the elder girl, asked.

Phoebe nodded. "I have invited him to tea this afternoon. But I am not certain he will be able to attend. You see, he has a houseful of guests…and there must have been a mix-up with your father's letter…" Goodness, she did not know what to say to lessen their disappointment. She had no idea whether the marquess could be trusted to show up. "He may not make it today, but—"

"He'll make it," Ella insisted.

Imogen nodded. "Yes, he loves us. We are the most important thing to him."

They seemed so certain that Phoebe did not know whether to be relieved or even more worried. These girls would be crushed if he let them down. They were so little and vulnerable, Ella only eight years old and Imogen two years younger.

What sweet girls they were, too.

"Then I know he will try his best, and if he cannot make it today, it will be because of dire reasons." She spared a glance at her own sister, who was still young herself at only fifteen. But she and Chloe had been managing well on their own at Moonstone Cottage and were easily capable of taking care of the marquess's nieces for the month, if it came to that.

Ella and Imogen cast her a patient look.

"He will be here," Ella explained in her sweet voice. "He would walk through fire for us."

Phoebe had difficulty understanding this man. Well, she really did not know him—nor did she wish to know him after their first encounter. But she would be polite to him for the sake of these girls. "Did he tell you that?"

Imogen nodded. "Always. He said we could always depend on him."

*Gad, the liar.*

Chloe shut the book she had been reading aloud to them and scampered to her feet. "If you girls are not too tired from your long trip, why don't we go to Mrs. Halsey's tea shop and pick up some special treats for us all?"

The girls nodded enthusiastically.

"We're not tired," Ella said, clapping her hands. "We sat in the coach for days, and Mrs. Grimble would not allow the driver to stop anywhere but at the coaching inns to change the horses. She was eager to drop us off and go visit her daughter. I hope she never comes back for us."

Imogen nodded. "She was always frowning at us. I'm glad she's gone. What an ogre she was. That's what Uncle Cormac called her, but our parents said she was vigi...vigi..."

"Vigilant," Ella said. "I'm glad she left us with you and went off. You are so much nicer than she was. I'm glad you're not vigilant."

Phoebe laughed. "Vigilant means keeping a close watch, but it does not have to be in a mean way. Chloe and I shall be that, but you will have fun with us. Have you comfortably settled in my old room? You are more than welcome to stay the month if the mix-up with your uncle cannot be straightened out."

"We won't stay with Uncle Cormac?" Imogen's eyes began to water.

Phoebe's heart tugged. "You might. Indeed, you likely will. I only meant that you should not worry if he cannot take you in immediately. Between your uncle and us, you will have a wonderful summer."

MOONSTONE COTTAGE'S CARETAKER, Mr. Hawke, took them into the village of Moonstone Landing in his wagon, which was a treat for the little girls. They enjoyed the bumpy ride in the rickety old thing, the four of them sitting on the wooden side benches and basking in the sun. Fortunately, they had all put on their bonnets to shade themselves from the bright rays.

The ride was most pleasant, for the sea breeze kept the temperature at a comfortable level, and the ride into town was filled with scenic overlooks and the fresh scent of woodlands and meadow flowers that mingled with the bracing air.

The girls were all giggles and smiles by the time they drew up in front of Mrs. Halsey's tea shop. The aromas of baked goods were heavenly, and the girls had fun picking out their favorite treats and the one they agreed would be their uncle's favorite, a lemon cake.

"That is Phoebe's favorite, too." Chloe smirked at her.

So what if it was?

That she and the odious marquess should share a love for the same cake meant absolutely nothing. Half the population of Moonstone Landing was enamored of Mrs. Halsey's lemon cake.

They placed their purchases in the wagon, then took a quick walk down the high street to the quaint harbor where several boats were still moored. Most of the fishing vessels were out to sea, so there were only a few boats, mostly used for pleasant afternoon sailing excursions, to be seen.

But the girls were fascinated because they had never seen such vessels up close before, nor had they ever seen a fish market. "Uncle Cormac doesn't like fish," Ella said, wrinkling her nose at the pungent odors.

"Oh, that is unfortunate," Phoebe said, and immediately bought two large haddock as an added course for their afternoon tea.

Chloe gave her a little swat on her backside as the girls moved ahead of them to the next stall. "That is mean of you."

"The man is horrid and vile, I assure you. His only redeeming quality is that he seems to adore his nieces. You will see for yourself soon enough, assuming he bothers to show up."

They rode back to the cottage, passing Westgate Hall along the way. It really was a lovely manor house, with a charming garden and spectacular views of the sea. All the finer houses in the area had their own private stretch of beach, and his was no exception.

In fact, his strip of beach adjoined theirs.

*Oh dear.*

She had better talk to the marquess about that. She could not have him cavorting naked with his tarts while she was on her stretch of sand with his nieces.

Well, it was one more thing she would have to discuss with him when he arrived.

If he arrived.

To her surprise, the clock in the hall had just struck the four o'clock hour when she heard the approach of a rider.

While Chloe and the girls were seated at the table on their shaded terrace enjoying lemonades, Phoebe had been running in and out of the house anxiously awaiting his arrival. She was now staring out the parlor window, and drew in a breath when she saw him. Since the windows had been left open to allow in the breeze, she was able to hear the pleasant exchange between him and Mr. Hawke.

"Beautiful bit of horseflesh," Mr. Hawke remarked as he took the reins of the marquess's stallion and gave the big black Friesian a loving pat. "The Duke of Malvern has one just like it."

"Yes, they are from the same sire. Got us through some fierce battles. His name is Hadrian. The old boy is getting on in years now."

Mr. Hawke laughed. "So are we all."

The marquess joined him in the laughter, his smile so surprisingly cordial and genuine that Phoebe was momentarily taken off stride.

Her heart was thumping as she rushed to the front door to open it.

Suddenly there he was, standing before her in all his magnificence.

And he was truly magnificent, exuding power and brawn.

The breath caught in her lungs. How had he sobered up so fast? And cleaned up so well?

Was it possible for a man to be this handsome?

He grinned at her. "Good afternoon, Phoebe. Are you going to let me in?"

She nodded lamely, unable to take her eyes off him, for she had never imagined such a transformation possible.

He cleared his throat.

She shook out of her daze and stepped aside. "Forgive me— do come this way."

Despite her attempts to appear elegant and unaffected, she was too busy gaping at him like a goose to watch where she was walking. She bumped into a side table, banging her hip against it.

His arm immediately came around her waist. "Are you all right?"

She cast him a wry smile. "I am fine, just behaving like a ninny. You startled me. Well, not startled so much as mystified me. How did you manage it?"

"Manage what?" he asked, his arm ever so lightly still tucked around her waist and making her insides tingle.

"You looked vile a few hours ago."

He grinned. "You like that word, don't you? Vile."

"You did look like a low creature. You know you did."

"And now?" He arched a dark eyebrow in expectation.

"You look heroic." She hadn't meant to compliment him, but how could she not? He looked splendid with his dark hair obviously freshly washed and his stunning blue eyes no longer bloodshot. He had shaved, and must have bathed, since his scent was divine, that hint of musk and maleness no longer hidden beneath a brandy-barrel reek, and now her heart was in even greater palpitations.

He wore buff breeches, a brocade silk waistcoat that matched the splendor of his eyes, and a dark blue jacket that seemed to enhance the breadth of his shoulders. His boots were black and polished to a shine.

"Heroic? No one's called me that in years."

She cast him a soft smile. "As you know, I am prone to speaking my mind. As you also know, I am quite opinionated. But I will tell you the bad and the good. Right now, you appear to be all good. We shall see how long that lasts."

She led him down the hall to the rear of the house and onto the terrace, where his nieces were seated with Chloe.

Since she hadn't taken her eyes off him, she saw the hint of pain along with the sparkle of love the moment he spotted the girls.

Phoebe was not certain what to expect, but it was never him suddenly bending on one knee and quacking like a duck. The girls shrieked with glee, bounded out of their seats, and rushed to hug him. "Uncle Cormac! Uncle Cormac!" they both shouted, and then began to quack like ducks as well.

"My ducklings!" He gave each of them a tender hug.

The three of them continued to quack and hug.

Phoebe and Chloe could not stop laughing.

"He seems to have cleaned up nicely," Chloe whispered as they watched this happy reunion. "Well, Phoebe. What do you think of him now?"

"I don't know. I am quite stunned by the transformation." Her mind was now awhirl trying to take in this side of him, this valiant side. This was a man who could be best friends with an honorable duke. This was the man who could be tender with his nieces.

But how much of it was real and how much was merely a façade?

And what of his behavior toward her earlier? He had been so brazen as to kiss her and then ask her to marry him.

She was certain he had been in jest and mocking her because she had blistered him upon their first meeting.

But what if he meant it?

No, it had to be a jest.

How could this man ever be a proper husband to any woman?

In any event, why would he want her?

More important, why would she want him?

# Chapter Three

C ORMAC FELT PHOEBE'S gaze on him as they sat outdoors and had their tea. What was it about her that he found irresistible? This girl simply drew him in. Perhaps it was not her at all and merely this perfect day. Well, it had not started out very well between them. But this afternoon was turning out to be quite nice.

The light breeze kept the annoying gnats away, and the bees were too busy pollinating the flowers to bother attacking their sweet cakes. The air was warm and filled with the fragrant scent of roses, which mingled with the salt of the sea. The sun was still strong in the sky and there were only a few clouds wafting by, most of them soft white puffs against the vivid blue expanse.

Imogen, her eyes wide, was digging into the delicious lemon cake and still chattering at him with her mouth full. He did not have the heart to chide her, nor did Phoebe seem to have anything to say about it. Her expression remained smiling and doting on his nieces.

He liked this about her. She was a bossy bit of goods, certainly had been with him. But she was gentle as a lamb with his girls.

Ella was the one who told Imogen to swallow before speaking, and then she took up where Imogen left off. "Mrs. Grimble was so angry when we got to your house, Uncle Cormac. She wouldn't let us go in and ordered the driver to take us here."

"Lord," he muttered. "You stopped at Westgate Hall first?"

The girls nodded.

"But you were sleeping in the altogether," Imogen said. "What does that mean?"

Chloe giggled. "It means he forgot to put his clothes on."

Phoebe kicked her under the table.

Imogen missed the exchange and continued. "Then she called you something bad, and then Ella told her to shut up and called her a witch."

Ella started to tear up. "She said I was a wicked girl and she was not going to stay with us another hour. She brought us here and left us. I know it wasn't right to call her a witch, but she was one, and... Are you very angry, Uncle Cormac?"

"Not with you, duckling." He reached over and took her hand in his. "Whatever happened was all my fault."

Imogen jumped down from her chair and climbed onto his lap. "Then we're not in trouble?"

He kissed her on the cheek. "No, not at all. As I said, it is all my fault. I must take full blame for this mix-up. And everything did get very mixed up, which is why I cannot take you home with me today. Will you be all right staying with Lady Phoebe and Lady Chloe for a couple of days? I will come by every day, I promise you. But I have a full house right now, and it will take a few days for me to get rid of my guests."

"Even the altogether ladies?" Imogen asked. "Mrs. Grimble said they forgot to put their clothes on, too."

Phoebe choked on her tea.

Chloe was snorting, trying to hold back her laughter as she patted her sister's back.

Cormac was waiting for the lemon cake to come flying in his face, for he had expected Phoebe to be furious with him. But she merely took a sip of her tea once her coughs subsided. Well, she had seen those ladies.

She had seen the worst of him.

He sighed. "I never liked Mrs. Grimble. She's a busybody."

Phoebe tossed him a cautioning look.

"Of course, I am not always on my best behavior, either. I'm sure she was just looking out for you girls. Ah, fish. My favorite," he remarked as Mrs. Hawke, the Killigrew housekeeper, brought out a platter of it.

"I thought you hated fish," Imogen said. "That's what I told Lady Phoebe."

"And she bought it anyway?" Lord, he was in danger of falling in love with the impudent chit. She was going to kick his arse from here to Sunday because she was still incensed over what had taken place this morning. "How considerate of her. But it does not matter. I am resolved to love anything Lady Phoebe dishes out."

Imogen smiled. "She's very pretty, isn't she?"

Cormac chuckled. "Yes, quite pretty."

"And so is Chloe," Ella tossed in.

"You are all beautiful in my eyes," Cormac said. "You want to know why?"

His nieces nodded.

"Because you are beautiful not only on the outside, but on the inside, too. And that is what is most important." He gave Imogen a little tickle on her stomach.

Ella immediately wanted to join in, so he tickled her, too.

Afterward, Chloe took the girls for a walk along the beach.

Cormac remained seated at the table while Phoebe and Mrs. Hawke cleared away the food and plates. He offered to help, but Phoebe would not hear of it. "You are our guest."

He arched an eyebrow, but did not protest.

At best, he was an unwanted guest. Although Phoebe did seem to be warming to him, no doubt because he was behaving himself and obviously doted on his nieces. Lord, to think his brother had entrusted their governess, that odious Grimble, to deliver the girls to him.

Phoebe soon joined him and took the chair beside his. "I think we must discuss your nieces. Chloe and I do not mind if they stay with us the entire month."

"That is generous of you, but my guests will be gone in a couple of days. A week at most. I would appreciate your keeping them with you until they are all out of my house. In the meanwhile, I'll come by to see the girls every day. Tell me what is convenient for you and I will accommodate your schedule."

She seemed surprised that he was being so obliging. "Won't you have your guests to entertain while they are here?"

"Phoebe, your disapproval is showing. Do not pass judgment on something you know nothing about. It isn't what you think."

She sat erect, her hands clasped on her lap and her kissable lips pursed, which were obvious signs of her continued irritation. "I am not thinking anything."

He laughed. "You have opinions on everything. You've told me so yourself. But I am serious when I tell you it is none of your business."

She stood up. "Well then, we have nothing more to say to each other. I will not stop you if you wish to leave."

"Gad, you are irritating." He took her hand and nudged her back into her chair. "We have lots to discuss. What do you need for my nieces? For that matter, what do you and Chloe need for yourselves? Charge whatever it is to my account."

"We do not require your charity."

"Now you are just being peckish. It does not suit you, Phoebe."

"How am I supposed to feel? You bewilder me."

He grinned. "Is that a compliment?"

"No, it assuredly is not." She shook her head, causing her dark curls to bob. Lord, she was a lovely thing. Beautiful, but in a warm and appealing way. She was the sort of woman one would never tire of holding in one's arms.

Not that he had ever bothered to simply hold a woman in his arms.

First of all, he was no longer capable of it, since he had only the one arm.

Even before he had lost the limb, he'd never spent time with his arms wrapped around a woman except in bed, and that was only for as long as needed to satisfy his sexual urges.

There was nothing he would call a romantic embrace. No cooing words of love. Just the raw act of satisfaction. Heat, grunting, the scent of sex on their bodies after a particularly wild tumble.

Of course, he made certain to pleasure the lady as well.

He did not know how much of their cries and moans of ecstasy were real or fake. For the most part, he assumed they were real, as they would not have sought him out time and again if they were not well pleasured. For the most part, he gave it little thought. His partners were not the sort of women he would ever consider marrying. Most were married already, or widowed ladies who enjoyed their independence. All of them were elegant and part of a faster crowd among the *ton*.

A few, like his former paramour, Lady Seline, had been unmarried when they first had relations. But she was not chaste even back then. She had been no virgin when he'd taken her to bed. Well, Lady Seline was married now, quite unhappily, to the Earl of Whitford.

It was a pity, for Whitford was a decent fellow, and she was going to give him a life of hell.

Women like Seline used sex as a weapon. Indeed, they used any wiles at their disposal because they craved attention and would never be satisfied, no matter how much attention was lavished on them. Nor would they ever be faithful to any one man.

Phoebe was nothing like these *sophisticated* ladies.

She was charming and compassionate, the sort who would be faithful and true. Therefore, she was certain to be far more dangerous to his heart than any woman he had ever encountered.

She could not be bought with trinkets, no matter how expensive. Nor would she accept anything less than full commitment and love.

Well, she had no idea just how damaged he was.

Not that the challenge would put her off. Indeed, he thought she would be drawn to him *because* he was a challenge. She had strength and determination, and he liked that about her.

"Would you mind if I came by each morning in time to have breakfast with my nieces? I could come by again around noon and take you all for an outing. A little something every day so they know I am here and thinking of them. As I mentioned, it may take me as long as a week to be rid of my guests."

"I see."

"No, I don't suppose you do. But I cannot tell you more, Phoebe." He also liked that she hadn't cringed when noticing his missing arm. He'd even held her up against him this morning, just grabbed her and pulled her to him. Not well done of him, but she hadn't flinched, even when her shoulder had rubbed against the stump of his arm.

She had no idea how much that meant to him.

Or how much he ached to take her in his embrace. Lord, he had to stop thinking he was still whole—one arm, that was all he had. One arm to wrap around her and hold her close.

"Very well. Join us for breakfast, and if the weather holds, we shall join you for a daily outing. It doesn't have to be much. These girls are happy just to be around you."

"I know." He flexed his shoulders and rose.

"Is your arm bothering you?" She rose along with him and walked beside him toward the cliff stairs that led down to the beach. They could see Chloe and his nieces, their shoes off and toes curling in the golden sand as they walked along the shoreline in search of seashells.

"Do you mean the one I am missing?"

She surprised him by placing a soft hand on that shoulder and caressing what remained of his arm. "Do you feel it still?"

He nodded. "The missing part? Yes, phantom sensations. At times I have to remind myself it isn't there."

"Then you get angry and refuse to come to terms with it?"

"I am not a starfish. I know that limb will never grow back." He hated speaking about his arm. "Change the subject."

"All right. Why do you think your brother sent the girls to you?"

"Is it not obvious? Because I am a complete and utter arse except when I am around them. I'm sure he hoped some of their sweetness would rub off on me."

She laughed. "Oh, dear me. No. I cannot imagine you as someone sweet. But I hope for your sake you stop being angry at the world. More important, I hope you forgive yourself and stop hating yourself for getting shot."

He gave a mock bow. "Ah, Lady Phoebe has ordered me to be happy, so I must be."

"I would never order you to do anything you do not wish to do, my lord. Well, I did toss a few orders at you regarding your nieces, but that was to protect them. You are a grown man, and no one is going to tell you what to do about making things right for yourself."

He laughed. "You would. You want to give me an earful right now but are holding back because I have been surprisingly on my best behavior, and you do not want to argue with me now that I am behaving."

She pursed her lips again, reminding him that he ached to kiss her once more. "I don't ever want to argue with you. But neither will I let you be a dolt around me or your nieces. Who is the real you? The man I saw this morning or the one in front of me now?"

"Both."

"Too bad. I did not like that drunken sot."

He laughed. "I do not like him much either. But he is me as much as the doting uncle. I'm not sure yet what I'll be as a husband."

She squirmed as he kept his gaze on her.

Finally, she sighed and looked up at him. "Are you referring to me? That ridiculous proposal you uttered this morning? But that was you just being stupid, was it not?"

"Ah, I do so love the way you describe me."

She managed a chuckle. "I warned you. I do not hold back my opinions."

"Nor do I ever want you to. I wasn't jesting. I want to marry you, Phoebe."

He saw the bubbling pool of passion heat up inside her... Well, perhaps it was more of a bubbling pool of irritation. "Do not bring that up again. The only reason you would want to marry me is to torture me with your misbehavior. Move your attentions to someone else who won't care what you do once you are her husband. As for me, I cannot think of anything more crushing to my heart than to be burdened with a faithless spouse."

"But it would be a relief if you did not love him."

Her eyes were now blazing. "That is the most pathetic, irresponsible, and vulgar thing I have ever heard in my entire life. I would never marry a man I did not love."

"Even if he were a wealthy marquess?"

"Are you referring to yourself again? I do not need your wealth. Some would consider me an heiress in my own right now that the Duke of Malvern has helped save our inheritance. Even if I did not have funds enough to support me, I would have to be desperate and on the verge of starvation before I considered you."

He glanced at his arm.

"It has nothing to do with that missing limb and all to do with your reprehensible conduct. How are you and Malvern the best of friends? I still cannot reconcile that friendship in my mind. He is a man of character. He would never consider cheating on my sister. He would jump into the bowels of hell to protect her and their children. Marriage for him is a salvation. Is that something so foreign to you? Can you not conceive of ever being such a husband?"

"Do you think I don't want this? To love someone so wholly and completely, to know they feel the same about me? But that is never going to happen for someone like me."

"You mean someone who is a stubborn clot and too stupid to see something good even if it slaps him in the face?"

He could not help but laugh.

She was so good at kicking his arse, and he very much needed someone who could put him in his place, especially with her gentle touch.

She inhaled lightly, her expression now heartfelt. "My lord, it will happen. But you'll never see it or appreciate it unless you first start liking yourself."

"Not like myself? Phoebe, I think *too* highly of myself. In fact, so highly, I cannot imagine any woman being adequate as my wife."

Her gorgeous eyes widened and her lips curved upward in the hint of a smile. "Oh, so you proposed to me because I was inadequate?"

"No, I proposed to you because I do not think I will find anyone *more* adequate."

"Be still my heart." She fanned her chest, which only served to remind him just how magnificent he considered her body. Especially those perfect breasts. "I do not think I have ever been spoken to so romantically. The great poets would weep if they ever heard your transporting words. *Adequate*. Oh, how greatly I've aspired to be...*adequate*. I do believe I am about to fall into a swoon."

Their laughter mingled.

"Are you through kicking my arse?" But he truly enjoyed being around Phoebe. She did not let him get away with anything. She was quick-witted and direct, eager to point out the absurdity of his thoughts and words.

Her smile was warm, and perhaps this was her greatest strength, to be able to put him in his place and somehow still come across as tender and caring. "My lord, I've hardly started."

She was lively, passionate, and achingly beautiful. For this reason, he wanted to be the one to bed her.

Of course, he would have to marry her afterward...perhaps

marry her first.

He shook his head. He had not come here this afternoon to seduce her. But heaven help him, he surely wanted this girl in his bed.

What he did not want was for her to claim his heart.

Well, maybe he did.

After all, he had asked her to marry him. Surely, that had to signify something.

His desperation for salvation?

Lord, he was a pathetic mess.

Perhaps she was right about him. How could he expect anyone to like him if he did not like himself?

Yet if anyone was to help him find his way, it would be this little lioness. Deep down, somewhere in the darkness of his soul, he knew if he ever stood a chance of finding happiness, it would be with Phoebe.

He'd known it the moment he first heard her name mentioned three years ago. Cain and Phoebe's sister, Henley, had come to him to console him when he first lost his arm. It was shortly before the pair married.

That loss had turned him into such an insufferable wretch, not even he could stand to be around himself.

Cain and Hen had jokingly described Hen's sister as that, a lioness, beautiful and fierce.

Well, it would take a lion's courage to deal with him, because he was such an arrogant arse and difficult to handle most of the time.

Was Phoebe up to the task?

# Chapter Four

P HOEBE WALKED DOWN the steps leading from Moonstone Cottage's garden to the beach and took an early-morning walk along the shore in order to think. She had tossed on a simple morning gown, a pale yellow muslin, and had not bothered to wear her shoes, since she liked the feel of soft sand under her feet. Bringing shoes along would only have given her something to carry while she dipped her toes in the cool waves lapping the shore.

Nor did she bother to properly do up her hair, instead leaving it in a loose braid down her back, since no one would see her, and she enjoyed this little freedom to do as she pleased.

It was shortly after six o'clock and the weather was unusually clear. Most days, a mist hovered over the water and did not disappear until several hours past sunrise. She had forgotten to mention the beach arrangements with the Marquess of Burness and was now worried he and his guests would brazenly cavort on his side of the beach in full view of his nieces if she dared take them down here later in the day.

Of course, she could mention it to him at breakfast, assuming he showed up.

However, she did not think he would arrive in time for breakfast. How did one drink and debauch all evening and then wake up bright-eyed and bushy-tailed at the break of day? Yesterday, he had barely been conscious when stumbling out of his house at noon with his shirt wide open, too drunk to see straight.

No, he wasn't going to show up.

She sighed and strolled along her beach, her gown raised to her knees so the fabric would not get wet in a rogue wave.

The Moonstone Cottage beach was separated from the Westgate Hall beach by a small outcropping of stones that had naturally formed over the eons and conveniently provided the neighbors a little privacy. The outcropping ended where the sand met the water, so it was fairly easy to breach if one wished to cross to the neighbor's beach, especially when the tide was out.

Of course, she intended to respect his privacy.

However, she strolled to the outcropping and stole a peek just to get a better look at his area of sand.

"Phoebe? What are you doing here?" a voice called from the water.

She was surprised when the marquess suddenly emerged, like Neptune rising from the sea. "Oh my heavens," she said in a whisper.

He wore no shirt but thankfully had kept his breeches on. Those were soaked and molded to his powerful thighs.

She squealed and darted back to her strip of beach.

"Phoebe, I do not bite. You needn't run away," he called out with a light chuckle. "What are you doing up at this hour?"

He skirted the outcropping as he waded out of the water and strode toward her. How was it possible for any man to be this beautiful?

"Um...I often wake early, since I go to sleep early and get a solid night's rest. The question is, what are you doing up at this hour? Or have you not gone to sleep at all yet?" It did not escape her notice that without his shirt to hide the missing limb, its lack was obvious.

Her heart tugged.

"I like to come down here early so no one sees me." He glanced at his missing arm. "Does this bother you?"

"No. Why should it?"

He cast her a mirthless smile. "Be honest with me. Most people grimace at the sight of me."

"Do you see me making a face? You know I do not hide my thoughts." In truth, her heart was wildly racing, for this man was utterly gorgeous. Wet and gorgeous. Muscled shoulders. Divine chest with a spray of dark hair across it and slightly downward to draw one's eye to—

It did not bear mentioning.

Firm, flat stomach.

Dark hair casually brushed back off his forehead.

Eyes that bored straight into her soul.

She felt small beside him, for he was a big man, and not having her shoes on seemed to make a difference. But she liked the size and breadth of him.

"Are you testing me again, my lord? Did you wake up early hoping to meet me and shock me?"

He grinned. "Hoping to meet you, yes."

"How did you know I liked to walk along the beach?"

"I didn't. I merely hoped you would. But I also came down at this hour for myself. You may not find this stump of mine repulsive, but most people do."

"I'm so sorry. It is a lack in them, not you."

He reached out and ran a finger lightly along the curve of her jaw. "Ah, Phoebe. I do not need your platitudes. Your little display of support does not make me feel any better."

"That is because you agree with those who would find you repulsive. That is your failing and explains why you do the debauched and depraved things you do. You are angry and you hate yourself."

"I was a wicked man even before I lost my arm. Losing it just gave me reason to continue being insufferable."

She laughed. "Well, at least you see yourself clearly for what you are. But I wish you would be a little nicer to others. And a little kinder to yourself. You might also gain by learning to trust people. We aren't all wicked creatures who wish to connive to take something from you."

He gave her cheek a light caress. "You wish for something from me, Phoebe. It is something I can never give you."

She frowned. "What are you talking about? I've asked nothing of you. If you recall, I went out of my way to point out that I am quite capable of taking care of myself. Nor do I need you to give me anything for the care of your nieces. They are sweet and undemanding. It is a pleasure to look after them."

"I wasn't talking about them. Nor am I speaking of monetary matters. However, I must insist on paying for everything while my nieces are with you. That includes any expenses you and Chloe have for yourselves. The matter is not open for discussion."

"Heavens, you are the most high-handed man I have ever met." A wave took her by surprise as she stood frowning at him instead of watching the water. She yelped and quickly hiked her gown well above her knees to keep it from getting wet.

The wretched man noticed immediately and brazenly smiled. "Nice legs."

She stepped further away from the water and lowered her gown to mid-calf, which she supposed was just as bad. It would not have made a difference even if she were covered down to her ankles, for he'd still be looking at her in that naughty, heart-melting way. "They weren't on display for you."

He shrugged.

"What did you mean when you said I wished to get something from you?"

"Is it not obvious? You want my heart, Phoebe."

She would not allow him to get away with that statement. He was the one making a thing of marrying her. She knew it was a farce. "I have told you already, you are the last man in England I will ever marry. So your heart is quite safe from me. Hide it away and keep it tightly locked up in that dark tomb of your chest so that it shrivels and dies. You may keep it all to yourself and share it with no one ever, for all I care."

She turned to walk away, but he caught her wrist and held her back. He was gentle as he turned her to face him.

His eyes held so much pain that she found herself coming undone. Was it real? Or was he merely manipulating her? She refused to be affected by him. He had to be playing with her feelings, although she did not understand why.

"What if I did want to share my heart with you?" he asked in a ragged whisper.

All semblance of humor fled, and she found herself in utter turmoil. "Then do so, for I will never purposely hurt you. Just be honest with me. I have no intention of becoming one of your conquests. If this is all you want of me, then leave me alone. What would it accomplish to seduce me, other than the boasting rights that you could do it? Cain would make you marry me, and I would refuse. It would leave me ruined, him hating you, and you truly alone, with no friends left to trust."

He released her.

"And another thing, what hour of the day do you and your friends plan to use your portion of the beach? I would like to keep your nieces far away from them. What do you say to allowing us the morning hours and after lunch until three o'clock? Then you and your friends can have the beach from three o'clock until darkness. Of course, you are welcome to use it beyond sundown, but I think it would be very stupid of you to swim at night when one can easily get disoriented and not see the shore."

"I'll keep my guests off the beach according to your schedule. I doubt any of them will bother to come down here at all. As for me, I'll come down whenever I wish and join my nieces here whenever it pleases me to do so."

"Do as you wish. Obviously, no one can control you. But it is not my intention to keep you away from the girls. I trust you with them. It is your friends I don't trust."

"They are not my friends."

She rolled her eyes. "Stop. They are with you. You are their host. I'll call them whatever I wish to call them. Good morning, my lord. Breakfast is in an hour."

She hurried up the stairs without looking back at him, but she could feel his gaze on her all the while.

What did he want from her?

Why was he paying her any notice?

She strode across the lawn toward her house, her heart still in palpitations. Her body would not stop responding to him. If she were honest about it, her body seemed to ache for his touch.

This was very bad.

She did not want this man stealing her heart.

He had already stolen her first kiss when he, in his drunken and dissolute state, had drawn her up against his body and planted his lips on hers. He hadn't even flinched when she punched him in the nose. She ought to punch him again now that he was more alert.

Did he even realize what he had done?

She always meant to save herself for the man of her dreams—whoever he might be—waiting for the right moment, the magical night and the perfect gentleman, and then this oaf had come along and simply presumed to kiss her. "Infernal, unmitigated clot."

However, as angry as she was about it, she resolved to be cordial when he joined them an hour later for breakfast.

HE STRODE IN with his typical arrogance, but his affection for his nieces was unmistakably genuine.

Those little girls worshiped him. Their eyes shone with love, and they had the broadest smiles whenever they looked at him.

"Good morning, my lord."

"Good morning, Phoebe. Good morning, my little ducklings." To his credit, he felt the same love for them.

He was kindness itself toward these girls. Funny and charming, too.

Why could he not be this way all the time?

Well, he wouldn't be him if he were pleasant all the time, Phoebe supposed. Around anyone else but those girls, he had a dangerous edge that some women found thrilling.

She didn't.

He had called her a lioness, but he was the dangerous lion who held the power to tear her to bits. He could easily break her heart if she ever allowed him close.

"Well, Phoebe? What do you say?" he asked, arching an eyebrow as he awaited her response.

The pulse at the base of her throat began to beat wildly. "Do forgive me—I was not following the conversation. Would you repeat your question?"

He grinned. Did he have to look so handsome when he smiled?

"I suggested we take a boat ride around the harbor this morning and then stop for ices at Mrs. Halsey's tea shop. Does this meet with your approval?"

"What about your guests? Do you not have to—"

"They won't be up before noon. Melrose shall steer them to the dining room for a late breakfast buffet. I won't be missed."

"I see. All right. That sounds like a good plan. What do you think, girls?"

Ella and Imogen cheered.

Chloe turned to her. "I promised Prudence I would help her at the church this morning. Would you mind terribly if I missed the boat ride and ices?"

*Drat.*

That would leave Phoebe alone with the marquess. But his nieces would be with them, so she supposed it was all right. "Give my regards to Prudence. I believe you met our cousin in London, my lord. She was with Hen and Cain when they married. She is now married to Cain's estate manager, Mr. Weston. Do you know him?"

He nodded. "A very good man. Send them my regards, Chloe."

Apparently determining that this conversation was settled, he turned to his nieces and emitted a playful roar that had them squealing in delight. "So it is to be just us and Lady Phoebe, my ducklings. Can she protect you from the big, bad marquess?"

Imogen jumped on his lap and hugged him. "You're not big and bad. You would never hurt us."

He kissed her on the forehead. "Of course I never would."

"You won't hurt Lady Phoebe either, will you?" She looked up at him with innocent eyes, awaiting an answer that was not immediately forthcoming.

Finally, he nodded. "You are all safe and under my protection. I'll do my best never to hurt her."

They finished breakfast, and the marquess agreed to meet them back at Moonstone Cottage within the hour. "I'll have my carriage brought around to take us into the village. Chloe, we can drop you off at the church if you like."

"Thank you. Yes, that would be perfect. I'll grab a ride home with Prudence afterward."

While Chloe ran upstairs to help the girls brush their hair and change into proper outfits, Phoebe walked him to the door.

"You are not happy with me," he stated while they waited for Mr. Hawke to bring Hadrian around.

"Should I be? Being pleasant around your nieces does not absolve you of all your sins."

"No one other than you would ever care or consider marrying a marquess a hurtful thing."

"That is their choice. I cannot marry for less than love."

"No, you cannot marry for less than a sacred promise from your husband never to stray. Most men stray. They are still good husbands who protect and provide for their families. You are punishing me for being honest about it."

"I am not punishing you at all. I am telling you I will never marry you, so you needn't concern yourself with my feelings. I shall never be your wife. Go find someone who wants you only for your wealth and won't care whose bed you warm." She grunted and shook her head. "This is so typical of you."

"What?"

"You act as though you are the one being put upon, but did you ever consider how you have imposed on me?"

"What do you mean?"

"I did not want to kiss you, but you went ahead and kissed me anyway."

"Women do not complain when I kiss them."

She frowned at him. "Well, I am lodging a complaint. Do you think I waited a lifetime for a first kiss only to be kissed by a drunk who could not even tell whether he was kissing me or the backside of my horse?"

He stared at her. "Your first?"

"That's right, and it should have been something special, something to treasure. Instead, it was you."

He grinned.

Of all the gall!

"Now I will have to blot it from my memory," she grumbled.

"No, you won't. You cannot because you like me more than you will ever admit. You also liked my kiss, although I truly am sorry I reeked of brandy. That was not well done of me. I'll kiss you again tonight, and I promise you will like it."

"Lord, you are dense. I mentioned it because I want you *not* to kiss me ever again." She pushed him toward his horse, not caring if he stumbled and the beast trampled him.

But he was too big and solid, so he hardly budged despite her shove. "Oh, Phoebe, now who is lying to themselves? I'll pick you up within the hour. I'll order a special ice for you at Mrs. Halsey's shop, a flavor just perfect for you...sour grapes."

She gasped and then looked up at him with her fiercest scowl.

He merely blew her a kiss and rode off.

Was he really going to kiss her tonight?

No, he was merely threatening the deed in order to tease her. Wasn't he?

So why did she now feel disappointed?

And why was her traitorous heart fluttering in anticipation?

# Chapter Five

"MELROSE," CORMAC SAID, stepping inside his house only long enough to check on his guests before leaving again, "have my carriage brought around. I shall be taking Lady Phoebe and my nieces for a sail around the harbor."

His butler nodded. "What shall I do with your guests when they wake?"

"Serve them breakfast and let them have at my stock of wine. Brandy if the men prefer. Otherwise, leave them to entertain themselves. I should be back by the time they really start to stir."

His comment met with a look of disapproval, for he and his guests had been waking late and staying up all night to engage in less-than-sterling conduct. However, this would now change for him, and had changed as of last night. He refused to be dissolute around his nieces. Perhaps Phoebe had something to do with his improved behavior as well, since he suddenly had no desire to touch anyone but her. He did not want to think about that.

"How is Lord Crawford?"

"Not good, my lord. I have assigned footmen to take turns watching him, for he remains distraught." Melrose cleared his throat. "Not even the ladies seem able to console him, if you understand my meaning."

Cormac ran a hand through his hair in frustration. "I promised his brother I would help him through this difficult patch. Do the best you can. I'll be back in a few hours."

If only his nieces had arrived at the end of the week instead of now. He had made a deathbed promise to Lord Crawford's brother, but he also had a duty to his own nieces. They were little girls, while this lord was a grown man, and yet he behaved worse than a child.

If ever there was a man in need of a strong woman's guidance, it was Lord Crawford. He had no leadership qualities, although he was not a stupid man by any means. *Scholarly* was a better description of him. The man cried out for someone smart, compassionate, and spirited—like Phoebe.

But not her.

Phoebe was his. He did not share or ever give up what was his.

No matter that Phoebe detested him. He would win her over in time.

He simply had to.

The impudent girl was meant for him, even though she refused to admit it yet.

He ran upstairs to look in on Lord Crawford, the new Earl of Crawford since the death of his elder brother, James, who had been Cormac's good friend. The two brothers could not have been any more different—James a soldier, fierce and brave, while Richard was little more than a scholarly mouse.

Relieved to find Lord Crawford sleeping, Cormac quietly stepped out of the young lord's bedchamber and gave a whispered instruction to the footman. "Do not disturb him. Let him sleep the entire day away if he chooses."

"Aye, m'lord."

Cormac did not bother to look in on his other guests, these friends of Lord Crawford he had mistakenly believed might offer him solace. One was an Oxford schoolmate by the name of Lord Harding who seemed nothing more than a grasping toady. No substance or character to the man. The two women brought along with him were nothing but elegant whores. Both unhappily married, one a countess and the other a viscountess, and each grasping for whatever they could claw from the distraught lord.

Their little party had indeed turned his home into a brothel, just as Phoebe had accused. But the blame lay squarely on himself for allowing it to happen.

And he was not proud of himself for partaking in the nightly pleasure games...well, until he had met Phoebe yesterday and his stupid heart would not permit him to touch another woman.

He found the lot of them tragically unhappy and a painful reminder of what he had become. That he was ready to make changes to his life did not absolve him of anything, for he had indulged in their stupid games and imbibed himself into a stupor right along with them—until Phoebe had stormed into his life like a little tempest.

Had it only been yesterday?

Until that moment, his life had been boring. Mindless. Empty.

The worst of it was, she was right about everything. None of his bad behavior offered him relief from his pain.

He did not know whether being good would either.

Figuring it out would have to wait for later, once he was rid of his houseguests. Unfortunately, he could not simply kick them out because of that deathbed promise to his dying friend. "Gad, James," he muttered to himself, "what did you have me do?"

Having them all here painfully revealed what all of them were, misfits who were in torment. How was he to fix others when he was nothing but an unhappy cripple himself?

Yet others saw something more in him.

James had asked him to take on the responsibility of guiding Richard as he stepped into the title of Earl of Crawford. For some odd reason, he'd trusted no one else.

How could Cormac refuse?

Now, the distressed young man was in deathly fear of his new responsibilities and could not stop bemoaning that James was dead.

Cormac had promised to give Richard a sense of purpose and

confidence to help him get over his dark feelings, and this was what he was determined to do.

However, all he had accomplished so far was to show Richard how wretchedly low they had all fallen.

He had to fix this, and would start tonight when the man woke up. His hours had gotten all mixed up, as had everything else since losing his brother.

Cormac walked out of the house and climbed into his waiting carriage.

Within ten minutes, the team was drawing up in front of Moonstone Cottage. His heart melted at the sight of his nieces in their pretty bonnets and lacy frocks. Phoebe had their pelisses in hand, for the weather would be cooler on the water and they needed a wrap to keep them warm.

She and Chloe climbed in and took the seats opposite his while his nieces sat beside him, the two of them so little, they hardly took up any space. Imogen climbed onto his lap. "Are you looking forward to our boat ride, my duckling?" he asked.

She nodded. "Ever so much."

Lord, how sweet she was, her big eyes so trusting and adoring of him.

He hoped circumstances would never turn his nieces into shallow, aimless women like the countess and viscountess presently under his roof. He shuddered to think of such a fate for these precious girls.

Perhaps Phoebe was not wrong in her insistence on a love match. He would demand no less for his nieces when they were old enough to marry.

As for himself, he could not be leg-shackled to someone he did not admire and respect. But once duly shackled, what then?

Even he, as thick a dolt as he was, understood some things had to change.

Within half an hour, they arrived in the village of Moonstone Landing proper. His driver slowed the team as they passed quaint cottages with their flowers in bloom and colorfully set out on display.

It was not long before they reached St. Peter's Church, the ancient stone structure within the vicarage of the same name where they were to drop off Chloe. The church was built atop a hill, and its spire was visible from almost everywhere one happened to be standing in the village. It was also easily seen by fishermen returning their boats to the harbor, serving as a landmark to guide them safely home.

After dropping Chloe off, he asked his driver to pull the carriage up in front of Mrs. Halsey's tea shop. From there, it was a short walk along the high street to the harbor. He hopped down and then lifted the girls out.

Phoebe was agile and hopped down on her own.

He took Imogen's hand while Phoebe held Ella's.

He ignored the warm feeling that came over him, for how could one be this content merely walking down a street? Perhaps it was the company he kept, for he certainly loved his nieces fiercely, and they gave his heart no end of pleasure.

Nor could he overlook the calm he felt having Phoebe by his side.

Not merely calm, but dare he say it...happiness?

He had forgotten what it felt like.

They passed the village green, and Phoebe paused a moment to study an inscribed stone monument placed prominently within the green.

"What is it?" he asked.

"A memorial in honor of our Moonstone Cottage ghost."

"Your cottage? Where my nieces are staying?"

"Yes, but he would never hurt them."

Cormac shrugged off her assurances, since he did not believe in ghosts.

"His name was Captain Brioc Taran Arundel, and he saved the children of this town. Of course, he was alive back then...unfortunately, this is how he died, saving all those precious lives."

Imogen and Ella were immediately interested.

"What happened?" Ella asked.

"Well, one day there was a village fair. There were games and treats and music. Everyone was having a lovely time. The local schoolmistress, Miss Gray, took her pupils for a boat ride around the harbor. Suddenly, it began to storm. Rain and thunder and strong winds came out of nowhere and pushed the boat onto the rocks."

"Oh no," Imogen said, her eyes growing wide.

"The rocks tore through the hull and the boat began to sink."

His nieces were rapt as they listened to the story, both of them now holding on to Phoebe's hands.

"Captain Arundel saw they were in distress. Despite the foul weather and impossibly roiling seas, he jumped into his own boat and sailed to the damaged ship to rescue all the children. He was able to save them all."

The girls cheered.

"Once he had them safely ashore, he went back for the stranded crewmen. But just as he rescued them and was about to climb back onto his boat, the mast cracked and hit him on the head. He tumbled into the water and was never found."

Imogen began to cry.

Phoebe knelt beside her and wrapped his sensitive niece in her arms. "But the story has a happy ending, little duckling. The captain's spirit remained very much alive, and he returned to his beloved Moonstone Cottage as a ghost. You see, it was his home, and he was happiest there. When my Aunt Henleigh bought the place, he fell deeply in love with her. From the moment he saw her, he knew she was the woman he would love eternally. He watched over her and protected her throughout her life. He waited for her, so they were happily reunited when she passed on years later. They were meant to meet and fall in love. Nothing, not time nor distance, could ever defeat their love."

"How do you know he loved your aunt?" Ella asked.

"Because my sister, Hen, and I met him, and he told us. He

was a very nice man—and quite handsome, too."

Imogen looked up at her. "As handsome as Uncle Cormac?"

Phoebe laughed. "Yes, as handsome as your uncle. Chloe was just a baby at the time and did not get to meet him, but I know he has spoken to her since. He watched over her as well. He protected all of us. We loved coming to visit our aunt, and now we own the cottage."

Imogen stared down at the harbor. "What if we drown in a storm?"

"We won't, duckling," Cormac said, giving her chin a little tweak. "The weather is beautiful, not a cloud in the sky. And you know I would save you. Didn't I promise always to protect you?"

She nodded.

"There, and I never break a promise."

"Will you promise to protect Phoebe, too?"

"Yes, Imogen. I will always protect Phoebe, too."

They walked on toward the harbor, but Cormac could not get the thought out of his mind. Uttering that promise to protect Phoebe had felt so right.

Yes, he wanted to protect this opinionated and vibrant beauty.

He wanted to be with her and hold her in his...hold her.

Damn it.

Why had he not met her when he was whole? Three years too late for that.

Phoebe knew all the local villagers, and they easily found a sturdy vessel to take them around. The captain was a young man by the name of Tobias Angel, a genial, talkative fellow who told them all about the town's history. "There are lots of us Angels living in Moonstone Landing," he said, winking at the girls. "My uncle is constable here. Another uncle manages the local bank. My cousin, Cara Angel, married a duke."

"My Uncle Cormac is a marquess," Ella said proudly.

"And that's why I am charging him double my usual fare," he said with a jovial laugh. "Only jesting, m'lord. We don't cheat anyone here."

Phoebe also thought the jest humorous. "Tobias, you really are a cheeky fellow. It is a good thing the marquess has a sense of humor. One of these days you are going to pull that jest on an important lord and he will impound your vessel."

"Nah, I can tell the nice ones from the humorless boors. You've got yourself a nice one here, Lady Phoebe."

"I can assure you, he isn't—" She must have realized the girls were listening to her every word, and she cleared her throat. "He isn't a humorless boor. Yes, he's quite nice. His nieces certainly think so."

Cormac grinned. "See how easy that was? Tossing that compliment didn't hurt at all, did it?"

"No, I suppose it didn't." She laughed softly, her eyes alight.

They spoke little for the rest of the ride, enjoying the breeze and the swell and dip of the boat upon the waves. Cormac held on to Imogen while Phoebe kept a firm grasp on Ella. Those girls were so little and light, they could easily be blown overboard with the slightest gust.

The girls enjoyed every moment of the ride, especially as they started to circle back to the dock. Dolphins surprised them by gliding alongside the vessel as it cut along the water toward the shore.

Ella and Imogen cheered and squealed in delight as the dolphins began to jump in and out of the waves beside them and put on a magnificent show just for the girls. "Twirl!" Ella shouted to them.

"Flap your tail!" Imogen cried.

The dolphins seemed to understand what the girls were saying, for they obliged, and then approached the boat to chatter at them in their own high-pitched squeals.

By the time the four of them walked off the boat, Ella and Imogen had the biggest smiles Cormac had ever seen on their little faces. Their cheeks were pink and their eyes sparkled with excitement.

Most beautiful of all was Phoebe, with her soft smile and sparkling eyes.

They walked over to Mrs. Halsey's tearoom, and the girls immediately began to chatter about their adventurous boat ride. The lovely proprietress listened patiently as they told her about the boat and the dolphins.

Imogen began to tell her about the ghost as well.

Cormac was not listening very closely until he heard Imogen say, "And Captain Arundel was on the boat with us and told me not to be scared."

He saw Phoebe turn pale. "Imogen, are you certain? Were you perhaps thinking of the story I told you earlier in the village square?"

Ella nodded. "We were thinking of it. That's why the captain told us not to be afraid, that you and Uncle Cormac would protect us. And if you couldn't, he would."

He saw tears well in Phoebe's eyes. "Girls, go to the cake display and tell Mrs. Halsey what you'd like for your treat."

While the girls were distracted, Cormac drew Phoebe aside. "Blessed saints. Now you have them seeing ghosts. Did you see him too?"

"No, but I wish I had. He isn't scary. We adored him growing up. I believe them when they say they saw him. I can hardly catch my breath knowing he was with us on the boat and standing beside your nieces. This is how he was with me and Hen when we were little. With Chloe, too."

She shook her head in dismay and looked up at him with imploring eyes. "If he is here, then it means my aunt is also still with us. They've been silent for so long, my sisters and I thought they had left us. I wish I could still see him and Aunt Henleigh. I hate to think I have closed myself off to dreams and childhood wonders as I've grown up."

"Phoebe, we cannot be certain... Indeed, how are such things even possible? To cross time and the barriers of space? You cannot believe in such nonsense."

She shook her head. "But I do. And it isn't nonsense. How could your nieces see him if he wasn't there? It does not upset me, nor should it trouble you. In truth, my heart is soaring now that I know they are still with us."

"Phoebe—"

"Don't you understand? This is what love is all about. Brioc and Aunt Hen. They must have felt I needed the reminder. He stayed with her. Protected her. Nothing could keep him away from her. This is the beauty in finding the one special person who is meant for you. The one who will understand you and love you as no one else can. Two hearts becoming one. Inseparable in life and in death."

"Blister it, Phoebe. Are you going to cry? Lord, don't you dare cry. Then the girls are going to start, too."

She cast him a tremulous smile. "I am not going to cry."

He took the handkerchief she had just removed from her reticule and used it to dab her eyes. "You have the prettiest eyes," he whispered. "Lord, you're a beautiful thing."

She laughed. "Careful, my lord. You may actually start to like me."

He handed her back the lacy handkerchief that had her initials embroidered on it. "I've offered to marry you. How can you think I do not like you? Are you feeling better?"

She nodded.

"Are you sure?" He gave her cheek a light caress.

"Yes...no... I don't know." She shook her head. "Yes, I will be fine." She took a deep breath and smiled. "There, I've fully regained my composure. I don't want to upset your nieces."

"Good." He cast her a rakish grin. "What shall I order for you? Ah, yes. I remember. You are to have a sour grapes ice."

She returned his grin with an impudent smile of her own. "And you are best described as an obnoxious crab apple. That's the ice I shall order for you, my lord."

He laughed. "Mrs. Halsey bakes a cake sinfully rich in chocolate, and she calls it a devil's cake. I think that devilishly rich chocolate better describes me."

"I think you have a tremendously overblown sense of your own importance. You are a crab apple and nothing more."

The bell rang over the shop door as more customers walked in.

Cormac escorted Phoebe to the table his nieces had chosen. Since Mrs. Halsey had no such flavors as sour grapes or crab apple, they settled on a more realistic order of tea and lemon cake, which was always a favorite.

He also ordered a slice of a decadent spice cake covered in melted chocolate that all of them devoured. His nieces, those two adorable angels, wound up with chocolate all over their smiling faces. Phoebe cleaned them off.

Cormac felt a tug to his heart, for the girls looked so happy.

Well, they were John's girls, and his brother always had the most pleasant disposition. Were he ever to have children of his own, they would be wild and uncontrollable brats, thoroughly arrogant and insufferable.

Although if Phoebe was their mother, they might turn out all right. She had more sense than he had, and a lovely, calm way about her.

Imogen fell asleep on his lap on the ride back to Moonstone Cottage. Ella was also drifting off by the time they arrived. Chloe had already returned from her church function, and she and Mrs. Hawke carried the girls upstairs for their naps.

Cormac now had a moment alone with Phoebe.

She smiled up at him. "I had a nice time today."

He nodded. "So did I."

She nibbled her luscious lower lip. "Then you are all right with your nieces having a ghostly encounter?"

"No, but there is little I can do about it. They do not seem troubled by it."

"They won't be. Hen and I weren't when it happened to us. Children are a lot more accepting of things out of the ordinary."

"I suppose."

"They are innocent and have not yet learned to close themselves off or be wary. This is the sad part of growing up, I think.

Learning not to trust, to always doubt. We lose so much of the magic life has to offer when we close ourselves off."

He arched an eyebrow. "Are you lecturing me?"

"No, I am merely making a general observation about what we lose when growing up. This applies to all of us, even me. I hate to think I have grown so cynical."

"You?" He laughed softly. "No, you still have that magic about you."

She shook her head "Hardly. But I think you might have gained a little of it back today. You were wonderful with the girls. I did not think you would last that long without turning surly."

"Is this all you think of me?"

"Well, I don't know you really. Considering the goings-on at your manor, I was sure the outing was going to be too tame for you and you would quickly grow bored."

"No, I am never bored with those little girls. I wasn't bored around you either."

She rolled her eyes. "Be still my heart. Another compliment from you. I did not bore you to tears. Please, you are making me blush with your flattery."

He put his hand to her cheek. "I did enjoy myself immensely. I like being around you. You make me forget who I am."

"No, I make you remember who you really are." She reached up on tiptoes and gave him a kiss on the cheek. "You were splendid today."

"Falling in love with me yet?"

She cast him an impudent smile. "It is early days yet, my lord. But I don't hate you nearly as much as I did yesterday."

"Ah, that's progress." He wanted to kiss that lovely pink mouth of hers but decided to save it for tonight. "I'll be back to tuck the girls into bed this evening."

He would tuck Phoebe into bed if she'd let him.

But that was not going to happen anytime soon. He did not wish to come on too strong with her.

In truth, he had enjoyed their time together, going about the village, taking the boat ride, and then stopping for ices. It was the sort of innocent day his brother might have with his wife and daughters. Yes, John always seemed to adore and thrive on these sort of days, these incredibly wholesome and innocent outings.

How different he and his brother were.

John found great pleasure in his family and was never one to behave like a hound, not even in his younger days, when anyone would have forgiven him for sowing his wild oats. Cormac had behaved badly enough for the two of them.

And yet he and John were as close as two brothers could be and loved each other fiercely.

Phoebe walked him to his carriage. "You needn't come by this evening. Do you not have your friends to entertain?"

"They will get along fine without me." Cormac shook his head and silently admonished himself for being an utter dolt. Perhaps his brother was onto something—this settling into family life and not looking at every beautiful woman as a potential conquest.

He had spent an entire day with Phoebe and not been bored at all. Not once. Even now, after hours of being together, he felt as though the time had passed too quickly. He could not get enough of her.

When had he ever felt this way about a woman?

Of course, this might all change tomorrow. But he did not think so.

"Very well," she said with a nod. "You are welcome to join us for supper, if you wish. I'll read to the girls for a little while afterward, then Chloe will get them off to bed."

"No, not for supper. But I will try to make it before Chloe takes the girls up to bed."

She smiled at him. "Ah, just in time to rile them so they will never fall asleep."

He held up his hand in mock surrender. "I shall be on my best behavior."

"No, just be yourself. This is what the girls adore about you. Besides, I shall enjoy railing at you if you get too far out of line."

He liked the sparkle of mirth in her eyes and her impudent

smile.

She was soft and sweet. Yet also a little lioness and not afraid to stand up to him. She matched wits with him and often bested him.

Some men might be offended by someone like Phoebe, but he relished her challenge. He was too often insufferable and arrogant. But that arrogance also too often turned to resentment, anger, and frustration over the loss of his arm.

This loss still haunted him and plagued him as though it were fresh.

Being around Phoebe eased him.

Not only was there a beautiful softness about her, but she regarded him as a whole being and gave no thought to the missing limb. Nor would she allow him to use that loss as an excuse for his misdeeds.

She blistered him whenever he took a step out of line, yet she had such a sweet way of doing it. Well, she did not mince words. But they were always delivered with caring and compassion. She wanted him to heal. She wanted him to find happiness.

He supposed that counted for something.

"Until later, then, Phoebe."

She nodded. "Until later, my lord."

He noticed she remained standing in the courtyard until his carriage rolled out of sight.

Well, he had been looking back at her, too. Did it signify anything beyond mere curiosity about each other?

He would also have to amend that "my lord" nonsense, for he wanted no formality between them. He was eager to hear his name on her lips.

*Cormac.* How soft and gentle it would tumble from her mouth. Lord, he ached to kiss her lovely mouth. He was going to kiss her again, of course. He hadn't changed his scoundrel nature all that much.

The question in his mind was, would she punch him again when he did?

# Chapter Six

C ORMAC WAS NOT surprised to find his guests already in their cups when he returned to his manor. They were drinking through his stock at an astonishingly fast pace. Not that he cared, for he could easily afford the expense of restocking his wine cellar. He looked around, concerned when he found only the countess, viscountess, and schoolmate toady in his parlor. "Where is Lord Crawford?"

The toady giggled. "Sulking in his room."

The two women approached him to rub themselves against him in blatant invitation. One cupped his privates. He drew her hand away. "Not now, countess."

*Not ever.*

As little as a few days ago, he would not have minded these advances and perhaps not hesitated to accept their invitations. For the life of him, he could not remember if he had taken either of them or where they had done the deed, assuming he had done anything in his state of inebriation. He vaguely recollected something occurring on the writing desk in a corner of the parlor. That could not have been comfortable. Perhaps it had been another desk in another room.

Gad, how had he fallen so low?

So had they all, he supposed.

He could not even remember the names of these ladies.

Oh, he knew one was Countess Rothmere and the other Viscountess Hopewell. But as for their given names? He simply could not recall. Had they bothered with names at all?

"Excuse me, ladies. I had better look in on Lord Crawford."

After all, that young lord was entirely the reason these wastrels were here.

The ladies did not bother to hide their disappointment.

"This is turning into a very dull week," the countess said, her expression prune-like.

"You are welcome to leave at any time." He glanced at the others. "That goes for all of you. As I mentioned last night, I will provide your transportation and inn accommodations back to London. My family has come to visit and forced my plans to change. As a gentleman, I allowed you to stay on for the week promised. But it seems pointless now, does it not? You do not care to be here, and I do not want you here. My carriage shall be ready if you wish to leave tomorrow."

The viscountess tipped her chin into the air and cast him a look of disdain. "You treat us as though we are disposable. Lady Seline warned us about you. Said you were bitter and deformed."

"How charming of her." He tried to ignore the verbal spear aimed straight at his heart.

But, to his dismay, these insults still managed to find their mark and wound him. It was quite irritating, really, to feel those wounds after all these years.

"If you are repulsed by my deformity, then pray, take your leave at once. I did not force you to take your clothes off or offer yourself up to me. It is a sad statement that we are all such low creatures. I have never denied what I am or tried to hide the loss of my arm from any of you."

Ah, Lady Seline.

What a gem of a woman.

She had called him deformed not only to her friends, but to his face.

Her look of revulsion was still vivid in his mind, the hurt still fresh, as was her look of triumph in knowing her aim had been true.

Dear, sweet Seline. She always knew how to dig her claws into a raw and open wound, make it fester and never heal. Losing her as a paramour had not hurt at all. In truth, it was a relief for him. That beauty and her brand of poison was the last thing he needed.

"Send my regards to Lady Seline when you next see her. The respect, or should I say the lack of respect, is mutual."

He walked out of the room, hoping they would not now destroy his parlor in their fit of pique.

"James, James," he muttered. "We've gone about healing your brother entirely wrong."

Part of the deathbed promise made to his friend was to help his brother lose his innocence. Richard, despite being of a manly age, did not have any experience with women and had come to Westgate Hall innocent as a lamb.

This week's house party was to serve a dual purpose. First, it was to make a man of Richard in the carnal sense, because that was the most easily accomplished. The second task was to turn Richard into a worthy earl and leader of men.

But Cormac had botched this deathbed promise from the start by giving Richard the choice of friends to bring with him to Westgate Hall.

Obviously, the man had chosen badly. How would he ever heal while in the company of friends like these? They were all users who held no particular fondness or loyalty toward him or each other.

Richard, now the new Earl of Crawford, was a sensitive man and thought these people actually cared for him when they were no more than bloodsucking leeches.

Cormac went upstairs to talk to him. Richard was in his early twenties. Cormac himself was only a few years older, not yet near thirty. But his years of battle and life experiences put them decades apart.

The drapes were drawn, leaving the room pitched in darkness as he entered. "Cormac, is that you?"

"Yes, I came to look in on you." It took a moment for his eyes to adjust to the somber lack of light.

"Well, I managed to dress. But that's about all I have accomplished today."

Cormac tried not to lose his patience.

His valet must have dressed Richard, who'd immediately afterward fallen atop his bed and remained stretched atop the counterpane, bemoaning his fate.

Cormac dismissed the footman attending him. "Come back in fifteen minutes."

"Yes, m'lord."

Now left alone with the fellow, Cormac crossed to the window and drew the drapes aside to allow afternoon sunlight to filter into the room. "Richard, have you noticed the view from your bedchamber. It is spectacular, is it not?"

"I hadn't noticed," Richard replied with a shrug. "Who cares about the view? My brother is dead, and I am to blame."

"Stop thinking like that. You did not force him to do anything he did not wish to do. The war is to blame, not you. If anyone is to be held responsible, it is Napoleon. He is the villain, not you."

"I wish I could believe that."

"You can and must. I know you are grieving, and I understand it is important for you to do so. James was a dear friend of mine. I miss him too. But I also know he had free will and made his own choices. He would be terribly overset to know you blamed yourself for something that was entirely his choice."

"He only chose to become a soldier because he knew I did not have it in me."

"He could have bought you out of your commission and paid someone else to take your place. But he did not do this because he wanted to join the battle." Cormac glanced at his arm. "Look at me, Richard. I made the same choice as your brother and lost an arm for it."

"But you survived."

"Hardly," he muttered, for Cormac would not call what he had been through over the last three years much of a survival. "You did your best to nurse him back to health, just as my brother did for me. His body simply was not strong enough to recover from his war wounds."

"Why are you absolving me of the responsibility? He was the heir. I was the one who should have gone to fight, not him."

He was tired of talking in circles with this pampered lord.

In truth, he wanted to haul him out of bed and beat sense into him.

Grow up.

*Punch.*

Stop whining.

*Punch.*

Face your responsibilities.

*Punch. Punch.*

That deserved two punches.

Instead, he remained by the window, resting a shoulder against the wall as they spoke. Phoebe would not approve of him smashing his fist into Richard's face. "The entire point is, both of you could have bought your way out. He chose not to. And who is to say he would have lived had he stayed in England? He could have fallen off his horse while fox hunting and broken his neck. You know he was always a reckless rider. Would it have been your fault then?"

Richard groaned. "My father was so angry when he enlisted. James did it because he was afraid I would die in my first battle. I'm sure he was right. He did it to protect me. And now, I am Earl of Crawford. How is this fair?"

"How is it fair that I lost my arm mere days *after* the war was over? I survived years with hardly a scratch and then one shot after truce had been declared sealed my fate. You dishonor your brother by shirking your duties as earl. He would not have made the sacrifice if he did not believe in you."

"You don't understand." Richard threw his arm over his eyes and began to cry. "I am a failure. I cannot handle the responsibility."

Cormac opened the window to allow in the sea breeze, for the room was too hot and beginning to feel like a tomb. "Have you even tried?"

"How can I? I am in mourning."

"The world does not stop because of it."

"Well, I want it to."

"There is not much you need to do, Richard," he said more gently, understanding his friend's pain and not wishing to make light of it. "Your brother was in no condition to actively participate in the management of the Crawford properties these past few years. This is why he hired good men to assist him. You do not need to do anything but meet with your estate managers from time to time and address whatever issues they raise."

Richard sat up and wiped the tears from his eyes. "How am I to do this when I have no clue what needs to be done?"

"This is why you employ them. They will tell you what requires attention and then handle the work themselves."

He appeared unmoved.

Cormac pressed on. "I assure you, if I can take on the role of marquess, you can handle being an earl. Whether the task is merely repair of a farmer's cottage or replenishing a field, purchasing more cattle or selling some off, your estate manager will know what needs to be done. All you have to do is give the nod and provide the requisite funds."

"Burness, you refuse to understand. I have no head for these things. I am a scholar."

"You are also a man of compassion and can do much good for England in your capacity as earl. I am the first to admit I am an insufferable arse, but even I know my duty and have taken it upon myself, along with other military men in the peerage, to do all we can for those who fought. It is in our power to make things better for those who cannot fight for themselves."

"All the more reason why I am not worthy to sit in the House of Lords. What can I do?"

"Lend your support to those causes in which you believe. You do not have to actively champion anything. Just support what is right and fair. What is so difficult about sitting in Parliament for an occasional vote? Then you can spend your days doing whatever you truly enjoy. Be no more than a figurehead, if that is all you can handle. You will not be the first earl nor the last to do so."

"I'll think about it."

The words sounded dismissive.

Indeed, Cormac knew they were, for he often said the same thing as a way of ending conversations. "Come to me if you ever need advice. I will help you. Richard, you cannot think only of yourself. Your sisters need you. The eldest will be ready to be introduced into Society next year. Do not leave her adrift."

"Now I am to be responsible for Arabella, too?" Richard covered his ears. "This is too much. You don't understand."

Cormac ran a hand through his hair in exasperation. Had he treated *his* brother this way? Worried him to death like this?

Despair could be a hideous and relentless feeling.

Yet even at his worst... Well, he could not recall just how bad he had been in those early days. He must have frightened his brother to no end. Even Cain, his best friend, had been worried to death about him.

Gad, looking at Lord Crawford only emphasized how miserable a burden he had been on his own family and friends.

It was a wonder any of them still talked to him. How on earth could they still love him?

Well, he would start with apologizing to Cain when he and Hen returned from Bath. As for his brother, he did not know how he would ever make it up to him. John was the best brother any man could have.

He stared at Lord Crawford, who had stretched back out on his bed and once more tossed an arm over his eyes.

Cormac had behaved the same way. Indeed, there were so many uncomfortable similarities between them.

Cormac had also defied his father's wishes and signed on for the army despite being heir. John should have been the one to serve, but he was a gentle soul and would not have survived the war years.

No, Cormac had done right in defying his father's wishes and signing on. John had done an able job of managing the Burness holdings in the meanwhile. It eased Cormac's soul to know John had made a good life for himself, a happy marriage, and had two beautiful daughters from it.

Unfortunately, the Crawford family was not faring as well.

He needed to turn this around, just as he had promised James.

Taking women to one's bed was not a mark of manhood. Yes, Richard was painfully naïve and needed to gain experience. James had insisted on it. But what Richard needed more than the knowledge of carnal pleasure was how to build character.

Cormac knew he would have to start from scratch, teach Richard to understand right from wrong. Teach him to hold to his principles and have the confidence to fight for them even if it made his life more difficult. Spur him to action instead of coddling his indolence. Teach him about the running of a thriving estate.

"Get out of bed, Richard. No more pitying yourself. You are coming with me." Cormac knew how to instill strength and purpose on a battlefield, but life in peacetime was a different matter. He hadn't won any awards for brilliance in that himself.

In truth, too often he felt lost and out of his depth.

Well, not in running an estate. But in every other aspect of his life, those that required sensitivity and feelings. He was terrible at that.

"Where are we going?" Richard asked as Cormac hauled him out of bed.

"Down to the beach. You need a dose of fresh air in your

lungs."

The man groaned. "No, I—"

"Utter another word and I shall knock you out cold and carry you down there myself."

This spurred the reluctant earl on. "All right. A short walk."

They marched downstairs.

Lord Harding and the two ladies were still in the parlor, no doubt bored and already drinking heavily. Cormac hurried Richard past them.

A glimpse in passing showed the toady, Lord Harding, leering at the countess while he ran his hands up the countess's legs. The viscountess was busy spilling wine onto Cormac's new carpet as she tried to pour the liquid from the bottle into her glass.

Melrose was at the front door, scowling at him.

"They are not my friends," Cormac muttered, as though this would absolve him of responsibility for their wretched behavior. He ordered the butler to shut the parlor doors and leave those lackwits to themselves.

"I need a drink," Richard said.

"It is the last thing you need." Cormac dragged him outdoors. "We're taking a walk. You can do what you wish afterward."

"I changed my mind. I hate walks."

"I don't care." He led the man toward the beach, keeping hold of him by the scruff of his neck as they descended the stairs, much like a dog would hold on to its pup. "Take a deep breath, Richard. Enjoy the sea air. Appreciate the bounty you have been given."

"I'd rather be tasting the viscountess," he muttered.

"I'm sure she'll be willing, assuming she hasn't passed out by the time we return," Cormac said with open disgust.

Yet was this not him as little as a few days ago?

Phoebe had been gentle when lacing into him the day they met. Was it only yesterday? It felt like forever ago.

Nor could he imagine being without her from this day forward.

Blessed saints!

What was he thinking?

He was *not* in love with Phoebe.

And even if he *were* in love with her, he knew the feeling would not last. When had he ever been constant in matters of love? For that matter, when had he ever been in love?

Never.

Not even close.

*Except for Phoebe.*

Well, he'd think about her later.

Right now, he had to find a way to get Richard to spill his feelings and somehow turn into a responsible man.

*Bollocks.*

Cormac really hated talking about feelings. Was he not always horrible in expressing his own?

They began to walk along the sand. The breeze had gentled and the sun was beginning to dip on the horizon. The sky took on the pink and gold hues of twilight. But it would be hours yet before the sun went down.

"Tell me what would make you happiest in life," Cormac said, thinking this might be something Phoebe would ask, because she cared about people. She understood warmth and compassion. He did not give a fig about most people.

Richard just gave him a blank stare.

Cormac tried again. "You said you were a scholar. What studies intrigue you most?"

They were alone on the beach with nothing but the sound of waves gently lapping the shore and the occasional caw of a gull to break the silence. One could even hear the soft hum of the wind as it surrounded them with its warmth.

"Richard?"

"It has always been my dream to go to Greece and study its ancient civilizations."

Cormac nodded. "Travel might do you good. I hear it is a beautiful land. The Minoan civilization particularly intrigued me.

How were they able to build the great palaces and temples they are known for at a time when most people were living in earthen huts and barely eking out their survival? They kept written records in a time when only a select few could read and write, and their craftsmen were true artisans, creating wonders beyond anyone's imagination."

"You surprise me, Burness. I did not take you for a scholar."

He smiled. "I enjoyed my studies."

"Yet you always struck me as a man of action."

"Yes, often stupid actions. My brother is the one with the level head. But some learning sank into that space between my ears. These ancient societies fascinated me as well. We think of ourselves as so advanced, but as we uncover ruins of the past, we see how great their knowledge was, how much they knew of the planets, mathematics, science, their knowledge of our earthly metals, the ability to forge them, to create works of lasting beauty. Pottery, jewelry."

"Weapons."

"Yes, this seems to be the nature of man. We are always finding reasons to fight. This is our greatest failing. Along with our desire to learn and advance, we are also burdened with sins. Greed, envy, a need to control and conquer. Perhaps one day we shall understand what makes men do the things they do. How do we reconcile these two parts of us? Why is it that the very intelligence that enables us to do great things also makes us cruel, murderous beasts?"

Richard nodded. "I don't know that we shall ever have an answer. Perhaps we shall discover more clues to ourselves as we unearth these ancient civilizations. I would like to visit Rome, Florence, and Venice. Perhaps journey to Egypt and Mesopotamia."

"Then do it. You have the means. You have the intellect to advance our knowledge. Talk to members of the British Museum. I'm sure there are expeditions they would love to have you fund. More important, that they would love to have you join as part of their research team."

"I always dreamed of doing exactly this. Discovering new civilizations, uncovering treasures that will change our understanding of the past and possibly provide guidance for our future. Do you think my brother would be proud of this?"

Cormac nodded. "I know he would be. Extremely proud."

Richard sighed. "I will think about it."

They had walked up and down Cormac's short strip of beach and were now back at the steps. "I have some books in my library that might interest you. It is far from complete, since I've only owned this house about a month. But I'm sure you will find one or two of interest. I will entirely stock the bookshelves eventually. There is much yet to do to fix up this house."

"I'll browse the bookshelves later…maybe." Richard laughed. "I don't have much of a head for reading at the moment. I'm in a sorry state and just want mindless sex with insincere lady friends who will flatter me shamelessly and tell me any lie I wish to hear. For this same reason, I keep Lord Harding on as a companion. I need someone to tell me I am droll and witty, and pretend to be my friend."

"You don't need any of them, Richard. I have already suggested they leave. I can toss them out at any time."

"No, I still want them about. Do you mind? These women are like sex-starved ferrets, and I am not all that adept yet. As for Harding…he is a witty enough companion. I worry about him. He would be homeless and starving on the streets if not for me. I know he is using me, but how else is he to survive? I know the difference between friends like him and worthy friends such as you."

"I am hardly worthy, but I hope to be someday," Cormac replied. "It took me years to work through my own despair, although I think I was more angry than ever despairing. But anguish is anguish, no matter what form it takes. Move at your own pace. Just keep moving forward, for this is what matters most. Forgive yourself for what you see as failings in yourself.

None of us is perfect. Do not judge yourself too harshly."

Richard stared at him. "What happened to you? In truth, you do not appear to be the same man you were even a few days ago."

"You noticed? Well, my nieces are here and serve as a reminder that there are people I treasure who rely on me. Perhaps this is what helps us heal. Knowing we are needed and important to some people in the world. Your sisters are in need of you. Do you not care for them? How can you let them down?"

"I'll take it under consideration," Richard said as they climbed the steps to return to Westgate Hall. "I do love my sisters, and they love me."

"Then you are a fortunate man, for few people will love you as dearly as your own family. And the eldest is now ready to enter the Marriage Mart. She needs you to protect her from all the scoundrels out there."

"Yes, I'll have to find all of them suitable husbands. Well, I suppose I could do with the distraction of marrying them off. You wouldn't be interested in one of my sisters, would you?"

"No." Cormac was about to add that his heart was already taken.

*Blessed saints.*

Richard noticed his expression and laughed. It was the first hearty laugh Cormac had heard out of the man.

"Perhaps I ought to find someone reliable for myself, too. Don't you think so, Burness? Surely there is a young lady out there who is similarly inclined and would enjoy traveling with me." He glanced up at Westgate Hall, the elegant manor that stood atop the red stone cliff. "Not like those lady friends. They serve quite a different purpose."

Cormac nodded. "You will find yourself bored with them soon."

"Perhaps. But I like having sex with them. They are quite...liberated in the bedchamber. However, I think they have had their fill of me. They found me amusing, at first. A young man, painfully innocent and naïve. I must have been quite a curiosity to them. Now, the curiosity has faded and they find me rather tepid. They much prefer you."

Cormac winced. "I am not interested. They'll return to London and soon find others to amuse them. This is what happens after these meaningless encounters. All is quickly forgotten by those involved."

"I expect so, although I don't think women forget *you* all that soon. They'll forget me for certain. I am not memorable."

"It doesn't matter. They were never meant to be permanent relations for you."

They slowed their pace toward the manor house. Richard was still eager to talk now that Cormac had finally gotten through to him. Cormac suggested taking a turn in the garden.

"Yes, that is a good idea." They ambled toward the flowerbeds. Richard was now pensive. "Do you think I will ever find a young lady who will love me?"

"Yes, but not among this fast *ton* set. You are more likely to find her in the museum halls or at a lecture. This is where you'll find the one who shares your love of history and travel. I'm sure there are several lovely ladies who will catch your eye."

"I only need one," he muttered. "It would be nice to travel together and perhaps keep a journal of the places we visit. I don't imagine we would ever grow bored with each other if we started out with so much in common. I wonder if there are any societies or lectures here in Moonstone Landing?"

"I don't know. It is a lovely village but still quite provincial. You will not find the intellectual stimulation you would find in London."

"Even so, I might remain here a little while longer." Richard clasped his hands behind his back as they continued to walk along the rows of flowerbeds. "I'd like to explore the area. Another week should not make much of a difference to my sisters or estate managers."

"Richard, my nieces are here and I must bring them to Westgate Hall soon. They cannot remain with my neighbors, lovely as those ladies are. I cannot have you or your friends—"

"Oh, our week here is almost at an end. Harding and the ladies will be gone within a few days, I assure you. I will tell them in no uncertain terms they must leave, if they think to linger."

"And you?"

"Please, Burness. Let me stay another week. Did you not promise my brother?"

Cormac sighed. "Very well, but I must have your word you will be on your best behavior. My nieces are precious to me, and I will flay you alive if you do anything to overset them."

"I never would. How old are they?"

"Six and eight."

"Ah, they are very young. I shall guard my language around them."

"No drinking, either."

Richard grinned. "All right. Not a drop."

He seemed sincere enough about it. "I cannot spend much time with you. My nieces are little and require my full attention."

"I never would have thought it of you. Perhaps you will make a fine father someday."

Cormac snorted.

"Then we are agreed, Harding and the ladies stay on for two or three more days. I will make certain they leave when their time is up. As for me, I stay on and busy myself exploring the area. A few extra days, perhaps a week at most, and then I will be off to join these friends in London."

Cormac nodded.

"You have no idea how grateful I am to you for all your guidance. You understand me as no one else does. Well, my brother did. But now, he is gone and left me in charge of the Crawford holdings. This still terrifies me, but perhaps a little less so now. He knew you were the right man to help me. I would never repay your kindness by upsetting your nieces."

Cormac was not so certain he wanted to bring them to Westgate Hall while Richard was still here.

He would discuss it with Phoebe later.

Richard seemed well pleased. "I think I shall head to the parlor now to indulge in some bad behavior while I have the chance. You don't mind, do you?"

"I am not your nanny. Do as you wish." After all, it was Richard who'd brought these ladies and Lord Harding here. "Try not to overindulge. Your friends are wastrels, but you are not."

Cormac was not pleased about Richard remaining for another week, but how could he shirk a deathbed promise to the earl's brother?

They'd had one good talk this afternoon, but more had to be done before Richard was truly on the road to recovery. The young earl would get there in time. Cormac had to think of ways to inspire him, give him enough confidence not to fall apart once he returned to London.

He was not convinced the girls should come to him yet.

First, because of Richard.

Second, if the girls stayed with Phoebe, it would give him reasons to see her every day. Phoebe sincerely liked his nieces and would not mind having them with her for a little while longer.

But he would not presume to know her mind. If she wished him to take his nieces, then he would reconsider what to do about Richard.

As the clock chimed the seven o'clock hour, he washed and dressed, eager to ride over to Moonstone Cottage and talk to Phoebe. It would not take him long to see his nieces and kiss them goodnight...kiss Phoebe, too.

Lord, he ached to kiss her.

He had said he would.

Not that she believed him.

After seeing them, he would return to Westgate Hall in time for a late supper with his guests. Of course, this assumed they were not already passed out in their drunken stupor.

Richard had returned to the parlor to join them. Was the

young lord truly ready to shake off these bad habits? It would be nice to have another conversation with him about these ancient civilizations.

Melrose, as always, was at his post by the front door and frowning at him.

"I am off to see my nieces. I won't be gone long. Send word at once if things get out of hand."

"They won't, my lord. Do you not hear the snores? Your friends are sleeping off the vats of wine they've steeped themselves in."

"They are not my friends."

Melrose ignored him. "All save Lord Crawford. He is no longer in the parlor."

"Where is he?"

"In your library reading a book."

"Really? He's actually reading?" He shook his head, knowing he ought not appear so incredulous. After all, this was exactly what he and Richard had been discussing.

This was a good sign, was it not?

"Look in on him from time to time, Melrose. He is still grieving, and I want to be sure he is all right."

"Of course, my lord." The butler nodded solemnly. "I will keep vigilant watch."

"Good man. I won't be gone long." Cormac did not know why he felt so on edge about leaving his guests tonight, especially Richard.

He ordered his horse saddled, and then poked his head in the library to bid Richard farewell. He was seated in one of the comfortable, overstuffed chairs positioned by the window, book in one hand and glass of wine in the other. "Burness," he said with a smile. "I've found this fascinating tome on the Phoenicians on your shelves. I had no idea you were such a discerning collector. This is quite a scholarly work. Have you read it?"

Cormac nodded. "I've read every book in this library."

"I'm impressed."

"Don't be. I am still an arse."

Richard chuckled. "We all have our strengths and weaknesses. Things we love to do and those we do merely out of duty."

"Enjoy your evening."

"Thank you, Burness. Enjoy your nieces. I really appreciate all you are doing for me. It is very kind of your neighbor as well. It is not my place to ride over with you now, but I would like to extend my appreciation to them. Would it be forward of me to ride over with you tomorrow?"

"We'll see. She may have other plans."

"She? I did not realize there was one in particular."

"There isn't."

*Outright lie.*

He did not like the idea of Richard meeting Phoebe.

It was ridiculous to be jealous of a pup like him, but what if Phoebe liked him? Was she not just the sort of woman a man like Richard ought to marry?

*No.* Phoebe was his. Richard would have to look elsewhere for his angel.

He rode to Moonstone Landing, his big Friesian eating up the ground beneath his hooves as Cormac gave him his lead. He was angry, and the horse sensed it.

But why should he be angry?

Just because Richard wanted to meet Phoebe?

He was being an arse again.

Indeed, he had to start courting Phoebe seriously.

But how did one go about such a thing?

He had proposed to Phoebe, but the offer of marriage had hardly been gracious.

No, what he had actually proposed to her was a marriage of convenience, the convenience purely for himself. He had made no vow to be faithful to her. Nor had he vowed to love and cherish her always.

All he had proposed was a marriage with no strings to bind him if he got bored and chose to wander.

Indeed, he was the biggest fool in all of England.

Why would Phoebe ever accept him on those terms?

# Chapter Seven

P HOEBE WAS READING a story to his nieces when Cormac arrived at Moonstone Cottage. They were in the parlor, the girls seated on the sofa while Phoebe was in a chair beside them with a book in hand. All three of them were rapt in the story he recognized as one of the Arthurian legends. "And then the wizard Merlin said to young King Arthur—"

She looked up and noticed him. "Lord Burness."

The girls immediately began quacking in greeting. He laughed and quacked back.

Lord, they had to stop this silliness. He could only imagine the uproar if Ella quacked at him during her Society debut.

"I'm glad I am not too late." He settled on the sofa beside his nieces. Imogen immediately climbed onto his lap and nestled against his chest.

Phoebe cast him a warm smile. "I'm almost done with the story."

Yes, she liked the way he was around his nieces. "Take your time. I enjoy the sound of your voice."

She blushed.

The girls giggled.

"Uncle Cormac likes you," Imogen whispered to her, apparently not grasping the concept that he was not supposed to be able to hear her.

"Yes, well...um...shall we continue with the tale?" Phoebe buried her face in the book and resumed reading.

When she was done, Cormac carried Imogen up to the bed-chamber the girls were using. He kept his pace slow on the stairs, since Ella had taken hold of his empty jacket sleeve while she walked up the steps beside him.

Yes, that empty sleeve.

That missing part of him.

When they reached the landing, Phoebe darted ahead and led the way. "This used to be my bedchamber."

He looked around and gave a nod of approval. "I'm sorry to have put you out."

"No, not at all. After Hen married, I moved into hers, since it is the largest and the view from its small balcony is magnificent. Captain Arundel designed this house and all its rooms to provide views of the sea from almost every one of them. Aunt Henleigh took over his bedchamber when she acquired the house."

"Then your sister took it over. You mentioned it to me the other day."

"Yes, it was her right, since she was eldest. And now me. We haven't changed a thing since Captain Arundel's day. It has a nautical feel, not feminine at all. But none of us ever wished to move his belongings. It simply did not feel right for us to change a thing about the room."

"Now I am curious."

"You wish to see it?"

He nodded. "May I? I'll merely poke my head in to have a glimpse."

"I don't mind. Have a good look, especially the view from the balcony. It is not to be missed. I'll help the girls into their nightclothes and tuck them into bed while you do."

He had not expected to be admitted into Phoebe's bedchamber and was not about to pass up the opportunity. Of course, it would have been nicer if she was in here with him and he was undressing her. But that was just him thinking with his privates and not with his head.

Phoebe was not going to be won over by his sexual prowess. She needed him to be a real man, one who would love and protect her, make a life with her.

He stepped into her bedchamber and looked around. It was as she had said, nautical and masculine, especially that big bed with its ocean-blue damask canopy and the dark wood headboard and footboard. Yet the room also had a feminine feel because she occupied it now. He caught the scent of lavender in the air...her scent.

He noticed her hairbrush and pretty butterfly hair clips atop the bureau drawer.

Although he should not have done so, he peeked inside her wardrobe.

She was a slender thing, and her gowns all looked so delicate. Most were of practical fabrics, muslin, wool, linen, but she also had her finer silks. He noticed her chemises neatly folded, and ran a finger across one of the sheer bodices, wishing very much to do the same with her in it.

This would not put him in her good graces.

He sighed, closed the wardrobe, and stepped onto the balcony. Indeed, one had a spectacular view of her garden and beyond to the glistening sea, especially on a cloudless day like this.

Phoebe's eyes were the beautiful aquamarine color of the sea and sparkled whenever she was pleased with him, which was not all that often yet.

As for the view, it was indeed breathtaking. She had not been exaggerating.

He must have been lost in his thoughts and staring at the water longer than he realized, for the next thing he knew, Phoebe was at his side and clearing her throat to gain his attention.

He turned to her.

She smiled up at him. "I never tire of watching the play of sunlight upon the water or the waves breaking upon the rocks. Every once in a while, dolphins enter our cove. The sunsets are so beautiful, no matter the season of the year. Your nieces are tucked in bed and awaiting a goodnight kiss from you."

He slipped his arm around her waist as they stood beside each other. "I promised you a kiss as well."

"I do not recall asking you for such a promise." She arched an eyebrow. "I think you have taken too many kisses from me. How about you try something different?"

"What do you mean?"

"Why don't you try asking if you may kiss me? Instead of *taking* from me, why don't you *give* me the chance to consent?"

He laughed lightly. "That would require me to be patient and considerate."

The comment put a sparkle of amusement in her eyes.

He loved that exquisite sparkle.

"Oh dear. What a chore that must be for you."

"Quite onerous." He grinned. "Very well, I'll give your suggestion a try. For you, Phoebe. Only for you. I'll do it because you ask it of me. Is that not a gallant gesture?"

"Yes, actually, it is. Try not to look so pained. One would think the effort was worse than having a tooth extracted." Her eyes were still twinkling, so he knew she was enjoying their exchange. "Also, do not make too much of your grand gesture. After all, it is only common courtesy, something quite foreign to you, I expect. I would hardly call it a noble feat. However, you might be pleasantly surprised by the results."

Patience and consideration were traits quite new to him.

However, Phoebe made his sacrifice more palatable.

Of course, it was not really a sacrifice. As she said, she was only asking for good manners from him.

He truly wanted to be a better man for her. The feeling was odd, but did not feel like a burden at all.

"Phoebe, I need to talk to you after I kiss the girls and bid them goodnight."

"Something serious? Is this why you are suddenly frowning?"

He nodded. "Something has come up, and my guests will not

be leaving immediately."

"I see."

"No, it is not what you are thinking. It has nothing to do with my debauched or depraved ways. I've told you, I have done none of that since I met you."

She cast him a dubious look. "All right. Let's go back to the girls, and then we can take a walk while you tell me the situation."

They returned to his nieces, and he took several minutes with each, listening to their thoughts about this day they had spent together and assuring them they would see him tomorrow as well. "You ducklings are more important to me than anything in the world."

They hugged him in turn, then closed their eyes and fell asleep with smiles on their innocent faces.

"They love you so much," Phoebe remarked as they returned downstairs and stepped outside to walk down to the beach. The sun set quite late at this time of year, so they had another hour or more before twilight was upon them.

Plenty of time for the two of them to talk.

They made their way down the sturdy wood steps and were soon on the beach. He offered his arm as they walked along the sand and was pleased when she did not hesitate to take it. "I think it is time I explained to you who those people are and why I need to ask another favor of you."

She looked up at him. "Go on."

"The one guest *I* invited is Lord Richard Crawford, the new Earl of Crawford. His elder brother, James, was earl and one of my closest friends. When Napoleon began taking over Europe, James joined my regiment and fought alongside me for years. He was a good man, and at that time a viscount, since his father was frail but still alive. Of course, as eldest son and heir, he was not expected to serve in the army."

"But neither were you. And yet you did."

He nodded. "James and I were alike in this regard. We each

had younger brothers who were gentle souls and scholars. This was my dread, that my brother, John, should go off to war and never return. He's the father of my nieces. Quite intelligent and capable, but not a fighter. Some men simply are not meant to be on a battlefield. He would not have survived a month were he sent over to the Continent. James felt the same about his brother, Richard."

Phoebe listened intently. "You said Richard is the only one you invited. Yet I saw others...a little too much of those others."

He groaned, recalling the state of undress of the ladies Richard had brought along with him. "Yes, I am getting to that. When the old Earl of Crawford died, James returned home to assume the title. But he returned plagued with injuries that never healed properly. He struggled for years, but did a good job of managing the Crawford holdings until he died last month."

She lightly placed her hand on his. "I'm so sorry."

He nodded, liking her brief, soft touch. "Before he died, he sent for me. I hurried to his bedside because I knew at that point there was little time left. It was then he made me promise to look after his brother, help him settle in as the new earl. He also asked me to... Those women you saw..." He shook his head and sighed. "I don't know any delicate way to put it. The new earl had no experience with women, so James begged me to invite a few along for the week."

"I see."

"They were for him, not for me. In truth, I do not know them very well. Richard and his companion, Lord Harding, are the ones who invited them."

Although he had participated. This was what he had been doing the several nights before he and Phoebe met, encouraging the young lord to explore the opposite sex. He had been satisfying his own needs with those ladies as well.

Meaningless.

Not all that satisfying.

But he had been drinking and debauching along with everyone else.

He wasn't proud of it now, wished he had behaved differently. But until Phoebe had come along, he was on a path of self-destruction and hellbent on crashing fast.

Phoebe was now frowning at him. "Those women might have been brought here for him, but will you deny your own participation in...whatever took place?"

"I do not deny it, nor will I apologize for what took place before meeting you. But I haven't been near them since I set eyes on you."

She laughed. "That was only yesterday."

"I know." He ran a hand roughly through his hair. "It feels as though I have known you far longer. You have been on my mind ever since Cain and Hen mentioned you to me shortly after I lost my arm."

"But that was three years ago."

He nodded. "Why do you think I purchased Squire Westgate's manor? And here is a hint...I did not purchase it to be closer to Cain or to take in the healthier air in Moonstone Landing."

She eyed him dubiously. "Are you suggesting you acquired it to be closer to me?"

"Yes, Phoebe."

"That is ridiculous."

"No, it isn't. You preyed on my thoughts. *Phoebe*. The little lioness. It was time I did something about you."

"So you turn up drunk on my doorstep and forget your nieces were coming to stay the month with you? That was a very good start."

He sighed. "Stop kicking my arse. I did not say I was perfect. I know I am far from it. But I was so tired of being angry at the world, of hating myself, and being a constant trial to my brother. Cain wrote to me about how much he enjoyed his life in Moonstone Landing and was constantly urging me to get out of London and move here. He would also tell me what you were doing."

She regarded him with confusion. "Why would he mention me?"

"Because I always asked about you." He settled on the sand and looked out across the sea. "In those dark hours, my darkest indeed, I would write to him. *Tell me about Phoebe. How is she? How is my lioness?*"

She settled beside him, tucking her legs under her shapely bottom. "I never knew."

"You weren't meant to. I purchased the house, had it furnished, and was about to start my new life. My *life*, because I was desperate to find a reason to go on living. Not that I meant to do myself in. I had no intention of it. I simply abhorred the path my life was taking and knew changes had to be made."

She said nothing, merely continued to listen.

"I know it was not fair to place this burden on you, for you owed me nothing. You had not ever met me until that disastrous encounter yesterday, and here I was deciding you were the only one who could save me."

He shook his head and paused a moment.

Waves lapped closer, but the tide was only now starting to come in. They could sit together a while longer before having to move back. "I had acquired Westgate Hall and was preparing to come out here when my friend died. I had given him my word to protect his brother, to make a man of him. Not only with women, although obviously... Well, that was easily attended to. But I had to keep my oath."

He glanced at her and continued. "How does one instill character in someone with a fragile heart? Having given James this deathbed promise, I invited his grieving brother along with me for this first week."

"Along with those ladies."

"Yes, those ladies that he, not I, invited. In truth, I was not keen on the idea of having them along, but he was so wretched and would not stop crying. His friend, Lord Harding, had already made plans to bring them."

"To *console* your grieving friend," she said dryly.

"Do not look upon me with disapproval, Phoebe. He needed... Well, it was part of the reason he felt so inadequate, not only in his relations with women but also in taking on his responsibilities as earl. As for the women, they are desperately unhappy creatures. Having felt my own pain and handled it badly, I am not one to judge them."

He leaned back in the sand, propping himself up by resting his weight on his one elbow. "Sometimes physical pain is an easier thing to handle. How does a broken heart or shattered soul ever heal? I sought relief in meaningless relations with the wrong sort of women. The partners were irrelevant. Perhaps it would have been wiser merely to drink myself into oblivion, but I never wanted my nieces to see me falling so low."

Phoebe scooted back as a wave washed close to their boots. "Move back with me."

He did so, once more settling beside her.

Life felt so much calmer when he was beside her, even though she obviously disapproved of his ways and was not shy about telling him so. He could not explain this feeling of peace that fell over him whenever he was with her. "I've probably botched the entire week. Lord Harding is a former schoolmate of the earl's and an utter leech. These ladies he brought along, despite their titles, have no scruples whatsoever."

He sighed. "I do not pretend to be a saint. Nor do I need you telling me how depraved we all are or how badly I have planned this week. My point in talking to you is that I will soon be sending these guests away. However, Richard has asked to remain with me another week. I think we had a bit of a breakthrough today, but he is not yet steady on his feet and could do with more time. I am torn, Phoebe."

She nodded. "Between duty to him and duty to your nieces."

"Yes, precisely. I will not have him in the same house as those girls. I cannot be sure he is recovered and do not want them near if he happens to have another breakdown."

"So you are asking me if they may stay here a little while longer?"

"Yes." He had been gazing out over the water and now turned to face her. The wind had picked up and was blowing a few wisps of her curls out of their pins and onto her sun-kissed cheeks.

She looked so lovely.

"But if it is too much of an imposition, I will understand."

"Your nieces are sweet and entirely too well behaved," she said with a lilting laugh. "Chloe and I don't mind having them with us at all."

"I will still come by every day to see them. I'll take them out and spend as much time with them as you wish me to spend. Both obligations fell on me at once, and…" He raked a hand through his hair once more in frustration. "Just say the word and I will take my nieces. They are most important. I'll figure out what to do with Richard."

"It isn't necessary. Chloe and I are fine with the arrangement. Do you wish us to invite your friend to—"

"No. I don't want him around any of you until I am certain he is truly on the mend. He completely fell apart when his brother died. Cried for days. Ignored his sisters and everyone else who tried to console him. I suppose his brother knew this would happen, and this is why he turned to me for help. For whatever reason, the Crawford family respects me."

"Well, you are not all that bad. They obviously saw some good in you."

He grunted in disgust. "I have done nothing to earn it."

"You are being too hard on yourself."

He caressed her cheek. "No, Phoebe. I've indulged myself, wallowed in self-pity, and behaved as I have all my life—like an arrogant arse."

"Perhaps in changing him for the better, you are teaching yourself to do the same. But you cannot expect everyone to forget what you were and suddenly adore you."

"I am still going to be arrogant and difficult, for that is too much in my nature. But I will also be kinder to those I love. Appreciate them more. Do my best to be more considerate of others in general. Most of all, I want to be a better man for you."

She paled, and her lips trembled. "Do not say this. You cannot say you are doing it for me."

"But why not? I am here because of you."

"Do not play with my affections or put that burden on me. It is not up to me whether you succeed or fail. Nor do I want to be just another bed partner for you, whether within or without the bounds of marriage. Those vows of marriage still mean nothing to you. But they mean everything to me. I am not like those ladies, the sort who can move on and forget you after you seduce me. I will not be a part of your game."

"You know this is not what I am suggesting. I want to marry you…a true marriage."

"And what is your definition of a true marriage?" She emitted a ragged breath. "You hardly know me. More to the point, I don't know you, and the little I have seen… I have no idea what to make of you."

"I'll accept that. I know your first impression of me was dreadful." He was trying to agree with her and accept responsibility for his actions, but this seemed to irritate her more.

He wanted to make things right, yet it all seemed to be coming out wrong, and he had no idea why until she frowned at him and said, "You stole my first kiss. You took that dream away from me, and I can never have it back."

*Bollocks.*

Yes, he had done that.

But it was just one kiss, and he intended to marry her, so what was so awful about it? "Phoebe, that is not fair. I just poured out my heart to you."

"And this makes everything all right?"

"Is it not a start?"

"Let us put an end to this conversation. I will keep your nieces. Visit them whenever you wish."

She rose and turned to run back to her cottage, but he rose along with her and caught hold of her wrist to draw her back to his side. "I cannot undo that first kiss."

"Because it never occurred to you that it might be something special to me, that—"

"Have I not just spent that last half-hour telling you how I feel and how sorry I am for hurting my loved ones? And as charming and well bred as you are, you are no docile flower. What is this really about? Are you afraid of me?"

"No, of course not."

"I don't mean in the physical sense, because you know I will never hurt you in this way. Are you afraid I will break your heart?"

"I won't let you do this to me."

"Nor do I ever wish to hurt you in this way. I intend to court you properly."

"Don't say that. You do not know how to do anything properly."

"Then I shall court you improperly. My point is, I intend to marry you and be a good husband to you."

"Do not tell me this."

"I need you, Phoebe. Probably more than you shall ever need me. Let me kiss you now, a proper kiss. If you hate it, I will never touch you again. You have my oath on it."

He was surprised by the pain he saw in her expression.

Well, this was what he seemed to do best. Cause pain. Upset his loved ones.

"I do not want your kiss."

He sighed again. "Are you that afraid of me? Because I have worked my way so deeply into your heart already?"

"No, not in the least." Her eyes began to tear. "All right. Kiss me again. I would rather have the memory of a sober kiss. I doubt I shall be kissing anyone else anytime soon. Nor do I intend to kiss you ever again after this."

"Duly noted. If you hate it, I shall never kiss you again. I gave you my oath and shall keep to it." Of course, she was not going to hate it. He had not earned his wicked reputation by being inept at seducing women. He was ridiculously good at it. However, if she wished to wipe the slate clean and start over, he was all for it. He wanted her to remember the softness and sincerity of this kiss.

He wanted her to think of him as a better man.

As for never again...that was not going to happen. He was going to kiss her until her toes curled. He wanted to make a life with her. Why could she not see this?

"Close your eyes, love."

Her eyelids fluttered closed. "I am not your love."

"Yes, you are. Put your hands on my shoulders."

Heat tore through him as she rested her delicate hands as he instructed.

He slipped his arm around her waist and bent his head to hers.

His lips met hers, and suddenly the world around him turned to magic. Of course, Phoebe was the precious source of this beautiful magic.

The world felt right whenever he was beside her.

Waves swept to the shore, *whooshing* across the sand.

The wind surrounded them in warmth.

His heart soared as he deepened the kiss, pressing his mouth to her soft, pliable lips. She tasted sweet as honey, and her body felt so soft against his.

Oh, how he wished he had two arms to hold her. How he wished to swallow her in his embrace.

But he had only the one, and it was all he could ever give her. He could not caress her cheek or run his fingers through her silken hair when holding her. Those were only possible in his dreams.

She moaned and surrendered to the plunder of his lips.

He wanted to devour this sweet girl.

In time, he would win her over.

He had to.

How long would it take for her to trust him? This was the greatest problem, getting her to trust him. He knew he could make Phoebe fall in love with him, for she was already strongly attracted to him—and not liking it one bit.

Perhaps she loved him.

Such things happened. Love at first sight.

He would not be surprised, for Phoebe was opinionated and quick to know what she wanted. How dismaying it must have been for her to realize *he* was going to be the man she loved.

Well, perhaps the man that she might love in time. He did not want to get ahead of himself in wooing Phoebe.

Let her deny her feelings for him all she wished, but she revealed everything in the way she clung to him and melted into his body. Desire was there—sweet, innocent, and heartfelt...only trust was lacking.

The kiss lasted longer than he had intended because he simply could not draw his lips off hers. She had given him a taste of magic, and he wanted to grab every possible moment, wanted to hold her against him and savor every precious sensation because she felt so soft and right.

Finally, he ended the kiss and stared at her for a long moment, wishing he could caress her cheek. But that would mean releasing her, and he was not nearly ready to let go of her. Would he ever be ready? "I love you, Phoebe."

She gasped and stared at him.

*Bollocks.*

Did he really just say that to her?

What a stupid thing to say.

And yet he had no intention of taking it back.

"Do not remark on it," he said, still kicking himself for allowing the thought to slip out. "I do not need a response from you and do not expect you to feel the same. Not yet, anyway. I know it is too soon for you to trust this feeling between us. It is new to me as well, this realization that someone is more important to me than my own arrogant hide."

He could feel the rampant beat of her heart against his chest. See the utter confusion in her gorgeous eyes.

"I know you want to punch me in the nose."

She nodded.

"Go ahead and do it."

"No, I don't want to hurt you."

Well, that was an improvement over last time. "What did you think of the kiss?"

His little lioness suddenly looked more like a wounded dove as she said, "How do you think I felt?"

"I made you tingle, didn't I?" He arched an eyebrow, warning her not to protest. "I know how to kiss women, Phoebe. I knew I was going to win this wager. I wouldn't have goaded you into it unless I knew you were going to enjoy it. Tell me the truth. What did you think of it?"

A thousand expressions crossed her lovely face.

She finally relented and cast him a reluctant smile. "It was a nice kiss."

Then she pushed out of his arms and ran toward the stairs.

He started after her, not intending to follow her into the house, because he'd given her too much to think about and she needed time alone to sort through her feelings.

He headed to the stable to collect his mount and ride home. To his surprise, she was waiting for him at the top of the beach stairs. "I did not mean to run away. Your admission scared me, my lord. I do not know what to make of you."

"Cormac. Do not be formal with me when we are not in company. Don't ever be scared of me, Phoebe. I will never hurt you."

"Yes, you will. Why did you say you loved me?"

"Because this is how I feel about you. I've never said this to any woman before."

"And you mustn't say it to me either. You really don't know

me."

He gave a harsh laugh. "My heart knows you. This is me finally growing up and maturing into a man."

"How long will that last?"

"Forever. I cannot go back to what I was. Wallowing, rude to my loved ones. Inconsolable, although I wasn't inconsolable so much as angry. I did not like what I saw in myself."

"And now you are changed? Just like that?" She snapped her fingers in demonstration.

"The change has been coming on for a while now."

"And what about Lord Crawford?"

"He has doubts about his ability to be a proper earl. I'll talk him through it. I've already told him he can come to me for guidance whenever he feels the need. But this is all new to him as well, and his pain is still raw. He and I are not fully alike in what we went through, but there are many similarities."

"As in wanting to toss the burden of running your estate onto your brother while you remained defiant and insufferable in your anger?"

"I was always competent enough to manage my holdings. I took over that chore from my brother as soon as I returned from battle. Yes, he helped me out in the months after I lost my arm, for I was still struggling with infections and delirious some of the time."

She looked pained. "Oh...I'm sorry. I suppose I just assumed... I'm sorry."

Of course, because she was too soft-hearted and knew her comment had hurt him.

"Taking over responsibility for my estate was never my problem. But you have no idea how it feels to lose an arm, Phoebe. Especially for a man like me. I cannot even button my falls without exertion. A three-year-old boy can dress himself or put on his shoes faster than I can mine. It is demeaning. Frustrating."

"I'm so sorry. Truly, I am." She now looked as though she wanted to cry.

"The one decent thing I have done since returning from battle is taking over the lion's share of the responsibilities for the Burness holdings. But I am also proud of my brother, for John was responsible for them while I was on the Continent fighting. He did an excellent job, as I knew he would. But this knowledge also allowed me to wallow in my misery for longer than I should have done. I have been a wretched ogre because of it. In time I hope he will be as proud of me as he used to be when we were children."

Now her eyes were watering.

Gad, did she have to be so sweet?

She emitted a breathy sigh. "I'm sure he never stopped being proud of you."

He shrugged. "I'm still an arse in many ways, especially when it comes to women. But I think seeing the countess and viscountess Lord Crawford brought along with him was a revelation for me. These are the sort of women with whom I dallied. Suddenly, I saw what they were and what I would soon become. Drunk. Bitter. Uncaring. Using people and then tossing them away. This wasn't me. I never wanted to become that man."

He shook his head. "I knew my dying friend did not mean for me to lead his brother down that path beyond...an encounter or two for the sake of experience. Well, I shall see how he behaves over the next few days. I don't know if he has it in him to become a leader among men. But he can still be a good earl and protect his sisters by putting the right men in place to assist with his holdings." He cast her a wry smile. "I had better get back home now. I'll see you tomorrow."

She nodded. "I plan to take the girls to St. Peter's Church in the late morning. They are putting on a marionette show for the children. Afterward, I thought to take them to Mrs. Halsey's tearoom for cakes and lemonade."

"And after that, back here?"

"Yes. This is our schedule for tomorrow. You'll know where to find us should you wish to join us. We'll return here by early afternoon, so just look for us either at the house or on the beach."

"I'll join you for the marionette show if I can. But don't wait around for me. I don't know what chaos will reign as my guests awaken...assuming they can pull themselves out of bed before nightfall. And who knows how Lord Crawford will be feeling? His crying bouts come and go."

"You could bring him with you."

He shook his head. "Absolutely not. He is not meeting you or my nieces until I am certain he is fit company. We'll see how he fares in a few days."

He took his leave and returned to Westgate Hall, disappointed but not surprised to find Lord Crawford in the parlor with his friends. They were already in their cups, including the young earl, and apparently had been awaiting his return to start their nightly revels. "No, I have work to do," he muttered, and strode into his study.

He shut the door with a slam and stalked across the room, sinking into the chair behind his desk.

It felt odd, this new page of his life.

Phoebe had refused his proposal, but he was not disheartened.

He was a marquess and used to getting his own way.

After kissing her—that kiss still innocent and tame—he did not want anyone but Phoebe. She had felt that kiss sear through her to her very bones.

She would be his eventually, but not before he tackled a presently insurmountable hurdle.

Trust.

This was the next campaign for him to wage, earning her trust. But how did one do this in the course of a week? This was something gained over time, over a course of years. He would never accomplish it if he reverted to his former self.

Phoebe would be watching him, waiting for him to make a mistake. One slip and all would be lost.

She wasn't trying to be mean about it, but she was afraid of her feelings now that she understood how desperately she could fall in love with him. This was what a good girl like her did—loved faithfully and wholeheartedly, and then had her heart crushed when the man she loved disappointed her.

For this reason, he understood it was easier for her to push him away than have faith in him and take the potentially heartbreaking leap to marriage.

After a few minutes, there came a soft knock at his door. "Enter."

Melrose walked in. "My lord, your friends are insisting upon your company."

"They are not my friends."

The butler's lips twitched in an almost-smile. "Nonetheless, they are asking for you. I fear they will destroy the parlor if you are not present to keep them in line."

Cormac set aside the papers he had planned on reviewing. How silly of him to think he could actually get some work done. "Blessed saints, they cannot leave soon enough. All right, I'll play nursemaid to them. How many more days of this must I endure?"

"It was to be two, but somehow has become three, my lord. Something about a carriage not being ready in time."

"Bother it. They cannot leave soon enough for me. Have any of them started packing?"

"Alas, no. I also doubt they will leave once they realize Lord Crawford is to stay on. How can they sponge off him while he is here and they are not? Nor can they sponge off you once you send them on their way." Melrose cleared his throat. "I speak for all your staff when I say we are ready to toss them and their belongings into your carriage and send them packing whenever you command. You have only to say the word."

"Very thoughtful of you, Melrose." Cormac cast the butler a wry smile. "But I made a solemn vow to Lord Crawford's brother, and I mean to honor it. You have my permission to toss out the others as soon as their week is up. They do not get to remain here a minute beyond."

"Very good, my lord. Do not hesitate to let us know if you wish to kick them out sooner."

Cormac shook his head and sighed. What choice did he have? A promise was a promise.

In any event, Lord Crawford's friends would occupy the young lord for the next few days, and this would leave Cormac free to spend more time with his nieces and Phoebe.

The last thing he wanted was Lord Crawford joining him and being around his little ducklings.

Or Phoebe.

He dismissed Melrose and strode down the hall to the parlor, cringing as he heard the countess's drunken cackle. Indeed, he could make out all four voices, all of them drunk and laughing.

So much for Lord Crawford's recovery. Well, healing was not going to miraculously happen overnight.

His heart sank as he watched the young lord.

He and his friends were playing cards, normally a fairly tame affair—except they were wagering articles of clothing, and the four of them were half-naked already.

Drunk and half-naked.

Cormac knew where this was going to lead.

But hell, so what if Lord Crawford enjoyed another night of debauchery? Sometimes a man needed to have his fill in order to then settle down with no regrets.

"Join us," the viscountess said, licking her lips in a suggestive way, as though that might ever entice Cormac. It was to his discredit that he had gone along with the sport those first few nights before meeting Phoebe.

The countess and viscountess were beautiful women, but he found little appealing about them despite their obvious good looks. These women were what he called hard beauties, not the sort over whom he could ever lose his heart. But that had not stopped him from participating in their games. Lord, he could not even remember what had gone on those past nights, which one he'd been with or what they had done.

Perhaps he'd been with both. He could not remember.

Yet he recalled every blessed moment with Phoebe.

Even his drunken moments.

Her lavender scent.

The sunshine in her smile and the slight upturn of her lips.

The blush on her cheeks.

The viscountess repeated her request to have him join their card game.

"I cannot." He used his arm as an excuse not to play. In truth, this *was* one of the many things he was no longer able to do. He could not hold his cards and easily discard the unwanted ones. Nor could he play billiards. Row a boat.

So many things were lost to him along with his arm.

He could not bear it if Phoebe were lost to him, too.

# Chapter Eight

P HOEBE WAS SURPRISED when the Marquess of Burness rode up to Moonstone Cottage the following morning in time to join them for breakfast. He also announced he would be riding with them to the church for the marionette show.

The girls were beside themselves with glee, running circles around him and quacking as he tried to walk inside and make his way into the dining room. "Ducklings, I'm going to fall atop you if you keep running between my legs." But his laughter was rich and heartfelt. "Good morning, Phoebe. Surprised to see me?"

"Yes."

"Pleased?"

She tried to stifle her tingles. "I'm not sure yet."

But that only earned her a wry smile from this exceedingly handsome man. She could not take her gaze off him even as she bent to pick up Imogen, who was still clinging to his leg.

He looked magnificent, not only because he was built divinely and had the masculine good looks to make any woman swoon. There was something different about him. He was smiling with genuine warmth, and his happiness was obvious.

Indeed, there seemed to be a lightness to his demeanor that she had never seen before.

She continued to stare at him.

He quirked an eyebrow and grinned. "What is it, Phoebe?"

She shook her head. "You ought to smile more often. It suits you. I mean...it is a genuine smile and reaches into your eyes. Dare I say it?"

"Say what?"

"You do not look angry. Indeed, you look happy, and I do not think you have felt this way in a very long time."

Her words clearly jolted him. He raked a hand through his hair and cast her a pained look.

Her own smile faded. "Oh, my stupid, big mouth. I should not have said anything. If only I'd kept my opinions to myself and let you enjoy the moment. I'm so sorry."

"No, it isn't your fault. I just... Come outside with me a moment." Without awaiting her response, he strode out onto the terrace and continued across the garden toward the beach.

"Girls, go into the dining room and wait for us. We won't be gone long." She left them in the care of Chloe and hurried after him.

Her heart ached for this proud, wounded man. His pain must have run so deep for him to forget the sensation of happiness.

"My lord..."

He paused at the top of the steps and shook his head. "Phoebe, you need to call me Cormac."

"All right...Cormac."

He gave a curt laugh. "Sounds nice."

A light mist hovered across the edge of the water, but the day was already turning warm and bright. There were more clouds in the sky than yesterday, but they were soft tufts of white, not the sort that brought on rain. The air held only the slightest trace of moisture as it swirled around them.

She took his hand in both of hers. "What I did to you a moment ago was not nice at all. You were happy, and I did not need to comment on it. Forgive me?"

He shook his head. "There is nothing to forgive. I was happy and still am. Being with you and the girls fills my empty heart. It is a new feeling for me, and I like it. The realization overwhelmed me for a moment."

"It is a nice feeling, isn't it?"

"Yes." He emitted a ragged breath. "I want this. I want you and I want the girls." He paused a moment and chuckled. "I suppose my brother will want them back, since they are his, after all."

She laughed as she nodded. "I would expect so. But I know what you mean. They are so lovely. Chloe and I are having such a good time with them. I can see why you do not want to give them up. We don't either. Your brother and his Lady Charlotte are very fortunate parents."

"Yes, and my brother is also the perfect sort of father who appreciates all he has. He's a good husband, too. His wife and those girls know he loves them with all his heart."

She still had light hold of his hand. "This is how I would want my marriage to be."

He nodded. "I know. You want a love that lasts forever."

"Yes, and that's just it, Cormac. True love does last. But I can see you don't believe it yet."

"I'm trying, Phoebe. I promise you, I am. Meanwhile, I am left with a rabble at my house and cannot think straight while they are about. I want to kick them all out, including Lord Crawford, but I must honor my promise to his brother. I will not break my word."

He slipped his hand out of hers and then wrapped his arm around her waist while he gazed across the water. "Lord Crawford and I had a good talk earlier yesterday, but by evening he was back to drunken revels with his friends. I was so disappointed in him. Yet how can I be angry when I was far worse? Not only before I lost my arm but for months afterward. I cannot expect miracles in a day."

"Did you join in?"

He cast her a wry look. "What do you think?"

"Well, since your eyes are clear, your shirt buttoned, and you do not reek of stale spirits, I would venture to guess that you did not partake. The more important question is, would I believe you if you had come here looking wretched? If you gave me your oath that you had not participated, would this have been good enough for me?"

He nodded. "I know I will never win you until you trust me. But I am a man of my word. Whatever other faults I may have, being a liar is not one of them."

She did not want to think about this matter now, since it was too soon for her to form any conclusions, so she gave him a playful poke in the stomach. "All well and good, but do not ask me to marry you again. Just because you claim not to be a liar does not make you perfect. I think we still have to work through arrogance, stubbornness, and insufferableness."

"Is that even a word?"

"Insufferableness? I'm sure it is. If you look up the meaning, it will have your name beside it. 'Insufferableness...behaving like Cormac Stockwell. Someone who is as profoundly irritating as Cormac Stockwell.'"

He laughed and drew her up against him. "Are the girls watching us?"

She gasped. "Yes, their faces are squashed to the glass, so you had better behave yourself."

"But then I would not be me. Someone who is profoundly irritating," he teased, tossing her words back at her. "I am going to kiss you, Phoebe Killigrew."

"Why tell me if you are intent on doing it anyway?"

"To give you the chance to run away if you do not want my kiss."

She groaned. "See, you are the very definition of insufferableness."

"And you, my sweet pigeon, did not run away when you had the chance. Admit it, Phoebe. You like me."

He brought his mouth down on hers, and she was lost. His lips felt so good, and he seemed to know just how to press them to hers. Not in a harsh or crushing manner, but in a firm, possessively melting way.

And his body.

*Blessed Mother.*

Why did he have to feel so good?

His scent was divine, that intoxicating hint of musk and muscles.

She clutched his lapels, clinging to them for fear her legs would not hold her up after his searing kiss. Yet he'd purposely kept the kiss soft. However, the smolder in his eyes warned his next kisses would not merely sear her.

They were going to scorch her.

She gasped once he took his lips off hers. "Don't look at me that way."

"How am I looking at you, Phoebe?"

"Like you want to set me on fire and make me burn for you."

He placed a light kiss on her cheek, hardly a touch, and yet it did not feel innocent at all. How did he manage it? "I held back for your sake. Yes, I want to scorch you, burn myself into you. Possess you. Conquer you. Kiss every inch of your delectable body. Taste your lavender-sweet skin. That is only the start of what I wish to do to you."

Heat rose in her cheeks, and her heart was now in palpitations. "See, you are still too naughty and unpredictable."

"I am not unpredictable. I do not pretend to be anything other than naughty," he said, casting her an appealingly rakish smile. "The only difference is that I am now willing to be naughty only with you."

She glanced at the house and groaned. "Now Chloe has her face pasted to the window as well. I can see them grinning at me all the way from here. Come on, you wicked man. Let's have breakfast. You must be hungry. And if you dare say you are hungry for me, I am going to kick you in the shin."

He laughed. "I would never say anything so trite."

"Oh."

"I don't need to say anything when my kiss should have told

you everything you need to know."

They walked back to the house, and she tried to pretend he hadn't just melted her insides with his delicious kiss—in full view of his nieces and her sister, no less. Of course, the ability to mask one's feelings was not a particular strength of hers, and she blushed throughout their meal.

She wanted to crawl under the table and hide when Imogen thought it important to tell Mrs. Hawke when she brought in a fresh pot of coffee. "Uncle Cormac kissed Phoebe."

He coughed, keeping his hand to his mouth to muffle his laughter.

The cad.

"Did he now?" Mrs. Hawke remarked. "And what did Lady Phoebe do?"

"She kissed him back," Ella added unhelpfully.

"Well, then. I suppose that makes it all right."

Phoebe's mouth gaped open. "Mrs. Hawke, it is not all right. He should not have... Never mind. Thank you for the coffee."

But she shook her head, now in a quandary. How was it all right for a couple who were not betrothed to take such liberties?

She sought out Mrs. Hawke once they had finished their breakfast. Chloe had taken the girls upstairs to fetch their bonnets and gloves, and the marquess had gone out to order the wagon brought around.

She took a quick moment for a word with her housekeeper. "Mrs. Hawke, I know he should not have kissed me. I will not allow it to happen again. I—"

"Lamb, he is in love with you. Do you think for a moment he will not ask you to marry him?"

She sighed, not wanting to tell her that he already had. In truth, she was surprised the servants at Westgate Hall had not gossiped about it. Perhaps Melrose, who had been the only one to overhear that ridiculous proposal the morning they first met, was being discreet about it. She would have to thank him next time she was there, which would not be anytime soon. She was not going near that house until his guests were gone. "How can you tell? I mean, how can I be sure his feelings for me are genuine when I don't believe he truly knows his own mind?"

"His heart knows, and this is what counts."

"I see. Thank you, Mrs. Hawke." But how soon before he had a change of heart?

It was too much right now to think about any of it, so she resolved to concentrate on the day ahead and nothing else. The girls scampered downstairs, Chloe right behind them. "Here, Phoebe." She handed over her bonnet, reticule, and gloves.

The girls were excited to be riding in the wagon again. Goodness, it was such a rickety, old thing, but they took such pleasure in every bump and rattle. Their uncle rode beside them on his stallion, seeming quite relaxed in the saddle despite the massive size of that beast.

The show was about to start by the time they reached the church, so the girls hurried to take their seats while Phoebe and Chloe offered to help the vicar set up the tables of treats for the children to enjoy once the show was over. "My lord, would you mind watching the girls while we set out the cakes?"

"They'll be so wrapped up in the puppets, I doubt they'd notice any of us missing," Cormac replied. "I don't mind helping."

"No, you'd only be in the way."

"I see." He glanced at his missing arm.

She inhaled lightly. "Not because of your arm. I didn't even think of that. I would have said the same to any man who offered. The ladies and I can get it done faster if we are left on our own and do not have to weave and dart around all the well-meaning bodies blocking our way. We work with military precision. Surely, you can understand this."

"All right. I will not take offense."

"We won't be gone long." She hurried to the rectory with Chloe. Since they had often helped out at various functions, they knew what to do, and quickly had the tables set up and loaded to groaning with sweets the children would love.

On their way out, she and Chloe noticed a young soldier sitting by himself on a front pew of the church and staring at the altar. He did not appear to be praying, just sitting there looking quite lonely.

"The poor man, he looks lost," Chloe whispered. "Should I invite him to join us? Oh, look at his leg. He must have injured it. And look, there is his cane beside him."

Phoebe nibbled her lip. "I don't know. We're here with the girls, and we don't know anything about this stranger. We would have recognized him if he were one of the local boys."

"We could ask the marquess. Leave the decision to him."

Phoebe nodded. "Yes, I like that idea. Let him be the one to decide whether the young man should join us. I expect he will invite him."

"Because he's injured?"

She nodded again. "He'll understand exactly what the young man is feeling. I'll fetch him." She hurried over to Cormac, who was standing with his shoulder casually propped against a shady oak a short distance from the noisy puppets and laughing children. "I need your advice."

He arched an eyebrow. "You can never go wrong with lemon cake. Put all of it out on the tables and the children will devour every last crumb."

She grinned. "I do not need your advice on what the children would like to eat after the show. There is a young soldier sitting by himself inside the church. He's wounded. Chloe and I wondered whether we ought to invite him to join us. Only for cakes and lemonade. I don't mean to invite him to spend the entire day with us. But we thought he might appreciate some company. He looks so lonely."

He glanced at his nieces and then nodded. "You have a soft heart, Phoebe. All right, lead the way. But I shall take the measure of him first. I'll only bring him over if I find him to be of solid character."

"Yes, this is why we came to you first."

He went in while she stayed outside and took his place under the shady tree. Chloe joined her a few moments later. The children's show ended about ten minutes later, so they took Ella and Imogen inside for some cake and strawberry tarts.

She, Chloe, and several other ladies had set up long tables and benches in the rectory. The children and their parents hurried to grab spots, although Phoebe knew there would be room for everyone.

The vicar motioned her over to a private table when he saw her walk in with Chloe and the girls. "Over here, Lady Phoebe."

"But Vicar Trask, there's room at the long tables."

He shook his head. "The marquess will not approve. Do sit here with his nieces."

Ordinarily, this special treatment would have annoyed her, for she and Chloe knew many of the villagers. They were kind and friendly to her and her sisters.

But there was also the young soldier to think about, for he did seem shy. "Will you join us, Vicar Trask?"

"Perhaps later. I have my flock to tend to," he said with a beaming smile at the parishioners who had turned out for the marionettes. "I wish my sermons drew this sort of crowd. Perhaps I will add puppets and strawberry tarts to my sermons."

He went off to greet the families in attendance.

While Chloe settled the girls in their seats, Phoebe brought over a plate of strawberry tarts for them to share. She had just taken her seat when Cormac approached with the shy young soldier. "Lady Phoebe, Lady Chloe, may I introduce you to Lieutenant Fionn Brennan?"

"A pleasure to meet you," Phoebe said, casting him a welcoming smile. "Please, do join us."

"My lord?" He glanced hesitantly at Cormac and muttered a thank you at his nod.

"These little imps are my nieces, Lady Ella and Lady Imogen. Move over, girls, and make room for the lieutenant."

Imogen smiled at the young man. "Uncle Cormac lost his arm. Are you going to lose your leg?"

Chloe gasped. "Oh, Imogen. It is not a polite question to ask."

"It's all right," Lieutenant Brennan said, taking the chair next to Chloe. "I actually broke the leg years ago. The doctors say I will always walk with a limp. Some days it is worse than others. I strained it a bit yesterday, which is why I am now using the cane."

Cormac settled beside Phoebe, but he engaged his nieces first. "What do we have here, ducklings?"

"Strawberry tarts, Uncle Cormac. They're delicious," Ella said.

"Hmm, then I think I must have three. Grab a handful for yourself, Brennan."

"Thank you, my lord."

"Lieutenant Brennan here has been assigned to oversee construction of an army hospital in the area. Moonstone Landing is one of the sites under consideration."

"It is only in the early planning stages. But the village already has an army presence and a good port that may need to be widened. It is definitely in contention, assuming the village council wants us here."

"The army's plans have been all the talk for quite a while now," Phoebe said. "I'm glad it is finally more than mere gossip. Do you have family in the area?"

Fionn blushed. "I have no family. That is...none that I have ever met. I grew up in a London orphanage, but left when they handed me over to a chimney sweep to work as his monkey."

Chloe gasped. "As one of those little boys small enough to crawl up the chimneys and clean them out?"

He nodded. "Many of them die within the year, so I ran away. I preferred my chances living on the streets."

"And now you are an army officer," Chloe said. "How did that happen?"

"I was doomed to a life as a street urchin until taken in one day by Viscount Brennan. I'm not sure whatever possessed him to take me off the streets and give me a chance at a decent life, but who would ever refuse such a generous offer? I had no surname of my own, so he insisted I take his. He saw to my education and paid for my commission. I owe my life to him."

"I knew him," Cormac said. "He was a good man. Unfortunately, the new viscount leaves much to be desired."

"Oh, then he's passed?" Phoebe asked.

The young man nodded. "Yes, recently. This is why I stopped in the church. I wanted to pay my respects. A quick prayer to honor him. Not that the viscount would ever hear me. Nor does it matter where I am when I think of him, I suppose." He shrugged. "I don't really know what led me to the church today."

Imogen set down her strawberry tart and looked up at him with her smeared little face. "I know why you came here."

He smiled at her. "You do?"

She nodded. "To meet us so we can be your new family."

He glanced at all of them, quietly stunned. "Ah...erm...that is very kind of you, Lady Imogen. But I would not dream of imposing. However, I shall be glad to consider you all my new friends. How is that?"

She gave her approval.

"And I shall be certain to stop in to see your uncle when I am back in Moonstone Landing. With your permission, my lord."

"Please do, Brennan," Cormac replied. "I do not give out invitations lightly. You are most welcome."

"Thank you."

Imogen cast her uncle the sweetest smile. "And maybe those naked ladies will be gone by then."

Phoebe choked on her lemonade.

Cormac burst out laughing.

Ella agreed, "Lady Phoebe did not like them because they were naked."

Dear heaven! Had the girls overheard her ranting that first day? What had she told Chloe? She really had been angry, because their uncle had been so despicable. Drunk. Arrogant. Ridiculous.

"No, Imogen...I—" She coughed. "It..." She coughed again. "I don't..."

She could not speak for trying to catch her breath.

Chloe was also laughing.

Cormac leaned toward the lieutenant. "Don't ask, Brennan. It is a long story, one I do not wish to tell. Unfortunately, it is not over yet." He turned to his niece. "Imogen, have you ever heard the expression 'silence is golden'?"

"No, Uncle Cormac," she said with heartwarming sincerity.

"What about you, Ella?"

His older niece cast him an equally honest, wide-eyed gaze. "No, Uncle Cormac."

He grinned. "Well, I'll tell you about it once I return you to Moonstone Cottage."

Phoebe knew her face was in flames, although it ought to have been the marquess who was embarrassed. But he seemed unperturbed. When Chloe and the lieutenant went with the girls to refill their plates, he turned to her. "Phoebe, are you all right?"

She nodded, trying to hold back her laughter, which came out in an unladylike snort. "You warned me they were little sponges."

"Indeed, they are." His beautiful eyes were alight with mirth. "Ah well. Nothing to be done about it now. The lieutenant spent at least ten years of his life on the streets, probably more. This is tame compared to what he must have seen and heard."

"You like him."

He nodded. "I knew his mentor, Viscount Brennan, as I said. I heard him speak a time or two of the boy. He far outclasses the viscount's relatives. Those heartless clots are a jealous lot. I'm sure they shut him out as soon as the viscount took his last breath. But he has brains, and his commission is secure. He'll go far, make something of himself."

"How do you know?"

"Well, nothing is certain in life. But it is easy to see a person's character. Little things always give them away."

"Such as?"

"Politeness. Small gestures of consideration. I can tell within a few minutes whether a person is someone I would ever trust."

"Can you do it now?"

"Yes, usually quite easily. Point someone out to me."

"That woman with blonde hair and wearing a dark blue dress."

He studied her for less than a minute. "No, I would not trust her."

"Why?"

"She denied the child seated across the table from her a slice of cake and ate it herself."

"Well, perhaps the child is not hers."

"Phoebe, would you ever deny a child?"

She shook her head. "No, but if that child had already eaten his fill and his parents did not want him to have more, then they would have been angry with me."

"First of all, you are too charming for anyone ever to be angry with you. Second of all, if you felt that child was hungry, you would have given him your slice and taken the reprimand. You would have denied yourself to feed him."

He was right about that.

"I never thought of it that way."

"I know. You are kind and compassionate. You stand up for what is good and right. This is how I can tell a person's character. We can talk more about this later. Oh, blast. Look at how many tarts Imogen has piled onto her plate. I know you had planned to include a stop at Mrs. Halsey's shop, but I think the girls are going to explode if they take in so much as another crumb."

She laughed. "I think you are right. Well, we'll eat a light supper if their stomachs are upset. Besides, as you have just pointed out, I cannot deny a child."

"A little discipline wouldn't hurt. But I am one to talk. Those little girls run roughshod over my heart."

"I've noticed, and I think it is wonderful." She glanced down at herself. "Oh, I've dribbled lemonade on myself and stained my gown. One last strawberry tart for the girls and then I'll take them home. We've had enough adventures for today, I think. A puppet show, a mountain of treats, and making a new friend. I'm sure Imogen and Ella will be exhausted by the time we get back. By the way, I ordered some sketchbooks and drawing pencils for them. Mr. Hawke went to pick them up for me after dropping us off at the church. I think Ella and Imogen will enjoy a quiet afternoon of drawing."

He nodded. "I'm sure they will. Thank you for thinking of them."

"They are a joy. Chloe and I like being with them. We'll take them for a walk on the beach to round out their day if they still need a little running around. I suppose you are eager to return to your home and see what is going on there."

"Westgate Hall?" He gave a mock shudder. "I dread it. The place has been overrun by gremlins, some of them naked," he said, tossing her a wink. "Seriously, I had hoped to be rid of them. But leeches cling tight, and Lord Crawford still wants them around."

"So you will give in to his wishes?"

"I don't know. I want to do the right thing, but I am out of my depth when it comes to him. I should be more compassionate and understanding for his loss, but I just want to wring his neck most of the time and tell him to get on with his duty. And yet *I* was such an arse when facing a similar situation. In truth, his loss is far worse. I lost an arm. He lost a beloved brother. I am not good with feelings, Phoebe. I usually suppress them."

"You only suppress the good ones. I've noticed that too often you let the bad ones overcome you. The loss of your arm is a constant source of frustration and enrages you."

He frowned. "It always will. You have no idea how it humiliates me. Not the wound itself, but all it denies me from accomplishing."

She reached over and placed her hand over his. "I know it is no small thing. I'm sorry if I made it sound as though it was. How thoughtless of me."

He laughed. "Don't apologize to me, Phoebe. I feel good whenever I am around you. I cannot explain why, for I never forget all the things I can no longer do, and that still infuriates me. As I said, it always will. But being around you...I just don't hurt as much."

He took her hand and put it to his lips, immediately drawing everyone's notice.

Phoebe blushed and hastily eased out of his grasp. "You shouldn't kiss my hand."

"Shall I kiss you on the lips, then?"

She sighed. "No. Now people will talk."

"I've come to the church with you and remained for the puppet show and treats. Speculation must be rampant among the villagers already. It has not escaped anyone's notice that we seem to be a very cozy family."

"You and your nieces."

"Everyone notices the way I look at you. More important, they also see the way you look at me."

She groaned. "Will you come around to Moonstone Cottage later today?"

He nodded. "Yes, I hope to. Assuming some calamity has not occurred with Lord Crawford."

The girls, Chloe, and the lieutenant came back with full plates, putting an end to their conversation. But the chatter around the table continued because they were all eager to learn more about the lieutenant's assignment and his early days as a child left to fend for himself on the London streets.

He did not reveal much that was truly personal. But he was engaging and patient with the girls, and appeared to enjoy his time with them. "My lord, I had better be on my way," he eventually said. "It was a pleasure to meet you all. Perhaps I will be fortunate enough to see you again before I leave Moonstone Landing."

"So you will be here a few more days?" Chloe asked.

He nodded. "I have several places to visit nearby, and I intend to use Moonstone Landing as my base while I scout the area. I'd also like to complete my report on the village before I head off to Devonshire next."

Chloe offered her hand. "Then I am certain we shall run into you again, Lieutenant Brennan. We are often in the market square."

He bowed over it and did the same to Phoebe.

The girls also held out their hands.

He grinned and bowed over theirs as well. "A pleasure, Lady Ella. Ever your servant, Lady Imogen."

"Hold on, Lieutenant Brennan. I'll walk out with you," Cormac said. "I think we are all ready to take our leave."

Phoebe tossed him a quizzical look.

"I'll be along in a moment. Don't wait for me. I'll catch up to you."

"All right." She took the girls by the hands as they all left the church.

Chloe and the girls scampered into the wagon with cheerful greetings for Mr. Hawke. Phoebe hopped in after them. Mr. Hawke greeted them with equal cheer and listened to the girls chatter about the puppet show and the new friend they'd made as he drove them home.

Cormac's expression was serious as he watched them ride off.

Phoebe wondered why he had remained behind to speak privately with the lieutenant. But it did not take him long to catch up to them, for his big stallion was a beast of a horse and could have galloped twenty miles without getting winded.

Cormac was quiet as he escorted them back to the cottage, kissed his nieces, and assured them he would see them later.

He merely nodded to Phoebe and Chloe. "Back soon."

While the girls ran inside to show Mrs. Hawke their new art supplies, Phoebe and Chloe remained in the courtyard to watch him ride away.

Chloe shook her head. "What do you think he'll find when he returns to his home?"

Phoebe shrugged. "I'm hoping he'll find a peaceful, happy scene. But it is more likely he'll encounter utter chaos. This new Earl of Crawford does not appear to be handling his brother's death well, and his friends are only making matters worse."

Chloe nodded. "With friends like that, who needs enemies?"

"Exactly. But the marquess is as much at fault for allowing those friends to stay. It is his home. Why can he not simply toss them out?"

"Would you?"

"I don't know."

"We should not pass judgment, Phoebe. We do not know the situation."

They locked arms as they strolled back into the house.

Phoebe gave her sister a kiss on the cheek. "Help me change out of my gown. I've spilled lemonade down the front. I hope Mrs. Hawke can wash out the stain."

"I'm sure she can. She's a marvel. It is a pretty gown. The marquess must have thought so. He could not stop looking at you in it." She cast Phoebe an impish grin. "Or was he merely trying to think of ways to seduce you out of it?"

"Chloe! It isn't like that between us."

"Really? Do you always kiss your friends as you did this morning?"

"It was nothing, just the marquess being his naughty self."

"Oh, I see. You were being polite by holding on to him as though you never wanted to let him go? I'm sure I detected flames bursting between you. Admit it, Phoebe. You like him."

"That is ridiculous."

"Well, it is obvious he likes you."

"He doesn't really."

"You do realize you are making no sense, don't you? If you and the marquess do not like each other, then why do you keep looking at each other in that ridiculously breathless way?"

# Chapter Nine

L ORD CRAWFORD AND his friends were just waking up by the time Cormac returned to his manor. It was early afternoon as the rabble sauntered into the parlor, preparing for yet another boring round of drinks and amusements. "My head is splitting," Lord Harding grumbled.

The others commiserated.

"Mine too," the countess said, and the viscountess nodded in agreement.

Lord Crawford did not look any better than his friends. All of them appeared green around the gills.

Cormac should have ordered his wine cellar locked. That would have chased them from his home. He silently chided himself for not thinking of it sooner. But it was merely wishful thinking. He wasn't going to be a surly host. In truth, he did not know what to do other than hope to distract them with entertainments that required them to be sober.

But his suggestions were shot down by all, including Lord Crawford. "Do you not even wish to take a ride in the countryside or walk along the beach?"

Lord Crawford at least considered it for a moment, then shook his head. "I don't see the point, Burness. It is too strenuous for the ladies, and Lord Harding does not wish to budge from that unopened bottle of wine beside him."

Cormac sighed. "My billiards table does not arrive until next month. Will you not even consider a walk down to the beach? A little sea air will do us all good."

Lord Crawford glanced at his friends then turned back to him with a sigh. "Seems cards and drinking are to be it for us."

"And delights of the flesh," Lord Harding added with a hearty laugh. "We mustn't forget that."

Cormac's stomach began to churn.

"Do not scowl at us, Burness," the viscountess said. "You did not mind it so much when we first arrived. What happened to turn you into a monk?"

"I've told you, my nieces are here."

"Ah, that's right," the countess remarked, her speech slurred, since she was still hungover from last night. "But what do you care? They are not in the house with us. They will not see what you do."

"I will know what I do."

The viscountess laughed. "Virtue does not suit you, Burness. Your reputation is far too wicked for that. You really ought to join us in our bad behavior."

"No, I am going to abstain. But a word of advice—numbing yourself to pain is not going to heal you. Do you not think it is time to face your own demons and overcome them?"

The viscountess snorted. "I am never going to overcome a lout of a husband, so spare me your lectures."

The countess agreed. "You have no idea how onerous marriage can be to a prig of a man."

He shook his head. "But you have wealth and security. You hardly see your husbands. Are they truly so odious you cannot tolerate them the few times a year you do encounter them?"

He could understand if their husbands were cruel men who beat them, but they were not married to such men. Nor were their husbands grotesque specimens. Yet these were profoundly sad women.

Lord, he did not want to hear more. He had all he could

handle with Lord Crawford.

Still, he was curious to understand what made a marriage unhappy. He needed to know this if he ever hoped to avoid such a fate and make a happy match with Phoebe.

This meant he would have to listen to these women spill their feelings. *Blessed saints.* He did not want to appear cruel or uncaring, but he really did not want them pouring their hearts out to him. Yet they had to. How else was he to know what had happened to make them so desperately unhappy?

He sighed. "You have my attention. What is it about your marriages that make you loathe your husbands?" It would destroy him if Phoebe regarded him as so bad a match that she had to drink herself into a stupor to face each new day.

No, that would never happen.

She would not destroy herself over him. It was more likely she would apply her sadness to doing good deeds for others.

"You have never been in love, Burness. You will never understand the pain of being apart from the one who is meant for you and can never be," the countess said.

"Then to see him move on and marry another," the viscountess added. "Do you think fine homes and jewels replace being in the arms of the one you love? Having to endure the touch of someone you care nothing for?"

"Then I am truly sorry." He did have some understanding of their sorrow, for having seen the love matches made by his brother and his best friend, he knew how happy these couples were and how devastated they would be if forced to part. "I suppose you were not given the choice to pursue your heart's desire."

The viscountess cast him a wry smile. "I had the choice. Marry a pauper I loved or marry a title? I would still choose the title if I had it to do all over again."

The countess agreed.

"But why?" Cormac shook his head. "Why knowingly enter into an arrangement that will make you unhappy? And since you would purposely make the same mistake again, why have you not reconciled yourself to it and made the best of the situation?"

"We are not all as strong as you, Burness," Lord Crawford said.

"Me?" Cormac shook his head and laughed. "I am an utter arse."

The countess approached and ran her hand along his chest. "But a handsome one, so you are forgiven all sins."

The viscountess laughed. "I'll have a turn with you next. Can you not see, Burness? We have reconciled ourselves with our lot in life. We are making the best of our unhappy situations by entertaining ourselves with men like you."

He moved away to peer out the window.

*Blessed saints.*

Had he fallen so low in his reputation?

A light breeze filtered in to cool his mounting ire.

Melrose must have opened the window earlier to air out the room from last night's drunken revels. He inhaled the refreshing breeze that carried the scent of the sea. "What of you, Lord Harding? You have said nothing about love."

The man shrugged. "What is there to say? You know what I am. If I can get through life in moderate comfort, then who am I to complain? I haven't a shilling to my name, but I can be witty and amiable, always ready to entertain the ladies…and the men, if that is their proclivity."

The ladies tittered.

Cormac truly pitied them.

They'd settled into their miserable but easy lives, and he was not going to change their outlook. "What of you, Lord Crawford? You have an earldom on your hands. Are there any questions you have of me? We had a good talk yesterday. What are your thoughts on the matter?"

"I have given your advice much consideration and am now more determined than ever to travel the world and study ancient civilizations. It is the thing I truly love, and you are all invited to travel with me," Richard said with a weak laugh.

Cormac shook his head. "And your sisters? Should you not see them settled first?"

"I mulled that over, too, and decided to leave their fates to my aunt. She will take them under her wing and make good matches for them. As for the expenses, I have not burned through my inheritance yet. If, as you say, my estate is in good order, then I can easily undertake the costs of their debuts. My estate manager shall see to the payments while I am sailing around the world. Do not look dismayed, Burness. I think my brother knew all along where this would lead. I just needed a wise head to guide me to it. You brought me clarity of thought while I was drowning in my fears."

This ought to have pleased Cormac, but it really did not. Running away from one's family and responsibilities was no solution. Well, perhaps everyone would be better off if he did get lost for years. Not all men were meant to be leaders.

But he did feel some remorse for the women in the Crawford family.

Then again, a shrewd aunt would do a far better job of finding suitable husbands for his sisters than Crawford himself ever could. For the sake of James, and to honor his memory, he would help out in any way he could.

As for these sad women before him, they were wrong about his not knowing love. He was in love with Phoebe. What he did not know was how long this feeling would last. This was what concerned him most.

He wanted to love her forever.

But what if he fell out of love with her a month from now? A year? Or ten years from now?

Or was love something that wrapped around your heart and fired your blood? Once found, was it as vital as the air one breathed into one's lungs? Was it a craving that never left your soul, not even after death?

He thought of the Moonstone Cottage ghosts, the sea captain

and Phoebe's aunt. Was such an eternal love possible?

"Burness, the day is too nice for all of us to be lost in morose thoughts," Lord Crawford said. "Feed us, and then I shall take a walk with you down to your beach. Happy now? I shall go with you."

"I think you will enjoy it," Cormac said.

"It is the charm of this barren outpost, is it not? Ladies, I agree with Burness. What do you say? A little fresh air and sunshine will do us all much good."

Lord Harding laughed. "My dears, do bring your parasols. The sun will be strong and burn your delicate skin."

"I shall pass." The countess turned to Lord Harding and motioned for him to pour her a drink.

"I do not enjoy the sun," the viscountess intoned, and gestured for Lord Harding to pour her one as well.

Lord Crawford shrugged. "Looks like it is just you and me, Burness. I'm game to venture down to your beach. But I do not know how to swim."

"You needn't go in the water. It is still a pleasant jaunt."

"Will you be swimming?" the countess asked, her ears suddenly perking.

"No." Much as Cormac would like to cool down in the pleasant waters, he would need assistance to remove his boots. He could manage the shirt himself, but then it would leave the stump of his arm exposed to their view in bright daylight. As for his breeches, he would have to leave them on, for it was too embarrassing to be seen struggling to put himself back in them after his swim.

He would not feel any such hesitation were he on the beach with Phoebe. She would never make him feel degraded.

Perhaps this was why he felt so strongly about her.

Not only did she make him feel good, but he trusted her never to hurt him. In truth, he did not think Phoebe had it in her to utter a vicious word.

Oh, she'd railed at him when they first met, but that was to protect his nieces. She railed at his bad behavior. Never even mentioned his arm.

She refused to see him as damaged because of it.

Come to think of it, she had never once looked upon it with revulsion.

This was what she was—fiercely protective and just as fiercely kind.

"Perhaps I will try learning how to swim," Lord Crawford said. "Not now, of course. A walk along the sand is enough for today."

Cormac was pleased to be making progress. Lord Crawford was not a stupid man. They would enjoy another conversation about ancient civilizations.

The two of them headed down to the beach soon after their meal, leaving the others to drink in the parlor. He and Lord Crawford had removed their jackets, waistcoats, and cravats, both of them of a mind to enjoy the walk in comfort, since there was no need for formality.

There was a softness to the afternoon, the wind warm and gentle, and the waves quietly lapping the shore.

The sun was strong, but Cormac enjoyed the heat seeping into his bones.

They helped each other tug off their boots, and then Cormac went to the water's edge and poured water on his hair. "Do the same, Richard. It will cool you down."

"All right." Richard imitated Cormac and soaked his head and neck. "Ah, that does feel good. Too bad the others don't appreciate this."

"Some people will never appreciate what they have."

"Yes, they seem to be locked in their own misery. I noticed how you were questioning them, trying to understand why they do what they do. Their answers surprised me. If one is miserable with one's lot, why knowingly take the same road if they are given the chance to correct their mistake?"

"The lure of wealth and title is too strong, I suppose. Their husbands are not bad men, you know."

Richard shook his head. "I am not acquainted with them. I suppose I will encounter them eventually, now that I am to be installed in the House of Lords. Perhaps I will be in London long enough to see one of my sisters launched into Society. The eldest, Arabella, is a pretty thing and ought to do well for herself. Are you certain you are not interested?"

Cormac laughed. "Quite certain."

They were now walking along the water's edge, allowing the waves to swarm about their bare ankles. They continued to walk and talk, going as far as the edge of his beach and then turning back to walk toward the outcropping that separated his property from Phoebe's.

Cormac wondered whether Phoebe had taken his nieces down to the beach. No, she wouldn't have them there now—it was after three o'clock. and she'd made quite a fuss about scheduling their beach hours so as not to interfere with his.

He would tell her tonight that the schedule wasn't necessary. His guests were not going to set foot outside of his house, except for Lord Crawford, who could be trusted not to cavort naked in the water, since the man did not know how to swim.

"I cannot tell you how much I appreciate this time spent with you, Burness. I was in a fog for weeks and do not think I would have emerged from it if not for you."

"You give me too much credit. I'm sure you would have pulled yourself out of it in time. You and I have had only one good conversation since you've been here. Perhaps this one will be the second."

"It is not only our chats that I appreciate. You stood by me as a friend and gave me the confidence to do what I must, not only for the good of the earldom but for myself. I will be contacting the Royal Society as well as the British Museum to look into their expeditions. Quite excited about it, in truth. I look forward to getting my plans underway, and the invitation is always open to you should you wish to join me."

"I shall politely decline. I've spent too many years away from home."

"But those were war years. It isn't the same."

"I know. However, I am looking forward to settling here and making a life for myself."

Richard laughed. "Then you do intend to marry. Have you found the girl yet? It cannot be Lady Seline, for she is now married."

"It was never going to be her."

He arched an eyebrow in surprise. "The gossip rags were touting how besotted you were with her."

Cormac laughed. "The information no doubt fed to them by Lady Seline herself."

"Then why not consider my sister? Arabella is smart and lovely."

"Richard, with all due respect, I do not want Arabella."

"Then who do you want?"

Before he could respond, a straw hat sailed over the outcropping between his beach and Phoebe's, landing at his feet. It was a child's hat. He immediately realized it was Ella's or Imogen's, so he picked it up. Were they on the beach? He hadn't heard their giggles.

In the next moment, Phoebe waded around the rocks with her gown hiked to her thighs. The breath caught in her lungs when she noticed them. "Lord Burness...do forgive me. But Imogen's hat flew off her head and the wind carried it from my garden to here. I was afraid it would fly into the water."

She hurried forward, grabbed it from his hand, and hastily waded back to her side without waiting for introductions to be made.

Lord Crawford stared at her retreating form. "Who is that angel?" Suddenly, he laughed and shook his head. "How stupid of me. She is the neighbor you have been so vigilant in seeing. No wonder you are eager to ride over there every day. You hound. You want her."

"She has my nieces."

"Then you are not interested in her? Are you blind, man? She is the most beautiful creature I have ever encountered. Eyes the aqua of the sea and lips as pink as roses. I shall have her if you do not want her. What is her name? She is magnificent."

"Enough, Richard. You are to keep away from Lady Phoebe." Cormac stopped Lord Crawford from following Phoebe and tossed him a warning scowl. "I mean it."

"Come now, Burness. You are behaving like a possessive ape. Just say so if you want her for yourself. If this is how it is, then so be it." Richard put up his hands in a gesture of surrender. "I am a gentleman and will keep hands off your lovely Lady Phoebe. But surely there can be no harm in my meeting her. I'll join you when you next visit her. Or are you the jealous sort who wants to keep her all to yourself?"

"I'll bring you over there in a couple of days," Cormac grumbled. "I need to be certain you are truly on the mend. I don't want you upsetting her or my nieces."

"Dear heaven, what sort of low specimen do you think I am?" But in the next moment, Richard shook his head and groaned. "Well, I see your point. I am presently mixing with an unsavory lot, even if they are considered *haute ton*."

"Precisely. You must understand my concern, especially while your friends are still here. I do not want Lady Phoebe or my nieces anywhere near them."

Richard went to the water's edge and poured more water onto his head to cool himself down. "Very well. Truce, Burness. I shall not approach her until my friends are gone. However, once they have left, you must introduce her to me."

"I will think about it."

"Fine, do so. Shall we return to the lovely ladies? They'll be quite drunk by now, and hot for you. Of course, since you won't have them, they'll take me. Who shall I have first?"

Cormac did not bother to respond.

It did not escape his notice that despite Lord Crawford's

gushing over Phoebe, he still wanted his friends around and was thinking with his lower parts rather than his brain. Even knowing it would take no more than a nod from him for Cormac to kick them out, he did not ask it.

This told him Lord Crawford was not truly ready to heal...or behave himself. Which meant Cormac was not going to let him anywhere near Phoebe, Chloe, or his nieces, no matter how vehemently the man implored him.

They returned to the house, and Lord Crawford rejoined his friends. "You will never guess what Burness has been hiding from us. Or should I say *whom* he has been keeping all to himself. But we are not to go near this earthly angel. I have given him my word."

Then why blab about it to his dissolute friends?

Cormac did not like this at all.

For all of Lord Crawford's pleasant manners and words of gratitude, Cormac was not certain he could be trusted.

Perhaps he was being too prickly about it. After all, the man had not uttered Phoebe's name to his friends, just left it as a vague tease.

Thankfully, his friends were too drunk to care.

He let out a breath of relief when none of them followed up with questions. In their condition, he doubted they could string two words together.

Still, Cormac did not like it.

Lord Crawford opened another bottle of wine, since the one beside Lord Harding was now empty. "Care for a glass, Burness?"

"No. I'll be heading off shortly."

"Lucky fellow. Are you certain I cannot accompany you?"

Cormac glanced around and motioned to his "guests." "I'm certain. You are not ready yet, and someone needs to entertain your friends. It isn't going to be me."

He marched upstairs to wash the sand from his body and salt water from his hair, calling for his valet to help him out. Although most peers retained a valet, the need still felt demeaning to

Cormac because he was now so helpless at so many tasks.

Gunyon was a good soul, and Cormac tried his best never to take out his frustration on the man who was amiable and went about his duties with due diligence. "How is that, my lord?" he asked, finishing up with a handsome knot of his cravat.

Cormac peered at himself in the mirror and nodded his approval. "Thank you, Gunyon. I shall call for you later."

"Very good, my lord."

Cormac headed downstairs, now fit to present himself at Moonstone Cottage.

As he strode past the parlor, Lord Crawford poked his head out and approached him. "Will you not reconsider my joining you?"

"Out of the question."

The man had not even washed the sand off himself, and Cormac was not about to wait around while he did. He found Lord Crawford's persistence quite annoying.

Or did he merely not like competition for Phoebe's affections?

# Chapter Ten

C ORMAC'S HEART LIGHTENED as it always seemed to do upon seeing Phoebe. She was standing beside her front door when he rode up on Hadrian, her arms crossed over her chest, fretting her pink lips.

He dismounted, handed the reins to Mr. Hawke, and strode toward her. "Good evening, Phoebe."

She cast him a hesitant smile. "Good evening, my lord. I wasn't certain you would show up tonight. The girls have had their supper and are now changed into their nightclothes. Chloe is in their bedchamber reading them a story. How angry are you with me?"

The notion surprised him. "Not angry at all. Why should I be?"

"Because I ran onto your side of the beach after my scheduled hour. I did not mean to, but Imogen's hat blew off her head while we were drawing in the garden. The wind carried it down the steps and onto the beach. I did not see the harm in chasing after it. It is a good hat and would have been a shame to lose."

"You are a frugal thing, aren't you?" He held out his arm to her and led her to the rear of the house to take a turn in the garden so they could speak privately. "I can buy her a dozen straw hats, if need be. Nor do I mind that you were on the beach. That schedule was your concoction, not mine."

"Because I could not risk the girls being subjected to your...friends."

He cast her a wry grin. "You mean my naked friends?"

Her smile in response was shy, but genuine. "I was relieved to find you both dressed."

"And Lord Crawford's eyes bulged when you came darting around the rocks with your gown hiked to your thighs. Do you have any idea how tempting you looked?"

"Oh, I did not realize. But I suppose it was rather brazen of me. I did not wish to get my gown wet. Besides, my legs were covered by the water."

He laughed. "Oh, Phoebe. The water is clear as a bell and your beautiful legs were on full display."

She looked genuinely distressed. "Then you and your friend saw too much."

"We are men, so to our way of thinking, we did not see nearly enough. Men need shockingly little encouragement. One glimpse of you and our bodies burst into flames."

She blushed. "I'm truly sorry. I was not thinking. Shall I apologize to your friend?"

"For being the one bright spot in his day? I don't think it is necessary. And Lord Crawford is not actually a friend. I've told you, none of them are."

"Fine, I shall refer to them merely as your guests. I don't know why you are so adamant about the distinction when you are housing them under your roof and not kicking them out. Were the others on the beach, too? In truth, I was so busy keeping my head down that I did not look beyond you."

"No. You needn't worry about encountering them down there. They seem incapable of moving from my parlor. All they do is drink and indulge in aimless pastimes. By evening, they are too drunk to stand on their own or hold their glasses steady. So they sit like lumps in their chairs, too deep in their cups to play so much as a round of cards. Life to them has become a numbing blur."

"Oh, you sound so angry," she said. "But it is a very sad thing for them, don't you think?"

"Forgive me if I show them little compassion. I've had my fill of their company. They think they are so high in the instep, but they are purposely letting their lives go to waste. The countess and viscountess have rich husbands and will never lack for anything. They have the ability to do so much that is worthwhile. Yet this is how they choose to spend their days."

"The gentleman with you, Lord Crawford, did not look so bad."

Cormac's heartbeat quickened, and he suppressed the well of anger that rose at the mention of the name. He wasn't angry with Phoebe, of course. Just at himself for allowing this simple remark to rouse his jealousy. Gad, he was hopeless. He wanted to keep this beautiful girl all to himself.

But he could not go through life behaving like a possessive oaf. "Lord Crawford is the one I brought here on the deathbed promise to his brother. He is coming around, but not quite there yet. I think in the end he will do something useful with his life."

Phoebe looked up at him with her sparkling eyes.

She really was exquisite.

"He's a scholar and enjoys studying ancient civilizations. He plans to return to London and organize an expedition to one of those biblical lands."

"That sounds fascinating. I would love to hear more. Why don't you invite him to come along with you tomorrow evening? Chloe and I would enjoy hearing him speak on the topic. Is he very learned?"

"No more than I am." Which was probably true, for he did know his history and had gained much of his military prowess on the battlefield by studying ancient battle tactics. "But I will decline the invitation on his behalf. I am adamant about this, Phoebe. He does not come over to see you while his friends remain here."

"Are you afraid they will come along, too? I thought you said they will not budge from your parlor."

"They won't. But I do not like that he still wants them around. It makes me wary, that's all."

"I see your point. The simple act of separating himself from his unsavory friends will count far more than a thousand promises he might make to you." She looked back at her house. "Shall we go up to see the girls?"

He nodded. "Of course."

"Be prepared, for they have drawings to show you. We spent the afternoon in the garden making sketches of whatever interested us."

"Did you draw as well?"

She laughed. "Yes, I am fairly decent at it, along with a host of other useless talents. Art lessons are a must if one wishes to become an accomplished young lady. I can sing, play the pianoforte, and embroider, too. Are you not impressed?"

He arched an eyebrow and cast her a warm smile. "Very."

"I wish I could do something truly important. You went off to save England. My talents are nothing outside of our privileged world."

"That isn't so, Phoebe. You have the ability to heal damaged souls. You've certainly done wonders for mine. Will you sing for me?"

"Oh, heavens. You really don't want me to do that." Her eyes glittered with mirth. "Perhaps tomorrow, when Imogen and Ella can join in. We might even coax you to sing along with us."

"Perish the thought." He groaned. "You do not want my croaking to mess up your song."

"I would not be surprised if you had a magnificent voice. But I suppose our amusements are too tame for you."

"No, Phoebe. Your company is a relief for me. I am so tired of the path I've been on for too many years now. I don't regret my past, nor will I make apologies for my rakehell ways. But it is time to move on."

"You do realize your decision is only a few days old."

"No, it was three years in the making."

"Well, we shall see how long it will last before you decide to unmake it." They walked inside and climbed the stairs to look in on the girls, who were sitting up in their beds. Chloe had just finished reading them a story about a talking frog.

"Uncle Cormac!" Imogen squealed.

"Uncle Cormac!" Ella cried out at the same time.

"How are my ducklings?" He sat at the edge of Ella's bed. Imogen immediately scrambled out of hers and clambered onto his lap. He kissed her on the forehead. "I heard you had a fun afternoon of drawing."

The girls began to chatter at him, each one eager to be the first to tell him what they had drawn. Chloe brought their pictures over to him. They were hardly more than stick figures, but he was touched to see how prominently they'd included him in each drawing—and actually depicted him as smiling.

They had also drawn themselves and Phoebe beside him.

Yes, it felt right that she should be shown standing alongside him. She did make him smile.

Even his little ducklings saw they were meant to be together. Indeed, they saw everything so clearly through their innocent eyes.

He kissed them each good night, gave them a tickle as he tucked them in, and then returned downstairs with Phoebe and Chloe. They had just settled in the parlor when Chloe made an obviously weak excuse and disappeared.

Phoebe sighed and sank onto the sofa. "I should not be left alone with you."

He took a chair beside her. "Everyone but you already has us paired. I understand your reluctance. You need to trust me."

"Actually, I do trust you." She searched his face as though she might find her answers in his eyes. "I am not the problem. You are the one who does not trust your feelings yet. Cormac, true love is not something that lasts a month and then fades. It lasts forever and becomes easier and more certain with each passing day, even through the difficult times."

"Phoebe..."

"I am not letting go of my heart until you are ready to believe true love is what you feel for me. Just let me know when you are confident this feeling will last a lifetime." She emitted a ragged sigh, a certain sign he'd disappointed her. "If we were to marry, you have to keep true to your vows. They have to mean something to you when you recite them. Only then will I begin to take your proposal seriously."

He knew what he felt for her was love, but he wasn't going to lie to her and make her promises he might not keep. He'd spent most of his life as a scoundrel. What if that part of him won out?

She took a deep breath and cast him a shaky smile. "What would you like to do with the girls tomorrow?" she asked, obviously eager to change the path of their conversation, since talk of love only seemed to upset her.

"I don't know. Let's see what the weather holds. We've had a string of nice days, so the rain has to arrive sometime soon." He shrugged and leaned forward. "And now let us speak of something more interesting than the weather."

She chuckled, and her soft, lilting laugh so easily seeped into his heart. "Dear heaven, are you suggesting the topic is dull?"

"Excruciatingly so." He smiled warmly.

"Are you also finding your reformed ways dull?"

"No, I like myself much better and don't mind behaving around you."

She nibbled her fleshy lower lip, the gesture sending a jolt of heat through him. "Can you see us spending quiet nights together like this?"

He could see hopefulness spring in her eyes. "Yes, Phoebe. I am never bored with you."

"Nor am I ever bored with you. I like having you around, although I should not admit this to you, for it will swell your head, and you are already too arrogant. Well, perhaps a nicer way of putting it is that you are confident in yourself."

He glanced at his arm. "Not as much now."

She shook her head. "No, that is something different. Your arm leaves you frustrated, but it does not make you less handsome or less intelligent. Or, dare I say it, less charming when you want to turn on the charm."

"I do not put on a false front with you," he said, now frowning because he'd given her a terrible first impression of himself—all of it true—and he had not considered it would be something he could never overcome.

Since that first encounter, he had laid open his heart to her...at least, he thought he had. Did she not understand this is what he was doing?

"I don't mean to suggest you turn your charm on and off whenever it suits you. Nor do I think you ever do this with me. I know you are trying to show me who you really are, and I like what I am seeing very much. But I've only seen three days of you, and I am eager to know more. Will you tell me something personal about yourself?"

He arched an eyebrow. "Such as what?"

She began to fret her kissable lips again. "Why did you ask me to marry you?"

"Because I find you beautiful, and you lighten my heart. Perhaps this is what love does to a man. It brings him joy. Peace. These are feelings I have not experienced in a long time."

"It is obvious, Cormac. Even now, I can sense you are not comfortable with these good feelings. You have grown used to being in turmoil."

"Perhaps it is built into me, but I am not angry or overset now. You are a calming influence—is it not obvious? I do not feel humiliated around you as I do around others. You are a lioness, and yet you have such a soft way when dealing with me."

"I have been so clumsy tonight in expressing my feelings, but I would never intentionally hurt you."

"I know, Phoebe. You see me as a whole person. I like that very much. But my missing arm is always on my mind. How can it not be on yours?"

"You are so much more than merely a missing part of an arm."

"I would like to think so, but I am constantly reminded of its loss. So many little things come up in a day that frustrate and anger me. You do not see my limitations. You do not recoil or remark on my failings. But I do. They smack me in the face and are a constant reminder of all the things I can no longer do."

"They are not limitations or failings in you."

"Phoebe, I cannot even cut a slice of beef with my knife. One needs to pin the meat down with one's fork and slice it using the other hand. I have no other hand. I cannot button my breeches without a struggle. I've ordered a billiards table for my house, and yet how can I play the game one-handed? It takes me forever to complete so many simple tasks."

He watched her face, took in her compassionate expression, and continued. "I cannot lift my nieces at the same time. Nor can I ever put my arms around you. Or ever carry you in my arms. I think I regret this most of all, knowing I shall never be able to hold you this way."

"Then I shall be the one to put my arms around you."

"It is not quite the same thing. My point is, so many stupid obstacles that I can no longer control or surmount crop up in a day. Each little thing destroys me. Yet it does not hurt so badly when I am around you. You never make me feel worthless. How is that for something personal? Now, your turn."

She cast him a heartfelt smile. "The naughtiest thing I have ever done is allow you to kiss me. Other than that, I have led a spotless life. How is that for boring?"

"Have you ever done anything daring or adventurous?"

"We've helped out Vicar Trask a time or two during storms. Very fierce storms. That was rather daring."

"What else?"

"Well, this is not really daring or adventurous…perhaps more about us suffering hard times. We were kicked out of our London home by our odious cousin, the new Earl of Stoke, after our father died. The title passed to that weasel, as did guardianship of us. But this did not stop him from kicking us out of our house."

"I know he gave you a very hard time."

"He tried to cheat us, as you know," she continued. "But Cain saved the day and then married Hen. We were never really in dire straits, so I don't suppose it counts, even though we were feeling quite desperate for a while. We've never really had to struggle. So I don't suppose that counts as anything. Certainly not daring or adventurous."

"Not everyone needs to live their lives in constant peril. You were raised in comfort, but you are not haughty, nor are you reluctant to come to the aid of others. There's fight in you, Phoebe."

She smiled at him again, her expression achingly soft. "Well, I hope I do not fight with my husband. That would make for a messy marriage. And what of you? You've faced danger every day of your life on the battlefield. How has that affected your outlook?"

"Darkened it. But also made me appreciate the good when it comes along. That's what you are, a shimmering, heavenly light."

She blushed. "Hardly, but thank you."

He leaned forward and took her hand. "This is what you are to me, Phoebe."

"Don't say such a beautiful thing to me or I will cry. Worse, I will fall desperately in love with you and then be shattered when you decide I am not right for you after all."

He bent closer and kissed her softly on the lips. "A light of heaven does not fade. This is what you are and shall always be."

And then it hit him, the realization falling atop him like a roof collapsing on his head. What he had just said was true.

He would never tire of Phoebe.

Nor could he imagine seeking fulfillment elsewhere when she was all he would ever want or need.

Was this not what she worried about most, that he would be unfaithful and crush her heart?

He was about to assure her it would not happen, pledge to her that he would not stray, when there came a sudden pounding on the door.

Phoebe jumped out of her seat, but he held her back. "Let me see who it is." He cast her a warning look to stay put and strode out of the parlor to open the door.

His butler stood before him, his face ashen. "Melrose? What the devil?"

"Countess Rothmere's husband is here, and he is livid. He has threatened to shoot Lord Harding and the Earl of Crawford."

Cormac uttered a curse in open disgust. "The fool waits till now to take offense at his wife's conduct? I would think he is about five years too late for that."

"Please hurry, my lord. I hope we are not too late now."

Cormac was about to call out to Phoebe to let her know he was leaving, but he almost knocked her over when he turned, for she was standing immediately behind him, a rifle in her hand. "I thought I told you to wait in the parlor."

"I did wait, then I heard Melrose and knew it was safe to come out." She peeked around him. "Good evening, Melrose. I am so sorry for the havoc these guests have wreaked on your orderly household."

"Certainly not your fault, Lady Phoebe."

Cormac ran a hand through his hair in frustration. "I have to go. I'll see you and my nieces tomorrow." Although he was not certain what his encounter with Lord Rothmere would lead to, especially if the man was enraged and took a shot at him.

He strode out of the house, thinking Phoebe was out of earshot. "Melrose, has he been disarmed?"

But the blasted girl had followed him out and was still behind him. She gasped. "Is he waving a pistol?"

His butler nodded.

"Oh dear. Give me a moment, and I will go with—"

"So help me, Phoebe—you take one step out of Moonstone Cottage and I will haul you over my knee and spank you until your backside is raw." Well, some women enjoyed that sort of thing. He had never struck a woman in his life, whether in anger or in sexual play. It wasn't something he could ever bring himself to do.

Phoebe clearly had no idea about such things.

Her expression was fierce. "He would not dare harm you if I was standing beside you."

"That is wrong on every count. A man enraged is not thinking straight. He is blind to his actions and does not see who is standing in front of him." Mr. Hawke had now brought Hadrian out of the stable. "Come on, Melrose. We had better hurry back before he shoots the entire worthless lot of them." He cast Phoebe a final warning glance.

She scowled back at him. "But I can handle this weapon."

"Have you ever killed a man? Because if you walk in pointing that thing at him, he is going to take it rather personally and try to shoot you first." Gad, she was going to be a handful when he married her.

And he *was* going to marry her.

He had never felt anything more fiercely or surely than he did now.

"But what if you walk in unarmed and he takes aim at you?"

"All the more reason for you to stay put. My nieces will need you more than ever if I am shot."

She gasped.

He loved her more than ever because she wanted to protect him. Yes, it irritated him, but it also made him immensely proud.

He intended to protect her as well, and would not hesitate to die a thousand deaths if this was what it took to keep her safe. She mattered to him more than his own soul.

He never thought to feel this way about any woman.

The lights of Westgate Hall were now coming into view as he rode home in the glimmers of twilight.

As he dismounted in the courtyard, he could hear the Earl of Rothmere ranting in the parlor. He still held its occupants hostage. A peek in the window revealed this included all Cormac's guests and two frightened footmen.

He entered the house, grabbed a decorative vase off the entry hall table, then dumped the flowers and water out of it. "Sorry, Melrose. Someone will have to clean this up."

"No worries, my lord. Do you have a plan?"

"Yes, this." Cormac hurled the vase into the parlor so that it smashed against the far wall.

Lord Rothmere turned at the sound. "What the...?"

When he turned back, Cormac smashed his fist in the man's face.

# Chapter Eleven

CORMAC GRABBED THE pistol out of the Earl of Rothmere's hand as the man crumpled to the floor. "Search him for weapons," he ordered Melrose, then turned to his two footmen. "Are you all right?"

The men nodded and muttered their effusive thanks.

"Good." He gave each a pat on the shoulder. "Assist Melrose. Check Lord Rothmere's boots. Feel along his jacket for a secret pocket. Once you are certain he has no weapons on him, tie him up securely."

"Must you do that?" Lady Rothmere asked, wringing her hands as she stared at her husband, who was now groaning and attempting to sit up.

"I would have been within my rights to make you a widow," Cormac snapped back. "What sent him here in a mad rage?"

She shook her head. "I don't know. I was too overset to listen to his rantings."

Cormac knelt beside the man. "Rothmere, what the hell were you thinking?" He did not appear to be drunk, so what had put him in a temper?

"You have everything, Burness. Must you steal my wife, too? I will not grant her a divorce. She will never marry you."

"Dear heaven, where did you hear such utter tripe? I did not steal your wife. Nor do I have any desire to marry her. I did not even know she would be here until she came along with Lord Crawford and his party."

The earl delicately rubbed his jaw to check whether it was broken.

Well, Cormac had given the man a hard punch, but had been careful not to hit him harder than necessary.

"The scandal is out, so you needn't deny it."

"What scandal?" Cormac asked. "I will deny it. I have no idea what you are talking about."

Lord Crawford now stepped forward. "Burness is telling you the truth. It is just a house party. A group of friends getting together to console me over the loss of my brother. There is nothing devious going on here."

"Someone played you for a fool, Rothmere," Cormac said. "Who told you this nonsense about me and your wife?"

Lord Rothmere refused to say.

"Must I beat it out of you?" Cormac wouldn't, of course. But the man did not know this.

"A reliable source."

Cormac itched to hit this dolt again. "Obviously not reliable. You might have killed innocent people in your outburst. And do not be so stupid as to challenge me to a duel. Even with one arm, I could easily best you. All that would do is make you dead."

"But my wife—"

"Drinks too much and has shockingly loose morals, but she is quite fond of her status and has no intention of ending your farce of a marriage. No, Lord Rothmere. You are stuck with her until you take your last breath."

"Really, Burness," the countess said. "Must you be so crude?"

"I am being the soul of reason. By all rights, your husband should be dead. No one walks into my house and points a pistol at my guests or staff without risking his own life. Your husband is alive now only because I am feeling magnanimous. Rest assured, if he ever thinks to draw a weapon in my home again, I shall shoot him between the eyes. Now, Lord Rothmere, answer my question. Who is your so-called reliable source?"

"I cannot tell you now. You might harm the lady."

"Obviously, anyone malicious enough to spread such rot is no lady. You need say no more. I know who you think you are protecting. Lady Seline, of course. She and I have a combative past, although it is beyond me why she should choose to malign me now."

"Indeed," Lady Rothmere said. "She dumped you years ago."

Ah, yes.

How politely she put it.

"A word of caution, Rothmere," Cormac continued. "You are better off keeping your distance from that viper. I can assure you, she did not care which of us would be hurt because of her lies. She is a nasty, spiteful thing who is happiest when hurting others."

"She does have it in for you," Lord Crawford acknowledged. "Does she not, Harding? We saw her recently at Lord Forster's ball and overheard her referring to you as a… Well, it was not a nice thing she called you."

Cormac tried to keep his temper in check, but he knew what Seline thought of him. "A grotesque cripple."

Crawford sighed. "Yes."

Was it not enough she had publicly ended their liaison after Cormac had lost his arm? Not only ended it, but went out of her way to humiliate him at the time. Apparently, she was not through with him yet.

However, he could not fathom the reason to resurrect their past, since she was now married to the Earl of Whitford and had done quite well for herself.

Of course, there was no marital bliss between the lady and her husband. Cormac knew she was already having affairs.

Had she also grown bored of the trail of men entering and leaving her boudoir?

Phoebe had the right of it, insisting on nothing less than true love.

The lot standing before him were so utterly pathetic. Their wealth and titles could not stave off their misery. Lord Crawford must have been thinking the same thing, for he turned to his friends. "I believe it is time for all of you to return to London. Lord Rothmere, take your wife home. But do me the favor of seeing Viscountess Hopewell safely delivered to her home as well."

"What about me?" Lord Harding asked.

"Lord Rothmere can drop you off at the Crawford townhouse. It is unoccupied at present, but fully staffed. You may stay there until I return. I'll be there in about a week." Lord Crawford turned to Cormac with a shrug. "I thought at the time my sisters would stay with me, so I kept the servants on. But they did not wish to remain beyond my brother's funeral. They prefer the countryside to London."

"Perhaps you ought to visit them there to make certain they are all right." Cormac arched an eyebrow. "Your estate is not far from London. You are earl, and it is important for them to know they can rely on you whether you are near or far from them."

Lord Crawford laughed. "Is that your polite way of kicking me out, too?"

"No, Richard. I will not make you leave. I made a promise to your brother to look after you and will hold to it."

Lord Harding shook his head. "You are the most honorable cad I know, Burness. I'm sorry if we gave you a hard time. You do have an awful reputation, you know."

"I know, but that is all in the past."

Lord Rothmere looked on in alarm as Cormac's footmen returned with ropes. "No need for that, Burness. I see now that it was an honest mistake. No hard feelings, old boy."

"None at all, Rothmere." Cormac turned to his footmen. "Tie him up. You will forgive me if I make certain you do not cause more harm. No hard feelings, *old boy*."

He thought Countess Rothmere might be overset by his treatment of her husband, for she had turned away and walked to stand beside the window. But he realized she was quietly laughing at her husband's predicament.

Ah, the joys of marriage.

Or rather, he thought sarcastically, the joys of a loveless marriage.

He ordered two footmen to guard Lord Rothmere, made certain his guests were not going to do anything stupid, such as try to release him from his bonds, and then rode back to Moonstone Cottage to assure Phoebe nothing was amiss.

He could have sent a messenger, but he knew she would not be satisfied until she saw him for herself.

Well, he needed to see her too.

His soul craved her.

There were no lights on in the house save for a lone lamp shining in the parlor, a sign Phoebe had waited up for him. How did she know he would return? He tethered Hadrian beside a yew tree, then strode to the front door, intending to rap lightly on it.

But Phoebe opened it before he had the chance to knock. "I saw you ride up. Come in. Would you care for a glass of port? Is everyone all right?"

He laughed, trying to get a word in edgewise.

"I'm so glad you thought to come back. I would have stayed up all night worried." She ran her hands along his body, suddenly realized what she was doing, and hastily dropped them to her sides. "I'm so sorry. I just wanted to be certain you weren't hurt."

"I'm fine." Rather, he had been fine until seeing her in her nightclothes, her hair down and tumbling over one shoulder in a glorious cascade.

He ached for this girl.

He strode in when she stepped aside to let him pass, his heart in a rampant roar. She looked so beautiful in her prim, plain night rail that probably hid an even plainer cotton nightgown beneath it. No sultry silk to tempt him.

Yet she could not have looked more tempting if she were wearing nothing at all. Gad, his heart would burst if she ever stripped for him.

It would not happen before they were married. He was not going to rush Phoebe into doing something she was not ready to do.

But if she ever *was* ready and willing? He would be all over her like a barnacle to the hull of a ship.

"Phoebe, you needn't fret," he said, his voice tight and raspy. "But thank you for worrying about me. You have no idea how good it makes me feel."

She smiled up at him. "Feelings, Cormac? Why, I do believe we are making progress."

"Perhaps." He gave her cheek a light caress. "I won't stay long. Lord Rothmere is nursing a bruised jaw. He's lucky I did not break it."

She led him into the parlor and motioned for him to sit beside her on the sofa. "What happened?"

He quickly related the tale to her, all of it, including Lady Seline's role in fomenting this bit of mischief.

Phoebe's eyes were wide and shimmering as she listened to him. "I am so sorry. Someone might have been killed because of her lies. What sort of low creature does a thing like this?" She paused a moment to stare at him. "She was the one you were involved with for years? You really have awful taste in women, you know. Has anyone told you that?"

"Everyone." He groaned. "My brother tells me all the time. But I purposely chose these awful women because there was no chance of my heart ever being lost to one of them. Imogen refers to them as my horrible ladies."

"Seems Lady Seline is living up to her reputation. Horrible, indeed."

He shook his head. "I haven't had anything to do with her for years. I don't know why she suddenly turned her venom on me."

"Do you think she will follow you out here to Moonstone Landing?"

"Doubtful. Her toadies are all in London. I have no idea what she would do with herself here. The quiet life bores her to tears."

"But you are here."

"And you think this will lure her?" He shook his head. "Phoebe, she refers to me as a grotesque cripple. She cannot stand the sight of me as I am now."

She inhaled sharply. "What a miserable and despicable thing for her to say. She is obviously blind. You are the handsomest man I have ever met. I cannot look at you without my legs turning to water."

"Is that so?"

"I... That is..." She blushed, sputtered some more, and then sighed. "Yes, it is so."

"I love that you are inept at hiding your feelings."

"It is not a loveable trait at all. I hate that you so easily know exactly what I am thinking or feeling. Or that I am too stupid to keep these thoughts to myself."

"It is a good trait. I'm glad you think I am handsome."

"You are smirking, and I can see your head swelling. It will soon be too big to fit inside this room."

He laughed. "I just saved the lives of my guests tonight. Will you not be a little kinder to me?"

"All right. In truth, I am very proud of you. And look, my hands are shaking." She held out the hands she had been clasping. "I was so worried for your safety."

"I know. This is why I rode back. I had to see you and let you know all had turned out well. Although Lord Rothmere is not too pleased to be trussed up like a Christmas goose. I am not untying him until he is in the carriage and on his way home."

"You must know you are splendid. How can anyone think you are not?"

"You are full of compliments for me tonight. The incident must have shaken you quite badly."

She nodded.

"Phoebe, love." He kissed her softly on the lips, making certain to keep it short and sweet. She had him on fire, but what was he to do about it when her sister and his nieces were just above them? "It will take more than a deranged husband to take me down. The man does not even love his wife. He was enraged because he thought she was going to divorce him. It was the shame of divorcing that turned him into a raging madman."

"Inconceivable. Utterly outrageous."

"That she sleeps with every man willing to make himself available does not bother him in the least. He probably does the same with the women of his acquaintance. Can you imagine anything more unpleasant than to be in such a marriage? They are both...but I suppose this is what I was, too."

"No, even at your worst, I do not think you would ever have settled for a loveless marriage. You have more honor than that."

He cast her a wry smile. "I was pretty bad, Phoebe. But I did set strict boundaries for myself. I never seduced an innocent. Had I seen you though, I probably would have broken all my rules and willingly faced the consequences. I cannot imagine myself—"

"Uncle Cormac," a soft voice came from the doorway, interrupting him as he was about to pour his heart out to Phoebe.

"Imogen? What's wrong, duckling?" He rose at once and took her into his arm.

She wrapped hers around his neck. "I have a tummy ache."

"You do?" He looked at Phoebe, for he had no idea what to do.

Her eyes widened. "Quick, follow me."

She picked up Imogen and raced into the kitchen. Then she grabbed a clean basin, set it on the long wooden table that stood in the center of the kitchen, and held Imogen over it just as she began to heave. In the next moment, the contents of every meal the poor little thing had eaten all week came out of her in liquid chunks.

He looked on, not knowing what to do.

Phoebe cast him a woeful glance. "She'll be all right. It was an exciting day for her, and her stomach couldn't handle it. There are some clean cloths in that drawer." She motioned to a cupboard near the sink. "Pull out a couple. Wet two of them and bring them to me."

He did as she asked, grateful for the moonlight casting slivers of light through the windows and allowing him to make out more than mere shadows. "I need to light a candle or I'm going to trip over things."

"Just bring in the lamp from the parlor. Or I can fetch it for us, but you will need to hold Imogen."

"I'll get it. I'm familiar enough with your house to avoid the obstacles." He returned quickly and held the lamp up to cast proper light in the kitchen. His breath caught again. The sight of Phoebe so gently tending to Imogen, both of them illuminated by the amber glow, had his heart in palpitations.

He did not think it possible to love Phoebe more than he did in this moment.

For a man who had avoided feelings for all his life, he was surely awash in them now.

He could not stop staring at Phoebe.

She was seated in one of the rickety kitchen stools, looking as magnificent as a queen on her throne as she cradled his niece on her lap.

Imogen rested her head on Phoebe's shoulder while Phoebe tended to her, cleaning her mouth and then gently pressing another wet cloth to her forehead. She smiled at him when he set the lamp on the table and knelt beside them. "She doesn't have a fever. It was just too much cake and excitement."

He tucked a finger under Imogen's chin. "Duckling, how do you feel now?"

"Better," she said, her voice soft and weak.

"Tell you what, Imogen," Phoebe said. "Why don't you sleep in my bed tonight so I can watch you if your tummy ache returns? Would you like that?"

Imogen nodded against Phoebe's shoulder.

"I'll keep a pot close if the need arises again," she said, now turning to Cormac. "She'll also be more comfortable knowing I am close. I'll wet a handkerchief and add a little cologne to it. This should help chase away any remaining nausea."

"Will you take me into your bed and nurse me like this if ever I fall ill?" he teased.

She laughed. "It would be too much like letting the wolf in among the lambs, don't you think?"

"You forget, you are Phoebe the lioness. I think you would easily defeat this wolf. Certainly claim his heart."

"Phoebe isn't a lion, Uncle Cormac," Imogen interjected.

He chuckled. "I know, duckling. I was just teasing her. Shall I carry you up to bed now?"

She nodded.

"Phoebe, is it all right? Lead the way with the lamp while I carry her upstairs. I won't stay. I just want to be sure she is comfortably settled." Lord help him, he was eager for Cain's return. He was so desperate to marry this girl, but could do nothing without his friend's consent. She was not yet one and twenty years of age and could not act on her own.

*Lord, how the mighty have fallen,* he thought. Never in all his years had he imagined himself being desperate to marry. Phoebe wasn't even trying to land him as a husband. He was lost to her anyway, no matter that she had not put the least effort toward catching him.

This had to be true love on his part, did it not?

Perhaps on her part, too.

She was naturally compassionate and kind. Was she feeling pity for him and mistaking it for love?

He carried Imogen upstairs while Phoebe led the way with her lamp.

When they reached her bedchamber, Phoebe pointed to the bed. "Set her down on the right side." She placed the lamp on her bureau beside a basin and ewer, then opened one of the bureau drawers to remove a handkerchief. She poured a little water from the ewer to moisten the handkerchief, wrung it out, and then applied some cologne to it.

The sweetly pungent scent filled the air. "I'm going to rub a little on your wrists and neck, Imogen. The scent of it will make you feel better. I'll also apply a little to your forehead. The water may feel a bit cool, but it will soothe you."

"All right." Imogen nodded and smiled up at both of them.

Phoebe sat beside her. "Do you think you can sleep now?"

Imogen nodded again and shut her eyes tight.

Phoebe looked up at him and grinned.

Cormac felt another hard tug to his heart.

This was what he wanted so desperately for himself. He had never understood why his brother was always so happy in his home life, even when his daughters were crying and his wife was relentlessly chattering at him the moment he walked through the door.

But he understood it now, saw how bonds grew stronger through good times and bad. His brother was loved by his wife and daughters, and smart enough to appreciate what he had.

"Goodnight, Uncle Cormac." His niece's eyes were still sealed shut and she was still smiling.

"Pleasant dreams, duckling. Phoebe has to come downstairs with me to bolt the door, but she'll be right back."

"Oh, I had better dump out what we left in the kitchen," Phoebe whispered as they returned downstairs.

He held the lamp while she hastily cleaned up Imogen's mess. Once done, she walked him to the door and laughed in surprise when he drew her up against him and kissed her hard on the lips. "I love you, Phoebe Killigrew."

Her smile turned impish. "You must if you still desire to kiss me after what I just cleaned up. Perhaps your sense of smell is not functioning."

"Everything on my body is functioning, which is why I had better leave before I put the naughtier parts of me to use." He kissed her again, pleased to see sparkles in her eyes. "I have so much I want to say to you." He glanced toward the stairs, expecting Imogen to scamper back down if Phoebe did not return to her soon. "But it can wait until tomorrow. I'll see you in the morning for breakfast. Lock up after me."

He left the house, but remained close until he heard the bolt click into place. Only then did he ride off. He rode slowly, hoping Hadrian had been back and forth enough times between the two houses to memorize the way, for it was quite dark despite the silver light of an almost-full moon.

It was not long before he saw the lights still blazing at Westgate Hall.

He patted Hadrian's neck again. "Good work, old boy. We've made it home."

Yet this was not quite true.

Yes, Westgate Hall was a beautiful estate, and he owned it. But no place would ever be a true home without Phoebe in it.

He gave his steed over to one of the grooms and strode into the house, which remained a hive of activity. "Melrose, what are all the servants doing up at this late hour?"

Of course, it was not considered late for him or his guests. These lords and ladies never stirred until noon. The servants, however, were up at the crack of dawn, and he had no intention of keeping them working day and night.

"We are assisting the ladies and Lord Harding in packing their belongings," Melrose replied.

Cormac laughed. "Can't be rid of them soon enough, can you, Melrose?"

The butler grinned. "They wish to leave, and we wish to make certain they do, my lord."

"And what of Lord Rothmere? Has he calmed down?"

"Yes, although he was not pleased when he realized you were serious about tying him to a chair all night."

"I was not too pleased he wished to shoot me."

"Quite so. We tied him up as you instructed, in one of the large, padded leather chairs beside the hearth. We kept his bindings loose, as you bade us to do. Truly, my lord, you have gone too easy on him. He'll manage a moderately comfortable night's sleep under the watchful eyes of my best footmen. If he complains come morning, then he can sleep it off in his coach on the way back to London."

"You did well, Melrose. Summon me if he gives them any problem. Indeed, do not hesitate to summon me for the slightest reason. I will not rest until that lot is gone." He then made a quick inspection of each room to be certain everything was under control before heading to his bedchamber.

He knew he would not get more than three or four hours of sleep, but he did not really need more than that to function. Morning could not come soon enough for him, not only because he wished his guests to be on their way. He was also eager to see Phoebe and his nieces, and looked forward to the day he could take the girls under his roof.

Phoebe, too.

But that would require a marriage license and a wedding ceremony.

Well, the girls would be with him soon enough. Another week of riding back and forth until his last guest departed.

"Blast," he muttered, wondering what he was going to do with Lord Crawford once the others were gone. He could not leave him to rattle about this big house on his own.

He supposed it was safe enough to bring Lord Crawford around to Moonstone Cottage to meet Phoebe, Chloe, and his nieces. But not first thing tomorrow for breakfast. That time was for him alone. Besides, he needed to make certain Imogen was not ill. Also, Phoebe might be exhausted if Imogen's stomach remained upset and she had to stay up all night with her.

His valet entered his bedchamber to assist him in undressing. "My lord?"

"Come in, Gunyon." Cormac scowled and remained scowling, for he hated to stand there like a child, incapable of managing the simplest tasks.

He knew he was behaving like a surly oaf, but this nightly ritual was demeaning, and he had never gotten used to his dependence on others. Three years now, and he still hated being treated like a child.

Gunyon cast him a worried glance as he set aside Cormac's clothes and helped him to wash up. "My lord, have I done something wrong?"

"No, I'm angry with myself."

"Why, if I may be so bold as to ask?"

"Look at me, Gunyon. I cannot even wrap a towel around my waist without your help. It gets to me sometimes...often, as you well know, since you are usually on the receiving end of my frown. It is not your fault, of course. The failing is in me."

Especially now that he wanted to marry Phoebe.

He did not like to think she would be marrying a helpless man.

More than anything, he hated the thought of Phoebe watching him struggle through this nightly bedtime ritual on his own. He wouldn't be so stupid as to ever try it. But he also hated the thought of having her watch Gunyon tend to him as though he were feeble and incompetent.

His valet was a good man, and now Cormac had him worrying. "My lord, we all need help in different ways. This is nothing. Are you not relieved you are not in the same circumstances as Lord Rothmere or Lady Hopewell's husband? Now that is cause for misery. Indeed, I expect the lords and their ladies are quite the unhappiest lot."

Cormac laughed. "That's true. Thank you, Gunyon. Don't mind me. This is no more than my constant grumbling. I'll see you at the usual time tomorrow morning."

"Very good, my lord." Gunyon gathered Cormac's clothes and boots and quietly left his quarters. The clothes would be cleaned and pressed by morning, and his boots would be polished to a shine.

This was what valets did, among other tasks. But Gunyon had also taken on the role of encouraging parent.

Cormac did not mind, but it also served to point out how

much the loss of his arm had taken from him. He'd lost so much of his self-respect along with his limb.

But as his valet said, everyone had problems and weaknesses. And most peers employed valets.

So why was he getting so bent out of shape over Gunyon helping him undress?

Cormac knew the answer. He was afraid Phoebe would take a look at him one day and decide he was the grotesque cripple Seline had called him.

The witch was not so far off the mark. There were days he thought of himself as exactly this.

How long before Phoebe thought so, too?

# Chapter Twelve

P HOEBE WAS RELIEVED come morning when Imogen appeared fully recovered. They'd slept later than usual, and Ella and Chloe had done the same. But it was well past time for them to stir, for the sun was arcing in the sky and it seemed to be another gorgeous day in the making.

Imogen, perhaps missing her mother after not feeling well last night, wanted to cuddle with Phoebe a little while longer. Ella came into her bedchamber. "What happened to Imogen?"

Phoebe scooted over so Ella could climb in with them. "Her tummy was upset, but she's fine now."

Ella looked at her with her big, innocent eyes. "Mine was upset, too."

"It was? Oh my. Then you had better get some cuddles, too," Phoebe said, knowing Ella was perfectly fine, for the girl had a big smile on her face as she nestled beside her.

Chloe walked in, washed and dressed for the day. At least one of them would be presentable when Cormac arrived. "Goodness, is there a party going on? Why wasn't I invited?" She jumped on the bed and had the girls squealing and laughing as she tried to snuggle in, too.

They were all laughing and making so much noise that they did not hear Cormac arrive. Well, the girls must have heard him, for they suddenly bolted out of bed and hurried downstairs barefoot and wearing only their little nighties.

She and Chloe tore after them.

Phoebe was halfway down the stairs before she realized why the girls had run off. Cormac now had one of his nieces in his arm and the other was clinging to his leg.

His mouth gaped open when he caught sight of her.

She was also barefoot, hair unbound, and wearing only her thin nightgown. She froze and stared back at him, her entire body warming under the heat of his gaze. "Heavens!" She *eeped* and ran back upstairs.

Chloe and the girls were laughing.

She really had to lecture her sister on proper behavior. Chloe should have been appalled, not holding her sides and laughing hard. "You needn't dress on the marquess's account. I don't think he minds at all," Chloe called up to her.

Phoebe popped her head out of her bedchamber. "Chloe! Come up here this instant."

Her sister was still grinning as she walked in.

"Honestly! You mustn't say such things. It isn't proper."

"Neither is the way the marquess was looking at you. I'm sure I tripped over his tongue on the way up here. I think you have ensorcelled him."

"Ridiculous. Help me lace up my gown and then help the girls get dressed. I'll do up my own hair." She took a deep breath as Chloe tied the final lacing on the dark green muslin, and inhaled the divine aroma of bacon frying in the pan and fresh scones just out of the oven. "Do you smell that? Mrs. Hawke has outdone herself this morning. I'm starved."

"So is the marquess—starved for you."

"Chloe! I am going paddle you if you don't behave."

Her sister laughed and gave her a big hug. "I'm just so happy. Two sisters in love, and you've both found the best men. I hope I am as lucky as you and Hen."

"No one has said anything about love." But Phoebe blushed, knowing it was not true. Cormac had told her several times now that he loved her.

She had not believed him at first. Now, she was beginning to think it was true.

Warmth flooded through her.

Perhaps he did love her and had come to realize it was a feeling that would last a lifetime. Not a month. Or a year. But forever.

She was now dressed and had just washed up when she heard playful shrieks outside her window. She had not yet brushed her hair or donned her shoes, but as Chloe ran downstairs to see what was going on, Phoebe went onto her balcony and looked down. "Run, Ella!"

She laughed and cheered as the two little imps ran barefoot on the grass, still clad in their nighties and enjoying their freedom. They made themselves dizzy while circling Cormac as he knelt in one spot and let out a roar each time he tried to grab them.

Goodness, those little girls were so riled and their stomachs still so delicate, they were likely to cast up their accounts. But they were having too much fun with their uncle, so she dared not admonish any of them.

He looked up at her.

Her insides melted.

Chloe now joined the girls.

Phoebe leaned over the balcony. "Wait for me!"

She ran downstairs and out of the house, wincing as she stepped on a pebble. Well, not even Chloe was wearing shoes, so why should she?

Ella and Imogen were now pretending to be the lions as Chloe circled them. Cormac appeared to be taking a break, smiling as he watched the girls frolic. But his gaze turned insanely hot when he looked at Phoebe as she walked toward them to join in the game.

Suddenly, he was prowling toward her, his voice a low, sensual growl. "Don't you look a tasty treat."

Tingles shot through her and her legs weakened.

Then her heart broke as he whispered, "I wish I could hold you in my arms, Phoebe. It is the thing I regret most and gives me the deepest ache."

She was about to say something warm and compassionate when he suddenly lifted her onto his shoulder and emitted a roar. "Sorry, love. It's all part of the game." He carried her to the girls as though she were a lamb for the lions' slaughter. "But I meant every word. It is my greatest regret."

He set her down, and the girls playfully jumped on her, pretending to be vicious predators. Though she did not think predators giggled or planted soft kisses on their victim's face.

Soon they were all exhausted and rolling on the grass laughing. Cormac stood looking over the four of them, his eyes alight and his smile affectionate.

When his gaze fell on her, the look in his eyes once again turned smoldering.

Fire tore through her.

She'd never felt anything like this before. The pulse at the base of her throat began to throb wildly. Her other pulses did, too. Including a few in places she did not know existed.

She looked at him, utterly bewildered.

Did he know how she was responding?

His shameless smile acknowledged that he did.

"Chloe, bring the girls. Breakfast is ready." She scrambled to her feet and ran into the house. Tears filled her eyes as she ran up to her bedchamber and frantically splashed water on her face. She needed to compose herself or she was doomed. Well, she was likely doomed anyway, for she could not look at Cormac without wanton thoughts crossing her mind.

And he knew it.

Dear heaven, everyone probably knew it except for Ella and Imogen, who were too young and innocent to understand such things.

She was still splashing water on her face when Cormac entered her bedchamber.

She gasped. "You cannot be in here!"

"Blessed saints, Phoebe. Everything shows on your face."

"I know. This is awful. Why did you have to cast me those hot glances?"

"Because I am in love with you." He grinned rakishly. "They were no different than the way I have always looked at you. You're the one who is responding differently."

"What do you mean?"

He caressed her cheek. "Your body has come alive, my little lioness. How can I put this politely to you so you will not slap my face? You want me in your bed."

She covered her face with her hands.

Her wet face.

And wet hands.

And the water was dripping onto her gown. "What sort of an example am I setting for Chloe? Her sister is a wanton."

"Hardly," he said with a soft chuckle. "Phoebe, calm down. I am not going to touch you outside of marriage."

She peeked up at him. "You're not?"

He laughed. "No, and it is not because the desire isn't there. I am racked with ache to explore your luscious body. But you hide nothing, and Cain is going to kill me the moment he returns. All he needs to do is take one look at you and he'll know I've touched you. So I am not touching you."

"But you've kissed me."

"That does not count. I will expire if you deny me that."

She nodded. "I enjoyed your kisses."

"I know, love. Come downstairs. Now that we've straightened this out, do you think you can compose yourself?"

She looked up at him.

"Blessed saints, you're tempting." He kissed her full on the mouth. "I'm riding to Bath and dragging Cain back here to get the marriage license. Phoebe, do you love me?"

"Don't ask me that question."

"Fine, but I have my answer. Your face shows it."

"Please, stop. Have I not made enough of a fool of myself over you?"

He laughed softly again. "And what of me? Do you think I ever imagined hearing those words out of my mouth? What you are feeling is desire. That just proves you want me to explore your body. And don't punch me! I know you would not be having these feelings of desire without also being in love. But I need to hear it from your lips. Do you love me?"

"It is your feelings I worry about. It is still too soon. What happens when you tire of me?"

The question went unanswered as Chloe came upstairs with Imogen and Ella. "The girls need to get dressed."

Cormac sighed. "And I need to wait downstairs. Hurry up, ducklings. Your uncle is hungry."

He heard the patter of little feet as they scampered into their bedchamber. Chloe bustled in after them.

He paused a moment at Phoebe's door. "Can you not say it to me?"

She wanted to tell him that she loved him. He knew it anyway. But saying the words aloud seemed so final. She wasn't worried about her feelings. As much as she'd tried not to fall in love with him, it was an utterly lost cause.

She loved him fiercely.

He'd called her a lioness, and this was how she loved him, with the pride and ferocity of a lion.

But she'd known him less than a week. Would he love her into next week? And the next?

He gave her a wry smile. "Funny how the words trip so easily off my tongue, but they seem stuck on yours. I see you still have doubts about me."

She hated to hurt him. "Cormac, wait."

He turned back and cast her a heartbroken smile as tears welled in her eyes.

"Love," he said gently, "you're crying. Don't cry over me. I know you care for me. Don't cry and don't start splashing water on your face again. I'll give you all the time you need to be certain of me."

She threw her arms around him. "Thank you for understanding."

He plunged his hand in her hair, his fingers soft as they slid through her curls. "Do I have a choice?"

"You could decide I am not worth the wait."

He kissed the top of her head. "You are silk and cream. I'll wait for you forever and beyond, if this is what it takes."

He released her and went downstairs.

She stared after him, trying to hold herself together as she absorbed his lovely words. Forever. He'd wait for her forever.

He'd made no bones about his desire to marry her, and was even willing to bring Cain home in order to get the license.

He'd bared his heart to her.

Told her he loved her.

And yet she'd held him off.

Worse, she'd pushed him away even though she did love him—and had felt this way from the day they met. Falling in love at first sight was a terrible thing. Falling in love deeper each time she saw him was mortifying. It was all happening too quickly, especially with a man like him, a rakehell with a most disreputable past.

Her body was in aching torment over him.

Her heart cried out for him.

So, what was she trying to prove? He knew how she felt, for this frightening desire she had for him could not be hidden.

He was wonderful.

She adored him.

She *loved* him.

Why could she not tell him?

# Chapter Thirteen

AFTER BREAKFAST WITH Phoebe, Chloe, and his nieces, Cormac rode back to his manor in time to oversee the departure of his unwanted guests. By the scowl on Lord Rothmere's face, he expected more vicious rumors to spread throughout the London ballrooms about him. Not that he cared what anyone other than those few he loved thought about him.

Removing himself from London was the best thing he could have done for himself. Only urgent business matters or sessions in the House of Lords would get him back there again.

Otherwise, his life would be centered here, and hopefully with Phoebe by his side.

Lord Crawford stood beside him as they waved the carriages off. "Lord Rothmere was not happy you left him tied up all night. But I did come down a time or two to make certain nothing was amiss and found him sleeping, so he could not have been all that uncomfortable. Since he and Lady Rothmere do not seem to like each other, I doubt he would have joined her in her bed had you permitted him other sleeping arrangements."

Cormac snorted. "More likely he would have spent the night with Lady Hopewell. Sleeping with another woman while his wife was right next door. Lord, what a miserable way they have chosen to live their lives."

"I see your point. It does leave an ill feeling in one's stomach."

Cormac nodded. "Theirs is truly a barren existence. I know James was hoping for far better for you."

"I know. Fortunately, he left the Crawford holdings in good stead, so I am free to marry for love. It is a relief not to worry about having to marry an heiress. However, I would not mind falling in love with one. Why not have it all, if one is fortunate enough to marry right?"

"Just do not rush into anything, Richard. Marriage is a lifetime commitment."

Lord Crawford shrugged. "Not necessarily. If it does not work out, we could follow the example set by Lord and Lady Rothmere and each live our separate lives. It is not ideal, and I cannot imagine myself sinking as low as they have done. I like to think I would show more respect for my wife and take pains to be discreet in my liaisons."

"Or you could find the right woman and make a happy marriage of it. Then you would never need to stray."

"Says the man who has made his way into half the female boudoirs in London."

Cormac stiffened. "That is all in the past. Come on. Enough of this conversation. We have work to do."

"Yes, let's train me to be a decent earl. I am in desperate need of guidance, since I've never looked at a ledger or ever dealt with matters of business. It really is much easier being the spare, especially when you have a generous brother who does not stint on your allowance. James was really very good to me."

Cormac nodded as they walked back inside. "Come into my study. I'll give you your first lesson on managing your assets."

As soon as they were in his study and had taken seats beside his desk, Richard spoke up again. "I really wish you would reconsider marrying my sister, Arabella. Then I could leave all my affairs in your capable hands and attend to my archeological discoveries knowing all would be handled properly. I cannot imagine anyone with more capable hands. Er..." He glanced at

Cormac's missing arm and sighed. "You know what I mean."

"I do, Richard. It is all right. But stop pushing your sister on me. It is not going to happen."

He made a gesture of surrender, waving a nonexistent white flag. "I understand your feelings, especially now that I have caught a glimpse of Lady Phoebe. What a magnificent pair of legs on the girl. Can you imagine them wrapped around your waist?"

Cormac emitted a low growl. "Watch yourself."

Richard's hands were still raised in surrender. "I'm just pointing out how convenient it would be if you preferred Arabella."

"And you took Phoebe?" Lord, Cormac should have sent the man off with the others when he had the chance.

"Well, the thought had crossed my mind. Do you think she would like to travel the world? As my wife, of course. I think I could be a good husband to her. I would not be inclined to stray if I were married to her."

"Put it out of your mind."

"All right. I'm merely suggesting you think about it. Arabella is also a lovely girl."

The man was as stubborn as a dog with a bone when he sank his teeth into an idea. "Enough. Let me show you how to read a ledger."

Cormac spent the next few hours educating Richard on matters of finance and farming. The man was obviously clever, just not at all interested. Still, it was important he make the effort to understand his holdings and how to protect them, or even his best workers would start to slack off. After all, if their lord did not care, then why should they?

Cormac closed his ledger book as noon approached, knowing Richard could not absorb any more about finances today. "I'll take you around to the Duke of Malvern's estate tomorrow so you can meet his estate manager, Mr. Weston. He's an excellent man and will walk you through the daily duties he undertakes on behalf of the duke."

Richard nodded. "I suppose that would be beneficial."

"It will be. Your Mr. Dowling is also a reliable manager, but I'd like you to see Mr. Weston in action so you can better understand Dowling's duties when he reviews the Crawford accounts with you. Also, you must go to your country estate to see firsthand how the farms are run. Tend to this first, before you design any grand plans for your expeditions."

He nodded again. "I see—take care of two birds with one stone. See to my sisters, as you've previously advised, and at the same time deal with matters of my properties."

"Exactly. And if Arabella is as clever as you believe she is, let her accompany you when Mr. Dowling takes you around."

Richard stared at him, obviously surprised by the notion. "But she's a lady."

"So? Who better to trust than your sister? I would not be surprised if she were already involved in running the Crawford properties. After all, she also benefits if they are well managed. A secure home. Perhaps a more generous dowry. An ample purse to cover the expenses of launching her into Society."

Richard shrugged. "Do you think James ever allowed her that much authority?"

"Why wouldn't he? Especially in giving her the running of the Crawford farms. He was not well enough to travel these past few years. You were not supervising anything. So why not rely on Arabella?"

Cormac pushed away from his desk and rose. "Care to be formally introduced to Lady Phoebe and her sister? They have invited us to join them for luncheon. You will also be meeting my nieces. I warn you now, do not dare take a step out of line around them."

Richard nodded. "I will be a proper gentleman."

Cormac was not pleased to have him along, but he could not avoid the formal introductions any longer. "All right. Make sure you are."

They rode over together and reached Moonstone Cottage in a matter of minutes.

Mr. Hawke came running out to take their mounts. "Good day, m'lord."

"Good day, Mr. Hawke. This gentleman is my friend, the Earl of Crawford."

"A pleasure to meet you, m'lord. Never you worry, I'll take good care of both beasts. Lord Burness, the ladies are on the beach with your nieces. I'm sure they'll be up shortly. M'wife has put on a lamb stew, and it should be ready soon. Shall I ring the bell to alert Lady Phoebe of your arrival?"

"Not necessary. We'll go down to them," Cormac said. "It'll do us good to stretch our legs after being cooped up in my study all morning."

They strode around the side of the house and descended the stairs leading down to the beach. The sun was bright, but the light breeze kept the temperature comfortable and the waters calm.

Cormac caught sight of the four of them, all wearing large straw hats to shade themselves as they built a large sandcastle beside the shore. His nieces were dressed in pink cotton frocks, digging their little toes into the wet sand.

When he reached the bottom step, Cormac noticed four pairs of dainty shoes lined up beside the step. In London, a young lady walking barefoot would cause quite the scandal. Here, it was a natural thing, and he was not about to make an issue of it.

He hoped Phoebe and Chloe would not fuss over the fact that their toes were also wiggling in the sand and visible to all.

The girls saw him approach and immediately ran over to him, their little hands full of wet sand, which they now slathered on his pants as they clung to his legs in greeting. They began to chatter at him at the same time. "Uncle Cormac, we're making a castle. Look how big it is!"

It must have seemed gigantic to Imogen, who was such a little thing. Ella was not much bigger. "An excellent job. Why, I'm sure it is as tall as the sky!"

They giggled.

Chloe and Phoebe scrambled to their feet and walked over to greet him and Richard.

Cormac's heart was as light as air and as bright as this Cornwall sunshine.

Seeing Phoebe and his nieces brought him a happiness he had not experienced in years. Too many years. Even a few hours' absence had him desperate to see them again. He quickly introduced them to Richard, who seemed quite charmed by all of them. Who could resist their big-eyed stares and welcoming smiles?

"We were just finishing up," Phoebe said, then turned to glance at the waves rolling onto shore. "Alas, the tide is coming in and will probably wash away all our hard work by the time we are through with our meal. Well, we'll rebuild tomorrow. Right, girls? I hope you came here hungry, Lord Crawford. Our Mrs. Hawke has prepared something special for us."

He nodded. "Looking forward to it."

She turned to Cormac and cast him a sparkling smile. "Shall we go up?"

"I believe we are to have lamb stew," Chloe added. "I can assure you, Mrs. Hawke is the best cook in all of Cornwall. It will be delicious."

Cormac eased his nieces off his legs and lightly tickled Imogen's belly. "As delicious as you, duckling?"

She giggled and threw her arms around him when he bent to give each of them a hug. "Up."

He laughed. "Do you mean, 'Uncle Cormac, please carry me up the stairs'?"

She nodded. "Yes. Up."

He rose with her tucked in his arm and started for the house.

Chloe took Ella's hand, and they scampered after him.

Phoebe gathered their shoes, which Richard immediately took from her hands. "Let me help you with those."

They walked up together, obviously sharing a jest, for the two of them were laughing. Cormac did his best to stifle his jealousy. It was ridiculous to think Phoebe was being anything more than polite to his friend.

But damn the man. He was doing his best to charm Phoebe.

Could nobody be trusted?

Well, he *had* to trust Phoebe. She was beautiful and sweet, and probably had half the single men in Moonstone Landing in love with her. There would always be men after her. And was this not the point of her reluctance to say those words aloud to him...*I love you?*

She refused to say them because she did not yet trust *him* to be constant.

And therein lay the foundation for a happy marriage...trust.

She did trust him in certain ways, just not this all-important one. Having spent years destroying his reputation with his debauchery, how could she ever believe he would keep faithfully to his vows?

It struck him that he'd never concerned himself with such matters before, because he had never cared for anyone the way he cared for Phoebe. Losing her would devastate him. But she was no society butterfly to flit from one man to the next.

When she loved, it would be forever.

This was the assurance she was also waiting to hear from him. She needed to believe he would be forever true. Forever in love with her.

But he was her first romance, so should he not also be asking questions? How could he be sure she was not mistaking infatuation with true love? Would she decide Richard was a better fit for her temperament?

Well, better he find out sooner rather than later.

"Uncle Cormac, why are you grinding your teeth?" Imogen asked, placing her little hand against his cheek.

"Am I? Perhaps I am hungrier than I realized. How are you feeling, duckling? You look much better than last night."

"I was already all right when you saw me this morning. I cuddled with Phoebe."

"Lucky you. Still feeling all right?"

She nodded.

Her big eyes just melted him.

She squirmed and tried to wriggle out of his grasp when they reached the top step. "I want to run on the grass."

He laughed and set her down.

She and Ella began to run around them, enjoying the feel of the soft grass under their toes.

But Phoebe had them sit while she wiped the sand off their feet and then helped them don their shoes. She handed Chloe hers, and then took a moment to wipe the sand off her own feet. "Girls, run upstairs and wash your hands before we eat."

She and Chloe excused themselves a moment to do the same.

Cormac was familiar enough with the house and their daily routine to lead Richard into the kitchen, introduce him to Mrs. Hawke, and ask for ale to be brought out to them. "Smells delicious, Mrs. Hawke."

"Thank you, m'lord. Make yourselves comfortable and I'll bring out the ale in a trice. My, your nieces are such delightful girls. What a joy it is to have them with us."

"They are having the best time. I don't think they'll want to go back to London when the month is up." He winked at her. "Makes me wish I was a little boy being tended by the lovely Lady Phoebe."

She laughed heartily. "You are a naughty man, and I'm sure you were a devil of a boy. She's such a sweet lass. But I think she would have handled you quite well. She may look meek, but don't be deceived. They are all fine girls and strong at heart, these Killigrew sisters. But Phoebe has the most inner strength of all of them."

He grinned. "She's got me handled, that's for certain. I've never behaved so well in my life...or enjoyed it more."

Mrs. Hawke nodded. "There's a magical quality about her."

"I know," Richard chimed in. "She has me quite besotted."

Mrs. Hawke glanced at Cormac and then frowned in disapproval at his friend.

He knew what she was thinking. Who the hell was this up-start to make a claim on Phoebe?

The lioness in question breezed into the kitchen, her cheeks pink and her smile captivating. "Chloe has the girls settled in the dining room. Shall we join them?"

"Ah, I did not realize the little ones were to eat with us," Richard said.

"Oh, yes, Lord Crawford. We do not hold to formality in this house. Besides, they adore their uncle, and I would not deprive them of the pleasure of his company. Please, do go in. I'll be along in a moment. Mrs. Hawke, do you need help serving the meal?"

"No, my dear. Mr. Hawke will help me out."

In the dining room, Cormac took his seat at the head of the table, Imogen on one side of him and Chloe on the other. Phoebe sat on the other side of Imogen, while Ella took a seat beside Chloe. That left the opposite end of the table for Richard, which placed him next to Phoebe.

The table was small, the leaves taken out to make for a more intimate setting.

Still, Cormac did not like Richard being seated so close to Phoebe.

Imogen looked up at him again with her big eyes. "Uncle Cormac?"

He stopped gnashing his teeth. "Ah, the food has arrived. Now I will not feel the need to eat you, my little duckling."

She giggled, always loving when he teased her.

Once they were all served, Phoebe asked Richard questions about archeology. The rest of the meal was taken up by his conversation, which Cormac might have found quite interesting if not for the fact that Phoebe also found Richard's holding forth on ancient civilizations fascinating, and that irked him to no end.

*Oh, Lord.*

Imogen was staring up at him again.

He sighed.

He could not help gnashing his teeth.

When the meal was over, Cormac extended his compliments to Mrs. Hawke. "Truly, one of the best meals I've ever had."

"Thank you, Lord Burness."

It had not escaped his notice that the lamb had been diced into small pieces so they did not require cutting. Phoebe must have requested this of Mrs. Hawke because the girl was a gem and thought of everything.

It was such a small thing, but a huge kindness to him. She knew he was a prideful arse, and having to sit there while someone cut his meat would have been humiliating for him.

Richard seconded the opinion and tossed Mrs. Hawke a flowery compliment.

"Very gracious of you, my lord," she said with noticeable stiffness. She had obviously decided Lord Crawford was not suitable for Phoebe.

Clearly, a woman of discerning taste.

Not that Cormac needed a team of supporters to help him woo Phoebe. It just irked him that Richard was not gentleman enough to step aside and leave the field clear for him.

Well, he would not have stepped aside either had Richard seen Phoebe first. Cormac knew he wanted her the moment he set eyes on her. He would have sprung on her like a lion on a gazelle.

Richard's efforts to gain her notice were tame in comparison.

Chloe took the girls outdoors and set out their sketchbooks and drawing pencils on the wrought-iron table. He and Richard followed them out while Phoebe discussed what was to be had for their evening meal with Mrs. Hawke.

She soon joined them. "They'll draw quietly for a while now. Chloe will watch them, not that they really need to be watched. They are such sweet, obedient girls."

Cormac laughed. "Sorry, I cannot get over how different they are from boys. I was a devil's spawn at that age."

She shook her head and smiled. "Not so different. From what I hear of your brother, he was an angel. Perhaps girls are able to sit quietly for longer periods and entertain themselves without spilling blood. But I'm sure we can be hellions, too. You were exceptionally difficult as a child, but I think you would have been the same whether you had been born a boy or a girl."

"Perhaps."

"No question about it," she said. "Perhaps as adorable as Imogen, but never as well behaved. More of an evil Imogen, if you can imagine such a thing."

Richard thought her comment incredibly witty.

Cormac stopped himself from gnashing his teeth again.

"Would you care to take a walk around our garden and grounds?" Phoebe suggested to them both.

"A delightful idea," Richard said, and immediately offered his arm.

She was standing to the left of Cormac.

He had no arm to offer her.

A stab of pain tore through him.

He silently admonished himself, knowing he was making too much of Richard's attention toward Phoebe.

"At Burness's suggestion, I am going to organize an expedition to Egypt, or perhaps to Mesopotamia," Richard said. "I also imagine spending time in Italy and Greece. Perhaps I shall let a villa in Sorrento for a few months on the way down. It overlooks the Bay of Naples. I hear it is beautiful there. I would do the same on my return, take a villa on one of the Greek isles. Which country do you think I ought to explore, Lady Phoebe? Egypt or Mesopotamia? Or should I be ambitious and attempt an expedition to both?"

"That would be quite a long trip no matter where you set your archeological explorations," she replied. "I'm sure your choice will become clearer once you speak to the Fellows in the Royal Society. Or perhaps the British Museum will commission you for a special project. One could spend a lifetime in any of those countries, and I am including Italy and Greece in this as well. They are all so rich in ancient history. Are you that determined to remain away from England?"

"I think the length of my absence would depend on my travel companions."

She nodded. "I expect you'll have several like-minded explorers who will be eager to join you."

"Yes, one or two Fellows in the Royal Society might. I would also hope to bring along someone more...permanent. It is my hope that I will be married by the time we are ready to undertake our expedition."

"That is quite a journey for a new wife. But I think you will find several young ladies currently on the Marriage Mart who will enjoy such an adventure."

"I am told you are quite adventurous, Lady Phoebe."

She paused to stare at him. "I am not afraid of adventure, but my home is here in Moonstone Landing. I cannot see myself going elsewhere."

"Not even with your husband?"

"Well, I would have to be deeply in love with a man before I would ever consider such a thing," she said. "But if I did love him that deeply, I suppose I would go to the outer edges of the world if this was what it took for us to be together."

Richard smiled broadly. "That is most promising."

She shook her head. "No, it is not. I would not leap at any offer of marriage, even if my heart knew he was the only man for me."

Cormac knew she was talking about him. Surely Richard had to understand her meaning.

But he seemed determined to overlook her implication. "Well, until you have made your choice, then any man can hope. Can he not?"

She ignored the question. "Tell me, what do you two have planned for tomorrow? Lord Burness mentioned he was taking you on a tour of the Duke of Malvern's property. It is excellently run. I think you will learn a lot from Mr. Weston. He is married to our cousin, Prudence. I've been meaning to invite her to tea. Perhaps you shall all come over after you are done. Please bring Mr. Weston with you."

They finished their walk and returned to Chloe and the girls.

Cormac knelt beside them. "What have you drawn, ducklings?"

To him, their drawings were similar to the stick figures they had drawn the other day. But Ella began to explain her artistic vision to him. "That's our mama and that's our papa and that's me and Imogen. That's our house in London. And that's our dog."

Cormac frowned. "You don't have a dog."

"Mama doesn't want us to keep a dog, so Ella and I have a pretend dog," Imogen explained to him.

"Ah, I see. And what is the name of your pretend dog?"

"Snuggles," Ella said.

Cormac's lips twitched upward in the hint of a smile. Lord, these girls were so sweet. If he'd ever had a pretend dog, he probably would have named it Hellhound or Apocalypse, and it would likely have had fangs. But that was just him, and he really had been an incorrigible child.

Phoebe stifled a giggle, but he saw the smile in her eyes and knew she was thinking exactly the same thing about him.

He chuckled and gave her a playful wink.

"Chloe says Phoebe can draw," Ella said.

"She says Phoebe is an artist," Imogen added.

Cormac was immediately interested. "Is this true? Do you have any works to show us?"

"She has a sketchbook full," Chloe chimed in. "I'll bring it down."

"No!" Phoebe cried, immediately blushing.

Chloe dismissed her reluctance. "You shouldn't be so modest about your talent. The girls are eager to see your work, too. Stop fussing. I'll run up and get your book. I know where you hide it."

"Chloe! I don't hide it. I tuck it safely away because I—"

Too late. Chloe was already bounding up the stairs.

Phoebe sighed. "Well, I've done a few sketches of the girls. One or two of you, Lord Burness."

Cormac arched an eyebrow in surprise and grinned. "Should I be worried?"

She blushed when Chloe returned downstairs and handed the sketchbook over to him. He paused a moment before flipping it open, intending to give Phoebe time to protest if she really did not want him to see what she had drawn.

But she seemed all right with it, although obviously shy about her talent.

The first were sketches of the view from her bedchamber window, lovely landscapes of the garden and the shimmering sea beyond it. The next few were of boats in the harbor. He drew in a breath when he got to the next set of drawings. "Phoebe, these are beautiful. Imogen, Ella, look."

She had drawn the girls, somehow managing to capture their sweetness and playful charm. He knew his brother would love these portraits. Phoebe had gotten everything right—their button noses, their little heart-shaped lips, the glimmer in their eyes, and the exact bounce to the curls in their hair.

Ella and Imogen were fascinated.

He turned to the next pages and saw himself staring back.

"Uncle Cormac, that's you," Ella said softly.

"I see that." She had caught his every nuance, down to the haunted look in his eyes. But it was not a dark, sullen drawing, for she had also captured the rake in him and his vitality.

Richard sifted through them as well. "Lady Phoebe, these are extraordinary. A talent like yours would add so much to my expedition."

Phoebe lifted the book from his hands. "No, my lord. You will find someone of equal ability without too much problem."

"Doubtful. You make these come alive. Have you had formal training?"

She nodded. "We had an art tutor when we were younger."

Chloe laughed. "The man detested me and Hen because we were such dreadful students. Our papa had to discharge him when he insisted on taking Phoebe to Florence to study the great Italian artists. He had developed an almost obsessive fascination with her, and our parents were afraid the man would run off with her."

"Oh dear. Nothing as lurid as that," Phoebe insisted. "He simply thought I had great promise as an artist and wanted me to study in Italy. But I had no intention of leaving England even back then. I knew my heart was here in Moonstone Landing. I knew it and felt it from our very first visit here after Aunt Henleigh purchased this house. Some things just get into your soul, and you know this is where you belong."

"But the world will lose out on your talent," Richard said in all seriousness.

"I assure you, Lord Crawford, the world will survive. I can put my artistic abilities to good use right here in Cornwall. Our eldest sister, Hen, is married to the Duke of Malvern. His manor house, which you will see tomorrow, is also neighbor to ours. We help Hen out with all her charitable works. These projects keep us busy, and some of them require use of my drawing talents. It does not go to waste."

Richard listened to her patiently, but Cormac knew he was not in the least put off by her resistance. "Well, I'll have the week to change your mind."

Phoebe took the sketchbook out of his hands and returned it upstairs.

While she was gone, Richard turned to him. "Burness, you really have to side with me on this. She is incredibly talented and would add so much to my expedition. Imagine the sketches she could prepare for me. And I'll take her to Florence if she wishes. We can spend a year there if it will help her learn her craft. And—"

"The decision is not mine to make. Nor is it Cain's, even though he is still her guardian. Phoebe does not want to go, and that's an end to it. Why can you not respect her wishes?"

"Would you if you were in my situation?"

"Yes, I would." Cormac did not want to continue this conversation in front of his nieces or Chloe, but Richard was not letting it go, so he carefully weighed his words. "Phoebe knows her own mind. She is clever and thoughtful. Yes, she draws with passion and love. But if her heart had been set on making a name for herself as an artist, she would have pursued it. She has a strong will and nothing will deter her. Perhaps it is a shame she views her gift as a diversion and not a dream."

"But this is my point, Burness. She could make it a dream. Why should she settle for something less? Why remain in this dull backwater when she could be regaled in the royal courts of Europe?"

"You are not listening to her. She is telling you that her heart is here in Moonstone Landing. This is where she wishes to put her efforts."

Richard turned to Chloe. "Can you not persuade your sister?"

Phoebe returned in time to hear his question. Perhaps she had heard more, for her eyes were blazing, a sign the lioness was stirred. "Do not involve my family in your schemes, Lord Crawford."

"I did not mean to—"

"Yes, you did. If you have a thought about my art, then say it directly to me. I have already told you my feelings on the matter and would rather not have this conversation with you again. As Lord Burness just told you, I know my own mind and do not need a man to tell me what to do or what to think. Nor do I need you condescending to me because you think my dream is lesser. It is not the same as yours, but it does not make it *lesser.*"

Cormac cleared his throat. "Phoebe, shall I ask Mrs. Hawke to set out coffee on the terrace?"

The blaze in her eyes softened as she turned to him. "Yes, that is a fine idea."

She took a deep breath and turned once more to Richard,

who now sat with his mouth agape. Well, did he think Phoebe would be biddable? She looked magnificent in her blazing glory, and that blaze was, for once, not aimed at Cormac.

"Lord Crawford, I do apologize if I was rude to you just now. I appreciate your admiration of my drawings, but I know what is important to me and what is not. Be assured, I will not let this talent go to waste. It will be put to good use right here in Moonstone Landing."

"I am duly chastened, Lady Phoebe," Richard said. "Still disheartened, but duly chastened."

"I mean it sincerely when I say there are young ladies in good society with a fine artist's hand who will share your passion for history and travel. I wish you extraordinary good fortune and fulfillment in your endeavors, and I will eagerly read your accounts when they are published. Please, do tell us more of your plans. I very much enjoy hearing of them."

"But you do not wish to be included in them," Richard said.

"That's right, my lord. I do not."

They strolled onto the terrace, and the girls went off with Chloe to toss a ball. Cormac watched them, his heart full of love for them. Poor Imogen—she could not catch that ball to save her life. But she was laughing and having too much fun to care.

Cormac watched them, but he was still quite aware and listening in when Richard drew Phoebe aside and quietly asked, "Tell me one thing: if it were Lord Burness instead of me asking to take you on his travels, would your answer be different?"

Cormac felt the full impact of her gaze now on him and noticed her begin to fret her lower lip. "I don't know. It is the only answer I can give just yet."

An honest one, because Phoebe did not lie, nor was she a practiced flirt.

He felt the pain of her honesty quite profoundly.

Was it too late for her to ever trust him? Having spent years destroying his reputation, could it ever be redeemed?

# Chapter Fourteen

T HE REST OF the week passed quickly, although not quickly enough for Cormac. He and Richard fell into the routine of visiting Phoebe and his nieces every day, as well as spending hours going over the duties of owning an estate. Westgate Hall was just a manor house, but Cain's neighboring property was much larger, encompassing several working farms and a grist mill. Those served as a good training ground for Richard.

They'd worked hard, but Richard was not content to spend his last night in Moonstone Landing behaving piously. They had taken to stopping at the Three Lions Tavern for rounds of ale and conversation with the locals most nights, but this was not enough for Richard on his last night here.

They had just left Phoebe's home and were now on their way to the tavern when Richard expressed his desire for female companionship. Cormac frowned. "Why now? You leave tomorrow. Can you not hold off for a few more days?"

"No, and I think you should give me a memorable send-off. Is this not what my brother urged you to do?"

"He wanted you to gain experience, but his request to make a man of you means more than simply learning how to pleasure a lady. He was speaking of building your character."

"Am I so terrible?"

"Of course not, but your enthusiasm for a thing sometimes

makes you act rashly."

"Are we speaking of Lady Phoebe? She is splendid, isn't she? But she has expressed her lack of interest in me quite clearly. So why not allow me to nurse my wounds elsewhere? The Kestrel Inn has an elite clientele, does it not? Let's go there tonight and see what we can find."

"You mean in the way of bored countesses?"

Richard nodded. "Where's the harm?"

"No, it is not for me."

"Oh, come on, Burness. You are not betrothed to Lady Phoebe. Even if you were, so what?"

Other than destroying any possibility of Phoebe ever trusting him? Sure, no harm. "You go on ahead. I have some work to do anyway."

"You really have sworn off women, haven't you?"

"Yes."

"But Lady Phoebe has given you no indication she will ever agree to marry you, so why turn into a monk?"

"She is worth the wait. Worth the hope."

"Yes, I suppose she is. At least she likes you. I don't think she likes me very much."

Cormac shook his head. "She does like you and quite admires your plans. But not enough to take that life journey with you."

"So what are you going to do, Burness? Spend the rest of your days here because this is where she wishes to settle? Will she be the one making all the decisions in the family? I cannot see you in that subservient role." Richard laughed and shook his head. "Nor can I see her demurely accepting your decisions. She may look like a kitten, but she scratches like a wildcat."

Cormac arched an eyebrow. "Why are you surprised? Did you not hear her railing at me that first day I met her? My ears are still burning from the scathing set-down."

His friend shook his head. "I was likely passed out. Too bad I missed it. She must have been magnificent, her beautiful eyes ablaze. Drat, I would have enjoyed seeing her take you down."

"Well, my point is that neither she nor I would ever be subservient. If I've learned anything—and believe me, I was quite dense about understanding any of it for the longest time—it is that neither party gives the orders in a happy marriage. The decisions are reached together. You each want to do it for the other, because seeing the other happy is the greatest satisfaction."

He leaned forward in his saddle and looked out upon Moonstone Landing as they rode over a scenic rise. The village looked beautiful in the fading light, its thatched roof houses quite golden and the sea beyond it a shimmering blue. "If you are ever so fortunate as to fall in love, you'll come to realize this. Many things will suddenly fade in importance."

"Not my travels. This is my life's quest, and I will not allow any woman to compromise my plans."

"Then look for a woman who shares your love of travel and exploration. If she cares for you, she will want to please you. If traveling becomes too much for her, which may arise if you have children, then she will be amenable to settling on a compromise. I'm sure your wife would not mind waiting for your return while basking in one of those Italian villas."

"Gad, no! And have her fall in love with some dark-haired Italian count? No, I'd ship her back to England for certain. Our dismal rain and wintery cold will do for her."

Cormac laughed and shook his head. "Ah, Richard. How can any woman resist you if you think like that?"

Richard grinned. "You are mocking me."

"I see myself in you, for this is something I would have said before meeting Phoebe. Anyway, have a care around the elegant women staying at the Kestrel Inn. Just because they are putting out signals they are available does not mean you can trust them."

"What do you mean?"

"I cannot explain it. It is just something you have to be able to sense."

"I still have no idea what you are talking about."

"I know. This is why I dare not leave you on your own yet."

Cormac sighed. "I'll ride there with you."

The inn had a good reputation, and Cormac doubted Richard would get into too much mischief so long as he behaved discreetly. A few lonely ladies might be looking for a night of comfort in his arms, for wealth and title were no guarantees to happiness. It was not unusual for those of rank to engage in casual liaisons. However, the man was still a babe in the woods. He could not accept just any invitation offered. With Richard's luck, the woman he chose would have a jealous husband hot on her trail who would not hesitate to shoot him when finding him in her bed.

Cormac decided the least he could do for his friend was point out who was safe to seduce and who was not.

*Blast.*

That sounded awful.

But these were not sweet lambs Richard was hunting. And was it not better to have him in the arms of a willing lady than to have him still sulking over Phoebe? The young lord was fascinated by her, and Cormac did not want him attempting anything foolish with her on his last night here. Phoebe was off-limits, and he would maim Richard if he dared touch her.

The inn had a private salon reserved for their Upper-Crust guests, although anyone willing to pay an exorbitant entrance fee was permitted to rub shoulders with the titled elite. The private salon was surprisingly crowded. "M'lord," the innkeeper said, bustling toward Cormac as they entered, "a large party came down from Bath just this morning. Some of them were asking after you."

"Is that so?" He did not like the sound of that. Although he was admitted into the best circles, he'd always sought out the fast set, preferring to amuse himself with those who misbehaved. No one of good moral character was likely to be asking after him.

"One lady in particular—quite beautiful, she is," the innkeeper muttered.

Cormac followed the man's gaze to one of the ladies seated

amid a host of admirers across the salon.

He silently uttered a string of expletives upon spotting Seline. "Lady Whitford?"

"Yes, m'lord. She's the one."

Richard's eyes widened. "Gad, she is even more stunning than the last time I saw her. Burness, you lucky man. Will you introduce me to her? She's never given me the time of day, but I am an earl now. Do you think she will continue to snub me?"

Cormac put a hand on his friend's shoulder. "She is a viper. You do not want to go anywhere near her."

Why was she here?

She looked up and saw them, her eyes taking on a menacing glow as she brushed aside her circle of admirers and walked over to him. "Burness, I knew you would come for me."

"Actually, I had no idea you were in Moonstone Landing until Mr. Egdon mentioned it just now," he said, referring to the elderly innkeeper. "What are you doing here?"

She gave a little toss of her head, no doubt aware of exactly how her curls would bounce and fall becomingly over one shoulder. "Bath was boring, and I heard this village was quite charming."

She must have encountered Cain and Phoebe's sister, who were on holiday there. They would not have said a word to her, but perhaps other acquaintances, who were unaware of Cormac's distrust of Seline, had spoken of him. Well, it mattered little how Seline had learned of his whereabouts. She was here and bent on causing trouble.

Had she nothing better to do than attempt to lay waste to his happiness? "I never knew you to enjoy charming things—unless it was to take pleasure in destroying them."

She placed her hand against his chest and lightly stroked it. "You are too cruel, my love. Will you show me around this lovely village tomorrow? I hear you've bought yourself a house on the outskirts. I would not mind seeing the view from your bedchamber."

He nudged her hand off his chest. "Go back to London, and take your toadies with you. There is nothing for you here."

"We'll see about that."

She ignored Richard, saving her malicious sneer for him alone, and returned to her admirers.

"That woman hates you," Richard muttered. "What did you do to her?"

"Went off to war and left her behind. Lost my arm. Not that its loss was any of her business. But I suppose she believes it is not punishment enough for my not asking her to marry me before I went off to fight Napoleon."

"Do you regret it?"

"Are you jesting? Not for a moment. I was never going to ask her, and she knew it. I took pains to be clear about it before I ever touched her. I do not lie about my purpose because it is important the lady knows my intentions and comes to me willingly."

"She may have hoped to change your mind. A woman's heart is a fragile thing, is it not?"

"Yes, but that woman has no heart." She was no innocent when he first touched her. "Indeed, she herself broke several hearts and gained quite a reputation before I ever came along. Richard, do not be a fool. She is never to be trusted. She thinks first, last, and always of herself. Just keep away from her, will you? Better yet, come back to Westgate Hall with me. You will recover from one night without a woman. But you will not recover from spending one night with her."

"What makes you think she will have me? She ignored me and spoke only to you."

"She will pounce on you if you give her the slightest encouragement because you are connected to me. If she hurts you, then in her mind, she is also hurting me." He did not give Richard the choice, just took him by the arm and urged him out.

They rode back to Westgate Hall, had a few drinks, and then retired. But Cormac knew his friend was going to do something foolish. It proved true when Cormac knocked on his door an hour later to check on him. The door was unlocked, so he looked in. "Bloody idiot."

Richard's bedchamber was empty.

He went downstairs and strode to the stable. The horse he had given Richard to ride during his visit was not in its stall.

"Bloody, bloody fool." He raked a hand through his hair, debating whether to go after him. "No," he finally decided. Perhaps the stubborn dolt needed to learn from experience. Cormac just hoped Richard would not be too badly burned.

WHEN RICHARD STILL hadn't returned by daybreak, Cormac went to the inn to fetch him.

"Good morning, Lord Burness. What can I do for you?" the genial clerk at the front desk asked with a beaming smile.

"Good morning." Good heavens, who could be so chipper this early in the day? "I'm looking for my friend, Lord Crawford."

"Ah." The young man blushed, and then glanced around to make certain no one was in hearing distance. They were the only ones at the front entry, since it was barely after sunrise and the well-heeled guests would not be up this early. "I believe he is visiting Lady Whitford."

A polite way of describing what those two were doing.

Richard was no longer innocent, but Cormac had no doubt Seline had taught him an eye-popping thing or two last night. "Send one of your lads to wake him. He is to return home to Crawford Hall this morning, and his carriage awaits."

"Very good, my lord." The clerk swallowed hard and then winced. "The lady has a bit of a temper."

"I have been on the receiving end of it a time or two."

"And survived unscathed?" The young man gave a nervous laugh. "I had better be the one to knock at her door. You see,

Constable Angel is my uncle. She may demand he be summoned to arrest me for disturbing her peace. He won't, of course. I am family."

"What's your name?"

"Thaddius, my lord. Thaddius Angel."

"Good to meet you, Thaddius. It seems everywhere I turn, I meet another Angel. The constable. The bank manager. The tavern owner. How many of you are there in Moonstone Landing?"

Thaddius laughed. "At least twenty, I should think. More if you count the surrounding villages."

"Well, I shall certainly stand by you if Lady Seline is so deranged as to demand you be arrested or discharged."

"You needn't worry about me. I'll be owner of this inn someday. Mr. Egdon is not going to discharge me."

"You are quite the enterprising lad." Cormac chuckled. "I'll be outside. Tell Lord Crawford not to keep me waiting."

WHICH WAS HOW the ridiculous rumor began, one that reached Phoebe's ears when Cormac joined her and the girls for breakfast a few days later. Richard had returned to his estate in Bedfordshire two days ago, so he was not around to dispel the rumor.

Cormac knew something was wrong the moment he arrived at Moonstone Cottage and saw the tension in Phoebe's eyes. She met him at the front door and would not allow him in. "We need to speak."

He nodded. "All right. Has something happened? Are the girls—"

"They are fine," she said, her lips tightly pinched.

"And Chloe?"

"She is fine. This isn't about them. Walk down to the beach with me."

"Of course." He could see her back was rigid and steps purposeful as she hurried past the garden and made for the stairs.

"Will you tell me what that look is about? Your face is so brittle it appears ready to crack."

She waited to respond until their feet hit the sand, then whirled on him and frowned.

"Have you not heard what everyone is talking about? You were seen leaving a lady's guest chamber at the Kestrel Inn."

He groaned. "Was the lady in question identified as Lady Whitford? That is Seline, my infamous former...whatever one would call such a woman. I can assure you, nothing of the sort happened, not with her or anyone else."

Phoebe studied his expression, obviously trying to search his face for answers. "You had a torrid affair with her. The two of you have a history together. Did you once pledge those same words of love to her as you have pledged to me? If you still love her—"

He laughed and shook his head—a bitter laugh, for this was what Seline always had him feeling. "I never loved her, Phoebe. Whatever affair we had has long since been over. She shut her door to me the day I lost my arm. Slammed it right in my face."

"Then she was the one who broke off relations?"

He sighed. "Yes, but we had both lost interest. It was only a question of who would bother to get around to it first. Her timing was particularly cruel, but true to form for her. I haven't bothered with her since that day."

"You were seen leaving the inn."

"Because I rode over there early in the morning."

"You were seen with her the night before."

"And now you think I am making a nightly habit of visiting her bed?"

"Oh, Cormac. I don't know what to think." She looked so anguished that he wanted to take her in his embrace and tell her how much he loved her.

Not that she would ever believe him now.

He raked a hand through his hair, uncertain what to say to make her believe him. He was no saint, but hadn't he been on his best behavior around her? Hadn't he poured out his heart to her?

He was incredulous that she would believe the rumors after all he'd done to put his old life behind him. "You cannot seriously believe I would go anywhere near that woman."

"I've seen her in town," she said in a strained whisper. "She is beautiful."

"Her heart is the ugliest thing imaginable. I was at the Kestrel Inn on the morning Richard left. I went there to fetch him. He was the one who, despite my dire warnings, spent the night with that witch. You know I want nothing to do with her. Just ask Thaddius Angel. He was the clerk on duty that morning. He will tell you the truth about what happened. It is exactly as I've just told you."

"You might have paid him to corroborate your story."

Her words felt like a slap to his face. She could not have hurt him more if she'd run a blade through his heart. "This is what you think of me?"

"Cormac, for pity's sake. I've known you all of two weeks. You've been in a relationship with this woman for a decade. How am I to know what your feelings are for her? And how am I to trust my own feelings for you? You're the first man I've ever kissed. The only man I've ever allowed to kiss me. Can you not understand how afraid I am of giving my heart to you?"

"And can you not take me at my word? I have never lied to you, Phoebe. Why would I ever want someone like her, especially now that I have found you?" He turned to leave before she saw the despair in his eyes.

Phoebe was a heavenly light.

Seline was a dark, ominous cloud.

He loved Phoebe so completely, not a doubt in his mind. Yet it suddenly felt like a hopeless love. She would never trust him because of Seline's schemes, never believe he could be faithful.

*Blast.*

He thought losing his arm had been painful, but it was nothing compared to the pain ripping through him at this moment.

He could not allow Phoebe to see him like this. "There is nothing more to say. Just tell the girls something urgent came up. I will see them another time."

The tide was out, so he took the opportunity to walk around the outcropping and take the shortcut along his beach up to his house.

His big, empty, lifeless house.

He had not made it very far past the outcropping before he fell to his knees in the sand, his heart in utter anguish.

Seline could never hurt him.

But Phoebe could.

Losing her...arrogant fool that he was, he had never seriously considered Phoebe might reject him. He had wanted her so desperately from the first that he refused to believe he could not win her heart.

But why should she love him? Or ever trust him?

What was he other than a grotesque cripple with a debauched reputation?

And now Melrose and his staff would see him crawling back home like the despicable creature he had once been. No, this was too much for him to bear. He took off his jacket and tore at his cravat, jerking the choking silk off from around his neck. He removed his waistcoat, not bothering to struggle with the buttons and just ripping them out.

He did the same with his shirt and tossed it onto the sand with his other clothes.

He was struggling to remove his boots when a slight shadow fell across him. He turned to look behind him and saw Phoebe standing there in tears.

He buried his face in his hand. "Damn it, Phoebe. Just go away."

"What are you doing?" She knelt beside him and put her arms around him.

"I am not trying to kill myself, if that's what you are worried about. I just needed to cool myself down. That's all. Assuming I managed to pull off my damn boots. It is almost impossible to manage with only one arm."

He tried to nudge her away, but she was not letting go of him.

She was torturing him with the soft lavender scent of her skin and the honey sweetness of her lips as she pressed them against his neck.

Her breasts felt pillow-soft against his shoulder as she leaned into him, her arms still wrapped around him.

"You idiot," she whispered.

"How am I an idiot? For hoping you could ever love me?" Since he had done a good job of tearing his shirt apart while removing it, there was no putting it back on to spare her the sight of his missing arm.

"It is not a question of love. And stop trying to hide your arm from me. It does not repulse me. Nothing about you repulses me." She kissed him again and again. On the cheek. On his jaw. On his lips.

"Stop kissing me, Phoebe."

"No."

He laughed. "Well, if you are going to insist on it, then do it right. No grandmotherly pecks will do."

She looked at him with a smile in her sparkling eyes. "Show me how I ought to kiss you."

"Like this, you irritating girl." He brought his mouth down on hers with crushing force, needing to swallow all of her up, needing to conquer her, for he wanted her so badly and was so afraid he would never have her.

He was angry that she was holding back her heart.

Of course, he did not blame her.

He'd spent a lifetime being an arse.

But he would never hurt her, not even in his anger.

Why could she not trust him? Why could she not believe she

was the most precious thing to him?

He ran his tongue along the seam of her lips to force those soft pink petals open. She did not resist and was obviously trying to gentle him by following his lead with a surprising willingness.

He thrust his tongue in her mouth, touching it to hers. Teasing hers. Probing and swirling it around hers. Mimicking the act of love, the very act he ached to complete with their bodies.

A rogue wave washed over them, causing Phoebe to wrench her mouth away and leap to her feet with a laughing yelp. She darted further back to avoid being knocked over by its force. Cormac merely let the wave surround him and soak into his skin.

As Phoebe had soaked into his soul.

"Now we'll both have to change," she remarked, staring down at her wet gown. "Come back to Moonstone Cottage after you do. Your nieces are expecting you. They'll be disappointed if you do not show up."

"And you?"

"I'll be happy to see you. How can you doubt it after that kiss? Will you be angry if I go into town later to talk to Thaddius Angel? You suggested it. I think I must."

"Yes...no...do whatever you please."

She sighed. "I don't think you would like me nearly as much as you do if I were a peahen who blindly believed everything she was told. I think the gossip is nonsense, Cormac. But I am not out of line for wanting to know all the facts before I dismiss those ugly rumors."

"After all I've told you about Seline, how can you think I would ever have anything to do with her? I give you my word of honor, Phoebe. I have not been anywhere near her or touched any other woman since meeting you. Why is it so hard for you to believe me?"

"Because men do stupid things all the time, do they not? Especially when their brains are controlled by that, um...organ between their legs. You cannot deny this was you a mere two weeks ago."

He shook his head and sighed. How could he deny it?

Only, he was no longer that man.

And yet she was not wrong to be wary.

"Having you give me your word on something as important and sensitive as this is not enough yet," she said, her words etched with pain. "But it will be in time. It is not fair of you to resent me for being cautious when you have not given me enough time."

He lay back on the sand and allowed the sun to soak into his bones. "I am not hungry this morning. Give the girls my apologies. I will come by later. I cannot do it now."

"Have I hurt you that badly?"

He shrugged. "Is this not what happens when one opens one's heart and has it stepped on?"

"Are you going to pout now?"

He laughed. "Yes, I suppose I am."

"Tell me this—had the rumors been about me and Lord Crawford, that he'd been seen coming out of my bedchamber, how would you have responded?"

"Do you mean before or after I killed him?"

She cast him a wry smile. "Spoken like a dolt. The point is, if you trusted me, then you would know those rumors could not possibly be true and poor Lord Crawford would be quite safe. So why are you angry with me for having a moment's doubt about you when you would doubt me, too? And I have a spotless reputation, unlike yours, which is completely besmirched."

"Do not be logical with me, Phoebe. It is truly irritating when you are right. I'll see you later. I have to retrieve Hadrian anyway. He's still in your stable."

"Are we all right, Cormac?"

"I'm still in love with you, if this is what you are asking."

She sighed. "I'm not sure what I am asking."

He watched her as she made her way around the outcropping of rocks and headed back toward her cottage. He remained stretched out in the sand, allowing the sun to beat down on him as he considered the gossip now floating around town.

He supposed he understood Phoebe's reluctance to take him at his word. She hadn't actually accused him of leaping into Seline's bed. She simply did not know what to believe and was trying to get at the truth.

He expected she would soon discover the gossip was nothing but lies concocted by Seline.

But this troubled him.

Why was Seline here? And why was she suddenly waging a campaign to destroy him?

# Chapter Fifteen

PHOEBE FELT AWFUL about having chased Cormac away this morning, but the gossip had unsettled her, and she had needed to speak to him about it. One look at him had convinced her of his innocence, only she had been too stubborn to let the matter drop.

Her lack of trust had devastated him. There was no mistaking the raw honesty of his feelings.

Now his nieces were sad because he hadn't joined them for breakfast. It was her fault, and she had to make it up to them. "Girls, would you like to learn how to swim? The water is calm and it looks to be another hot day. Won't that be fun?"

Ella appeared more enthusiastic than Imogen, but they both nodded.

Chloe was also eager for a dip. "The Duke of Malvern taught us how to swim several years ago after our eldest sister, Hen, almost drowned on his beach. He insisted we all learn. And now we'll teach you. Believe me, you'll enjoy it."

She ran upstairs with Ella so the two of them could change into their shifts. Chloe's shift was designed to be something of a swimming costume made of sturdy fabric that would not turn sheer when wet. Phoebe had the same, and now ran upstairs to change into hers. But the girls only had their light shifts, which would have to serve for now. If they took to the water, Phoebe would arrange for bathing costumes to be made for them.

Imogen looked up at her. "Must I go into the water?"

Phoebe took her hand. "Don't be scared, duckling. I'll hold on to you. And I won't make you dip so much as a toe. You'll let me know when you are ready. Until then, we shall play in the sand. But you'll see, it will be lots of fun if you decide to venture in. I wager you'll be swimming like a dolphin by the time the month is through."

The little one nodded. "Will Uncle Cormac join us? Why did he go away? Doesn't he like us anymore?"

The breath caught in Phoebe's lungs. "He loves you always. That will never change. You and Ella are the most important thing in the world to him. It is my fault he left. I said something to him that hurt his feelings."

"You did?" Imogen looked up at her again with big, innocent eyes. "Why?"

"Well, it is not so easy to explain. You see, I heard he did something bad, and when I asked him about it, he said he didn't do it."

Imogen nodded. "Uncle Cormac doesn't lie."

"I hope not."

"No, he never lies." The girl had an impudent frown on her face. "You have to believe him."

The little one was too innocent to understand...or perhaps Phoebe had allowed her own grownup feelings to cloud the truth little Imogen saw so clearly. "Come on, take my hand and we'll go build our sandcastles. Your uncle will come around later, and I will apologize to him then."

They tossed their robes and towels into a large bag, put on their straw hats, and headed down to the beach in their bare feet. They all enjoyed the freedom the privacy of their beach allowed.

Since Imogen was reluctant to go in the water, Phoebe remained with her by the water's edge and helped her fashion all sorts of silly sand animals, along with another woefully unimpressive sandcastle. But it looked magnificent to little Imogen, who was beaming at all the sand art they'd created.

Chloe had gone in with Ella and was now teaching her to float on her back. Chloe was only waist-deep and not about to take Ella any further, but Imogen was still worried for them and constantly looked over to see what they were doing.

"Imogen, would you like to try it?"

The little girl shook her head. "No."

"All right. We'll keep playing right here."

Suddenly, Imogen scampered to her feet. "Uncle Cormac!" She ran toward the outcropping with her arms outstretched.

Cormac had been carrying his boots in his hand but tossed them aside to scoop the little one up. "Did you think I had forgotten you?"

She nodded.

He kissed her cheek. "I never would. You know that, duckling."

Phoebe now reached him and cast him a hesitant smile. "Chloe and I thought to teach the girls to swim. But Imogen doesn't want to go in the water."

"Will you go in with me, duckling? You know I would never let you come to harm. Nor would Phoebe. You can trust her to always keep you safe."

"I know. But she isn't as big as you," Imogen replied.

Cormac smiled. "She's the perfect size for a Phoebe. And you are the perfect size for an Imogen. I'll take you into the water, if you will let me. All right?"

Imogen nodded.

They walked in silence back to the castle they had built. It looked little more than a lump of sand piled high, but Cormac dutifully complimented his niece on its grand design and remarked kindly on the animal shapes around it.

"You are a master builder, Imogen," he said, giving her a kiss on her dimpled cheek.

Phoebe had picked up his boots and now set them beside their bag containing the towels and robes.

Since he had merely tossed on a work shirt instead of donning one of his fancier Savile Row shirts of softest lawn—and nor had he bothered with cravat, jacket, or waistcoat—he now removed the shirt and handed it to her, along with Imogen's hat. "Weigh them down with my boots or they'll fly off in the breeze."

She did as he asked, although there was hardly any breeze.

And hardly a ripple on the water. It was almost as smooth as glass. The waves were tiny and hardly foamed as they gently broke along the sand.

Phoebe watched him with his niece. Imogen had such trust in him—she did not show a trace of fear as he waded into the water. Nor did she show a trace of revulsion at his missing arm. This was her beloved uncle, and she was going to love him no matter what.

Tears stung Phoebe's eyes as she watched them together. The joy they each felt being together was palpable and magnificent.

Cormac's body was also magnificent, but she could not allow herself to be distracted by that. But heavens, those broad, tanned shoulders. That manly chest. The flat ripples of his stomach. All of him glistening and wet.

He spared her a glance. "Come join us, Phoebe."

She wiped a stray tear from her eyes. "All right."

He kept tight hold of Imogen as they both watched Phoebe swim. She did not go out very far, just a little beyond them before she turned and swam parallel to the shore. Chloe was also holding on to Ella who was studying her movements as she glided over the water. "I want to do that," Ella cried.

"You will," Chloe assured her, and returned to teaching Ella to float on her back. Soon, Chloe was teaching her how to tread water.

Imogen was still clinging to her uncle and watching wide-eyed.

Phoebe swam over to her. "See, Imogen? You'll soon be able to do this." Certainly Ella would, for she took to the water like a fish and did not even hesitate to dunk her head beneath the surface.

It would take a lot more to get Imogen comfortable enough to do that. But she made a little progress, even enough to trust Phoebe when her uncle handed her over so he could take a swim. She'd thought he would have difficulty now that he had only one useable arm, but that did not appear to be the case.

He still managed to cut through the water with ease, his body beautiful and powerful as he skimmed along the surface, swimming the length of their beach and back toward them. He swam the last stretch beneath the water and came up behind them with a playful roar.

Imogen squealed with delight.

Phoebe's body melted as he shook the water off him and brushed back his hair by raking his fingers through his dark mane. His eyes were a stunning, crystalline blue, and his smile was simply breathtaking.

Had he forgiven her for doubting him?

No.

She saw the shadow creep across his eyes as he glanced at her.

Since there was nothing she could do about it now, she pretended not to notice and simply concentrated on helping Cormac's nieces learn to swim. The water was warm, and so was the light sea breeze, which made for an idyllic outing.

It also did not hurt to have Cormac beside her. Neptune could not have looked more magnificent. There was nothing soft about his body—it was all hard, wet muscle.

But his touch, the few times he stood close enough to touch her, was achingly tender. His arm grazed her chest as he took Imogen from her arms to carry the little one out of the water. Phoebe dared not follow them, ashamed of the tingles coursing through her body.

She needed to splash water on her face to cool herself down from his touch.

Thank goodness she had an entire sea at her disposal.

She took a deep breath and swam underwater until she could

no longer hold her breath. When she came up for air, she began to swim hard along the length of the cove. By the time she returned to her starting spot, everyone else was out of the water and watching her.

Yes, they were all watching her, but it was Cormac's gaze she felt boring into her soul.

He came toward her with a towel as she waded out of the water breathless from her exertion. "Bloody hell, Phoebe," he said in a ragged whisper. "Wrap this towel around you before I rupture an organ. I cannot afford to lose any more parts of my body."

"What do you mean?"

"Your bathing costume hides nothing of your body."

She glanced down at herself. "I don't see—"

"It clings to your every curve, and I am going to burst into flames if you do not cover yourself up right now."

Her eyes rounded in surprise. "Oh, you weren't looking at my sister, were—"

"Lord, no! I averted my gaze as any gentleman would." He glanced back at the three girls standing by their belongings, towels wrapped around all of them. "But I cannot seem to take my eyes off you. My brain simply doesn't function when I am near you. Nor can I keep my hands off you... Well, the one hand. Do you have any idea how tempting you are? Or how naughty my thoughts are right now?"

His voice was low and raspy, his desire barely leashed—and this excited her. "Oh," she said with a groan, "I need to splash more water on my face."

He laughed and helped her wrap the towel around her body. "It will not help, Phoebe. We are lost to each other. Even you, Miss Temple of Virtue, feel it. We are meant for each other."

The bell sounded just then to alert them their lunch was ready.

Chloe herded the little ones up the stairs and called out to Phoebe, "I'll leave our supplies for you and Lord Burness to carry up. Don't tarry. Girls, wasn't that fun?"

Cormac's two nieces nodded as they waddled like little ducklings after Chloe.

After a moment, Cormac turned back to Phoebe. "I'll help you carry your things back to the house, but I dare not join you as I am."

She shook her head. "The Hawkes will not say a word about it. They know we've all been swimming. Just toss on your shirt and we'll dine outdoors. You won't ruin those wrought-iron chairs. Unless you will be too uncomfortable with your trousers wet. I can give you some of Captain Arundel's clothes to wear. We have a trunk full of them, and I think he must have been about the same size as you."

"I appreciate the offer, but I cannot."

"Why? I don't mind if you return the clothes to us later. We are in no rush to have them back. And the girls will be so disappointed if you miss another meal with us."

He emitted a ragged sigh. "Do you not understand?"

"Apparently, I do not. What is wrong with my suggestion?"

He sighed again, or perhaps it was more of a groan. "It will take me forever to dress myself. What takes you a minute with two hands takes me ten with only the one...and I cannot manage anything that requires lacing. I could not even wrap you in your towel by myself. All these little things require two hands. You don't even notice, but I can assure you, I feel the lack acutely."

She stared at him.

How could she have been so stupid? She was not thinking merely of their morning swim or sitting for their midday meal.

Oh, how utterly stupid she had been!

A man as proud as Cormac would never sleep with Lady Seline. Oh, perhaps he would have been amenable to a quick romp that required him to undo a button or two. But to spend the night in her bedchamber? To undress himself? And undress her? Then put himself together sufficiently to walk out the next morning?

He could not do it.

Nor would his pride allow him to rely on someone like Lady Seline, who was not above mocking or ridiculing others. He had to fear she would do the same to him.

Of course she would. Yes, she would utterly destroy him as she watched with malicious amusement while he struggled to don his clothes and boots.

He'd referred to the woman as a viper.

She gasped. "I'm so sorry, Cormac. Can you ever forgive me?"

He frowned. "About my not wanting the sea captain's clothes? What is there to forgive?"

"No, not that." She stared at him, feeling quite anguished for her inadvertent cruelty. But he did not appear to know what she was talking about. "The rumors...they're all lies."

He arched an eyebrow. "I told you that. You didn't believe me. What has suddenly changed?"

"I wasn't thinking straight. I am so, so stupid."

"Phoebe, stop. Why are you beating yourself up?" Then he inhaled sharply. "My garments. That's why you believe me now. Because you've suddenly realized I am as helpless as an infant when it comes to dressing myself."

"And too proud ever to allow someone as ruthless as Lady Seline to see you struggling and vulnerable." She took his hand. "Come upstairs with me. I'll help you."

He laughed. "Are you mad? If you are caught with your hands on my falls, you'll be ruined."

"And you will save me by marrying me. Is this not what you are hoping for?"

"Lord help me, yes. I'm aching for the day we exchange wedding vows. But are you all right with it? Don't you need more time?"

"No. And you can thank Imogen mostly. She adores you."

"And I love her, as must be obvious. My nieces are the most precious things to me, as you well know."

Phoebe nodded. "She is as wise as any ancient sage. She told me quite plainly that you do not lie. So if you say the gossip is not true, then it isn't true. She is right. And I was a fool to ever doubt you."

"No, love. Not a fool." He caressed her cheek. "Just too scared to love someone with a past as wicked as mine."

She looked up at him, just stared at him while her heart opened up and allowed him in. "But in asking me to marry you, you are trusting me with your most intimate fears. All these little things that frustrate and anger you at every turn. That wound your pride. You are letting me in because you know I will never hurt you. Cormac, I am not scared anymore."

He kissed her lightly on the mouth. "Then you'll marry me?"

She nodded when he ended the soft kiss. "Yes."

"Well, blessed saints." He smiled and kissed her again with tender urgency.

The sun shone down on them, and the air felt fresh and light.

Allowing herself to love him was the most wonderful feeling in the world.

She now understood how much he loved her, for he would not have revealed his private shame to anyone else. Oh, as a practical matter, others would realize his constraints. But to actually be in the room with him, assisting him...that was something too much for his pride to take.

Yet he was allowing her in. Not only did he love her, but he trusted her never to hurt or shame him. He was sharing his vulnerability with her, and it was no small thing for him to do.

It was the purest act of love.

Phoebe was happier than she had ever imagined possible. She had been so caught up in her own doubts, too blind to understand how devastating a blow losing an arm had been to his independence.

"Phoebe, are those tears in your eyes?"

She nodded. "But good tears."

"Is there such a thing?"

"Yes, shedding a tear for happiness is always a good thing."

"All right, if you say so."

He held her hand as they walked to their belongings, but released it as they started to gather them up. "Cormac..."

"Yes, sweetheart?"

She smiled at him. "I love you."

# Chapter Sixteen

T HE NEXT FEW days brought on a constant rain, but it did not bother Cormac in the least. As far as he was concerned, the sun shone brightly in his heart, and it had not been there for a very long time.

Seline was still in town with her circle of toadies, and they amused themselves by spreading malicious gossip about him, some of it so ludicrous that the Moonstone Landing locals quickly saw through it and began to place wagers on what lies she would spread next.

"My lord," Mrs. Halsey said, approaching him when he entered her tearoom to pick up sweets for afternoon tea with Phoebe, Chloe, and his nieces. Cain's estate manager and his wife were to join them as well. "What can I get for you?"

"A lemon cake, of course. Perhaps two. Yes, make it two, Mrs. Halsey. The first will be devoured within five minutes of our tea. I'll also have a dozen strawberry tarts."

The woman laughed. "For Imogen, of course."

He smiled. "She is very fond of them." He added a few more items, and was just about to leave with his boxes of delights when Seline and her friends sauntered into the tearoom.

All chatter in the place immediately died down.

Mrs. Halsey cleared her throat. "Good day to you, my lords. Lady Whitford. Let me show you to a table."

"Not necessary," Seline responded.

Ah, so they were here for him, Cormac realized. They must have seen him entering.

The rain had stopped earlier in the day and the sun was now shining, but his former paramour was like a dark cloud hanging over his head.

Her malicious little ploys were nothing more than an annoyance for him, but Phoebe would be meeting him here in a few minutes, and he did not want her to encounter Seline and her toadies. She had stopped by the local dressmaker's to make an appointment for his nieces to be fitted for new outfits. Specifically, pretty gowns befitting their upcoming role as the littlest members of their wedding party.

They had kept the news of their betrothal quiet, since nothing could be officially acknowledged until Cain returned and gave his consent. But it did not stop them from quietly preparing for the event.

Seline purred as she rubbed against his chest.

She thought she was being seductive, but he only thought of her as a mange-ridden cat. Indeed, she was giving cats a bad name. He ignored her and tried to leave, but her friends blocked the door.

Cormac rolled his eyes. "Seldon, you little lizard. Step out of the way before I squash you."

The man stared at his missing arm and sneered. "Are you speaking to me, Burness?"

"I can see your confusion, since the place seems to be crawling with Seline's lizards—or should I refer to you all as toads? I suppose it matters little. Yes, I am addressing you. Get out of my way. I will not ask politely again."

The man ignored him.

Well, Cormac did not really *want* to hurt Lord Seldon, because the man had reason to detest him. After all, he had been intimate with the man's wife back in his wicked days. Lady Seldon hated her husband enough to openly mock his failings in the pleasuring-your-wife department. Cormac knew the man was...*flaccid*...to put it mildly. But he would never be low enough to now land such a hurtful blow, no matter how much Seldon deserved to be brought down.

Also, he was not about to start a fight in Mrs. Halsey's charming tearoom.

He turned back to the proprietress and handed his boxes to her. "I'll retrieve them in a moment. Seldon, step outside."

He gave the man no chance to respond, knocking him aside with his shoulder as he strode out and waited for the dolt to follow.

"Are you going to let him do that to you?" Seline said, goading the dolt.

She had walked in with Lord Seldon and two other lords Cormac did not know very well, but he expected they were of low reputation, or they would not have come here with her. They certainly should not have remained in the village once they realized how dull it was or what Seline's purpose was in coming here.

Why involve themselves in a confrontation that was only going to see them humiliated? Well, Seline was Lady Whitford and had the means to pay these men to do her loathsome bidding. He would not be surprised if their pay included a romp in the sack with her, although to Cormac's thinking, Seline had lost the bloom of her youth. Her once-beautiful face was beginning to show signs of wear, and there was nothing soft or sweet about her to redeem it.

The three men finally mustered their nerve and rushed out after him.

Seldon cursed at him, his language shocking several ladies who happened to be passing by. "Fight me, you coward," he said, then took a swing at Cormac. "I demand satisfaction."

Cormac easily avoided the fist. "You are making an arse of yourself, Seldon. I have no wish to fight with you. However, beware. Insult me again and I will lay you low."

Why on earth were these men coming at him in broad day-light in the middle of the high street? This was a respectable part of town. Ladies walked along here with their children.

Well, he understood Seldon's reason. But he'd had no en-counters with the wives or sisters of these other men. Why would they risk serious punishment for striking a marquess?

The promise of sex did odd things to a man's brain.

None of them were trained for fighting, something he could easily tell by their hesitation in approaching him.

Thaddius Angel came running out from the Kestrel Inn, which was just across the way. "I'll fetch my uncle," he said, and took off at a run.

The three men now moved to surround Cormac. Seline stood at the door of the tearoom, a smirk on her face.

Cormac was itching to teach these idiots a lesson, but he had never fought one-handed and was not certain whether his lack of an arm would throw his balance off. Well, hopefully it would not come to that. Constable Angel was an amiable fellow, but he would not tolerate anyone disrupting the peace in his town.

"Coward," one of Seldon's companions muttered with a snarl.

Seriously? Had all Cormac's years of battle and the loss of his arm not proven his worth? Where had these sniveling toadies been while war raged? Definitely not on a battlefield, or they would never have tossed the insult. Soldiers knew better than to talk to their brothers in arms this way.

"Brougham, is it? You are the Duke of Anston's nephew, are you not?"

"What's it to you, Burness?"

"I was just curious. I like to know the identity of the man I am about to knock unconscious."

"Ha, you just—"

Cormac slammed his fist into the man's face.

The man toppled and then lay groaning on the ground.

Seline shouted at the other two, "What are you waiting for?

He's a lousy cripple."

Ah, the woman was such a delight.

He easily knocked the other man down when the fool lunged at him—another haughty lord who had no understanding of what it meant to fight for one's life or one's country, and how that experience trained one for survival.

The two of them were now rolling on the ground, groaning as they nursed their bruised jaws.

He turned toward Lord Seldon and came to an abrupt halt.

*Damn it.*

"Put down your pistol, Seldon. It will be the gallows for you if you shoot me. You are not a peer. No one will protect you, least of all Lady Whitford."

"You humiliated me. We'll see who gets the last laugh." Seldon raised his weapon and was about to fire when it was suddenly ripped from his hand.

What the...?

The pistol fell to the ground with a clatter, thankfully not going off and injuring any innocent witnesses. Well, the street was deserted at the moment, for everyone had scrambled to take cover in the nearby shops until the incident was over.

Everyone but Phoebe, who had grabbed a rope attached to a grappling hook from the nearby mercantile and apparently knew how to handle it as capably as she knew how to draw. She'd swung that grappling hook and caught Seldon's arm with it. She now gave it a firm tug and dragged him to the ground.

Seldon growled as she stepped forward to unwind it from his arm. "Do not move, you idiot," she said. "The hook will cut your hand."

He ignored Phoebe's warning and angrily stormed to his feet. "Why you bi—"

Cormac punched him solidly in the jaw.

Seldon crumpled beside his friends.

"No one insults Lady Phoebe," Cormac muttered, retrieving the pistol before Seldon could get his hands on it again. He was relieved there were no more men left to hit, because his fist was sore and he'd probably break a bone in his hand if he needed to throw another punch.

Seline, realizing her sport had come to an end, began to sidle away.

"Oh no you don't." Phoebe had just freed her grappling hook and now swung it again with flawless aim, wrapping it around Seline's ankles and tripping her. She landed with a grunt in a muddy puddle beside her toady friends.

With another expert flick of the wrist, Phoebe unwound it and handed it over to the mercantile owner who had worriedly followed after her. "Thank you, Mr. Bedwell. I do hope you don't mind my borrowing the implement."

"Not at all." The man laughed. "Always a pleasure, Lady Phoebe."

She now looked every bit the lioness as she stalked toward the foursome with fists clenched and a fierce expression on her lovely face.

Cormac was never one to allow a lady to fight his battles, but Phoebe... Lord, she was magnificent as she drew in a breath to fill her lungs. "You despicable vermin...*wonk, wonk, wonk*...loathsome, slime of the earth...*wonk, wonk, wonk*. If you are not out of here within the hour, I will personally come after you...*wonk, wonk, wonk*. Believe me, you'll be sorry when I kick the living daylights...*wonk, wonk, wonk*...shoot you right between the eyes."

He loved this girl with all his heart.

He did not think it was possible to love her more deeply than he already did, but watching her in all her magnificent fury made his heart open up to her even more.

He slipped his arm around her waist and held her back as Seline and her companions were hauled away by Constable Angel, who'd arrived on the scene with several of his men. "Do not go after them, Phoebe," Cormac warned.

"Why not? They tried to hurt you. They spread despicable

lies about you."

He grinned at her. "But it is over, my beautiful lioness. Constable Angel and his men will take care of tossing them out of town within the hour."

Thaddius Angel followed close on his uncle's heels. "Are you all right, my lord? And you, Lady Phoebe? I hope they did not distress you." He turned to Cormac, noticing he had his arm around Phoebe's waist. "Did she faint? Does she need smelling salts?"

Cormac laughed. "She is fine. She thinks she saved my life."

Phoebe gasped. "Thinks? Why, you arrogant dolt, I did save you. Lord Seldon had that pistol pointed straight at your heart."

"And would have done little damage at that distance, assuming he was even able to properly aim his shot. I assure you, his hand was shaking too much. Despite his bravado, I don't think he had it in him to actually try to kill me. But that does not diminish your bravery in coming to my rescue. I am so proud of you, Phoebe. This arrogant dolt very much wishes to kiss you."

She frowned at him. "You may kiss me, but not before you admit I saved your life. Admit it, you wretched man, or next time I shall let that miserable Lord Seldon fill you with holes."

"All right, you win. You saved my life." He was not going to belabor the point. After all, it was always possible the man might have gotten off a lucky shot. However, Cormac was never going to just stand there and wait to be taken down. He'd grown fairly adept at dodging lethal weapons aimed at him in battle—until one mistake after a truce had been called cost him his arm. "I love you, Phoebe."

He kissed her gently on the lips.

"That's better," she grumbled, giving him a tender smile as a crowd began to gather around them. "Where are the cakes? I'll really be angry if they destroyed them."

"No, love. Mrs. Halsey has them safely tucked away for us."

Thaddius stared at them.

"Ah, you must be wondering about that kiss and my calling

her by that endearment." Cormac cleared his throat. "I have asked Lady Phoebe to marry me, and she has accepted. However, we would appreciate the matter being kept—"

Thaddius let out a whoop and ran into the tearoom. "Mrs. Halsey! Mrs. Halsey, have you heard?"

A moment later, they heard Mrs. Halsey's joyful shriek.

Her daughter tore out of the tearoom and ran into the neighboring shop.

More shrieks were heard.

Cormac sighed. "I don't suppose we'll be keeping our betrothal quiet any longer. I had hoped to wait until Cain and Hen returned to make the formal announcement."

Phoebe shook her head. "Not a chance of it now. Do you mind?"

"No, love. I meant it when I said I was proud of you. You were magnificent in coming to my rescue. But please, don't ever risk your life for mine. Our children can do without me, but never without you."

"Children? Are you not getting a little ahead of yourself? We don't have any yet."

He tossed her a wicked grin. "I shall have to rectify this oversight, won't I?"

# Chapter Seventeen

S INCE THE ORIGINAL fittings for new gowns for Cormac's nieces had been cut short by the Lady Seline incident, Phoebe rescheduled it for the following day. As dawn broke over the horizon to signal this new day, she quietly rose from her bed and opened the doors onto her small balcony to peer across the water.

A mist still hovered over the sea, but she saw a faint glow from beneath the surface of the water. This glow somehow managed to cut through the mist. She had heard the lore of the moonstones and their signifying true love.

She laughed and turned away to prepare herself for a busy day.

After breakfast, she was helping the girls into Mr. Hawke's wagon to head to the appointment with the town's modiste when Cormac rode up on Hadrian. "Let Chloe and Mr. Hawke take the girls to the dressmaker's," he said with a smile that had her melting. "You and I have urgent business which must be attended to at once."

She gazed at him in bemusement. "What is going on?"

"Cain and Hen are back and unloading their carriage as we speak. I just ran into Mr. Weston, who told me." He nudged his stallion closer to the wagon and leaned over to kiss his nieces. "Ducklings, I need Phoebe for a few hours. She cannot go with you right now."

Chloe was all smiles as she hopped in the wagon beside the girls. "I can manage their fittings. I'll order a lovely gown for me as well."

Cormac laughed. "Thank you, Chloe. We'll catch up with you later."

Phoebe shook her head as he reached his hand down to her. "Are you not being a little hasty? They've hardly set foot in their own house."

"I've waited a lifetime for you. I am not waiting a moment longer. Put your foot in the stirrup. There you go." He lifted her onto his lap and tucked her securely against his hard body. "Behave yourselves, ducklings."

"They are angels," Chloe said with a laugh. "You are the one who had better behave himself with my sister."

He winked at them and spurred Hadrian on.

Phoebe held tightly to him as he rode off with her on his lap.

It was not long before St. Austell Grange, the beautiful estate of her brother-in-law, the Duke of Malvern, came into view.

The ducal carriage was still in the courtyard as they rode up, footmen busily unloading all their packages and a second carriage that held all their trunks.

"Hen!" Phoebe called out, delighted to see her sister standing on the steps by the front door. "You'll never guess!"

Her sister laughed and ran forward to give her a hug as soon as she dismounted. "We know all about it! Lord Burness wrote to Cain asking for permission to marry you. It seems he could not wait for Cain's return. But Phoebe, are you certain about this? You haven't known him very long, and..." She looked over at Cormac, who had just handed Hadrian's reins to one of the Malvern grooms. "He does not have a sterling reputation."

"I know. Quite a horrid reputation—and he lived up to it, believe me."

Hen was shocked. "Then why are you agreeing to marry him? Oh no! Phoebe, did he compromise you?"

"No, he's been an insufferable gentleman about *that*. He

knows Cain would kill him if he touched me outside of marriage. Let's go in. I want to see the babies. Let me kiss them, and then I'll tell you everything that has happened while you were away."

Hen's infant twins, a son and daughter, had been tired out from their travels and fallen asleep in the carriage as it neared their home. "Their nanny has taken them up to the nursery for their naps. Let's join the men in Cain's study while our staff brings in the last of our belongings. We can look in on the children afterward."

Cain, a big bear of a man, came around his desk to greet the pair as they walked in. "Phoebe, your sister and I long ago jested about you to Cormac, but we never dreamed the two of you would ever marry. Are you sure about this?"

She nodded. "Yes, not a doubt. Has he told you all that went on while you were in Bath?"

"He started to," Cain said with a wry smile. "I have a feeling Hen and I missed all the excitement. Have a seat and tell us the rest of it."

She and Cormac took turns filling them in, ending with the incident with Seline and her despicable friends outside of Mrs. Halsey's tearoom.

Cormac was still shaking his head about it. "Cain, I know you taught Hen and her sisters how to swim, but did you also teach them how to use a grappling hook?"

"No. Why on earth would I ever do such a thing?" Cain stared at Phoebe. "Who taught you?"

"No one."

Cormac began to pace in front of her. "See, Cain? She will not tell me. I had hoped you could shed light on it. Phoebe, love. Why the secrecy?"

"It isn't a secret. Only you will all think my wits are addled if I tell you." She sighed. "Hen will understand because…because she's also seen our Moonstone Cottage ghost, Captain Arundel."

Hen inhaled sharply. "Brioc is here?"

"Yes, with Aunt Hen. Cormac's nieces saw him when we

took them on a boat ride in the harbor."

Cain frowned. "Did he frighten them?"

"No. He was kind to them, just as he was to me and Hen when we were children. But I'm sure he's the one who must have guided me as I used the grappling hook. I could not have done it myself. I've never even held one before. But I couldn't let that horrible Lord Seldon shoot Cormac." She turned to Cormac. "I couldn't tell you. I was afraid you wouldn't believe me. I also thought you would be livid if I admitted I'd never held one before."

"Blessed saints," he muttered, raking a hand through his hair. "I ought to be. Phoebe—"

"This is exactly why I needed to wait until Hen returned. I knew she would understand."

"Love, I would have believed you."

She arched an eyebrow. "Truly?"

He sighed. "Maybe not. I'll admit I was rattled when my nieces spoke of him. But I did not think they had made up the story. Nor do I doubt you. I don't care how you learned to swing that grapple. You were brilliant, and I have you to thank for taking down that arse. Although I suppose I would have been furious if I realized you were a novice at the time."

"What I still don't understand," Cain said, "is why Seline came after you the way she did. What happened between you to set her off?"

"I have no idea." Cormac shrugged. "You were there shortly after I lost my arm. She dumped me and ridiculed me. I thought that was the last I would ever hear of her. Not that I minded in the least. She was an anchor around my neck, and I was glad to be rid of her. However, I would have been far kinder in ending our liaison if the situations were reversed."

"Your *illicit* liaison," Phoebe added. "She was married at the time."

He winced. "She wasn't married when I first went off to fight Napoleon. She married a few years later. Unhappily, that much is obvious. I don't know what she thought would happen on my return. She was enraged when I came back wounded and about to lose my arm. Ever the compassionate creature, she cut off all connection to me once she knew it had to come off."

Cain absently took hold of Hen's hand as he spoke. "That happened three years ago. It still doesn't explain why she followed you here and harassed you now."

Cormac shrugged once more. "Truly, I have no idea what set her off."

"I think I might," Hen said.

They all turned to her, eager to hear what she had to say.

"There were rumors circulating in Bath that her husband intends to divorce her."

Phoebe's eyes rounded in surprise. "Divorce? But her husband is an earl. Would he do this and destroy all hope of siring a legitimate heir? Would the church sanctify a union if he remarried?"

Cain shook his head. "Possibly, if he can convince the church to grant him an annulment. He may have found the grounds."

"Goodness." Phoebe turned to her sister. "Go on, Hen. I'm sorry. I did not mean to interrupt you."

"Well, apparently one of the things he mentioned—and I've heard this third-hand, so please take it for what it is—is that they were screaming at each other quite loudly and overheard by their servants. We all know how they sometimes gossip. Well, we had let a townhouse in the Royal Crescent, and it was not far from theirs."

Phoebe leaned closer. "Go on."

"One of the maids in their household happened to be the sister of one of ours, and she repeated everything to me. It appears Seline's husband was furious over one of the latest of her cruel antics. He said he should have realized what a cold… I cannot repeat what he called her. Anyway, he accused her of being cold as ice and cited her response to Cormac when he came back wounded as an example." She turned to Cormac. "Whitford considered you a war hero. Apparently, he is a great admirer of yours."

"So that's what set her off? Gad, how could Whitford not hate me? I gave not a thought to his feelings." Cormac groaned. "Well, my encounters with Seline mostly occurred before they were married. I wasn't at my rakehell best when returning with a shattered arm. Then it became hopelessly infected and had to come off."

Phoebe reached out and took his hand.

Cormac gave a mirthless laugh. "Since I wasn't at my best, I suppose Seline took on other lovers. Her indiscreet infidelities must have added to Whitford's humiliation. By that time I had my own struggles to contend with in trying to save my arm, and was not among the parade of men who warmed her bed."

Hen pursed her lips and frowned. "That is nothing for you to be proud of."

"Indeed, I am not proud of it at all," he said with a wince. "It shames me more, since he held me in high regard. A war hero? I did nothing more on the field of battle than a thousand other men did throughout the war. Every soldier who fought deserved the same honors. More so, because they were more valiant in their daily lives than I ever was."

Hen shook her head. "You and my husband are surprisingly modest in this regard. Quite surprising, considering how arrogant you are in most things."

Both men chuckled.

"Cain is always humble when people come up to him and call him heroic." Hen cast her husband an admiring smile. "You are both valorous men and deserve praise for your deeds. But Seline's husband specifically made mention of Cormac. This must have left her with quite a bitter taste, especially if the divorce rumors prove true."

Cormac shrugged. "He is well rid of her. That woman is poison."

Phoebe emitted a sigh. "I think she must have been in love

with you. Even if you were honest about your intentions not to marry her in those early days, a woman can still dream. Even one as casual about her liaisons as she obviously was. You are irresistible, you know."

He kissed her on the forehead. "I am a stubborn idiot who does not deserve someone as fine as you. But I am sure as hell not letting you go. You are a gift to me and I will treasure you always."

He turned to Cain. "I meant what I said. Will you give your consent to marry Phoebe?"

"I love him, Cain," Phoebe added. Despite their being best friends, Cain would refuse the request if he had any doubts about Cormac's qualities. He took his responsibilities as guardian seriously.

She held her breath, awaiting his answer.

No one knew Cormac better than Cain did, and this could work against them.

But she needn't have worried, for Cain grinned and walked over to slap Cormac on the back. "When do you intend for the happy event to take place? Blessed saints, I cannot believe it. Well, I can with Phoebe. She's a gem. And you had better be good to her."

Cormac winked at Phoebe, his smile breathtaking. "She'll keep me in line. I wouldn't want to be on the receiving end of her grappling hook."

"I would never…" She laughed and shook her head. "Mr. Bedwell is afraid to allow me back into his shop."

"Phoebe and I discussed it," Cormac said, once more taking her hand. "My brother and his wife will arrive next week to pick up their girls. We'd like to marry once they are here. I won't drag you from home today, but I hope you'll come with me tomorrow to obtain the license. We can discuss terms of Phoebe's settlement tomorrow as well. I'll make it easy for you. Write up whatever terms you deem fair. Make certain she is generously provided for when I am no longer around."

Cain's grin broadened. "Come by after breakfast and we'll ride to the parish church together. But there's another thing we have to think about, and that is Chloe. She cannot live alone at Moonstone Cottage."

"Oh." Hen exchanged a glance with Phoebe. "Cain and I will take her in, of course. He is her legal guardian, so it makes the most sense. But I hadn't thought of a Killigrew no longer living there. It will feel odd to have the house empty."

"Nor had I," Phoebe admitted. "We'll figure out something. We met a lovely young man in town a few weeks ago, a soldier assigned to scout locations for an army hospital. Not that I would want our beautiful home torn down, but it might serve the wounded soldiers in some other useful way. Just for the few years until Chloe is old enough to reside there on her own. However, the house must stay intact."

"Agreed," Hen said. "And we mustn't ever sell it. Brioc and Aunt Hen are there, and it wouldn't feel right to abandon them. But does it not strike you as odd that our aunt and Brioc have remained? I think they must have a purpose—perhaps to see us all happily matched first?"

"Yes, that must be it. I know they are going to look after Chloe and protect her." Phoebe grinned at Cormac and Cain. "Not that she won't have plenty of protection with you two ogres scaring all her suitors away. As for now, we are also happy to have Chloe settle in with us at Westgate Hall. She may not want to because Cormac and I will be newly wed. But we'll set aside one of the nicest bedchambers for her so she can stay over whenever she likes."

"She loves you both," Cain said. "I'm sure she'll split her time between her two sisters. But I think Moonstone Cottage is the place she considers home. Do not be surprised if she asks to move back there the moment she comes of age."

Phoebe and Cormac did not remain long afterward, since her sister and Cain still had a lot of unpacking to do and were likely tired from their trip. They decided to ride into town to see how his nieces were getting along with their fittings. Also, she was eager to relate the good news to Chloe and the girls.

Of course, they were aware of the couple's desire to marry. But it was nice to be able to officially proclaim their betrothal.

Not that it very much mattered, since the entire town now knew of their feelings and had simply accepted they were betrothed.

Cormac was unusually quiet as they rode toward Moonstone Landing. Hadrian ambled at an easy lope, his big hooves muffled as they struck the damp earth. Phoebe remained comfortably tucked against Cormac's chest.

But she turned to him when he suddenly drew Hadrian to a halt. They had just reached the scenic rise overlooking the village and the sea beyond.

He dismounted and then helped her down.

"Is something wrong?" she asked, for he suddenly looked quite serious.

"No, love." His voice was thick and raspy. "I just wanted a moment alone with you."

He wrapped his arm around her as they stood together and admired the view. Her breath caught when she glanced at him and noticed his eyes tearing. She wanted to ask him what was wrong, but there was something in his expression that stilled her tongue.

After a moment, he let out a ragged breath and spoke. "One loses sight of beauty when your face is flat against a muddy, blood-slicked ground and cannons are firing all around you. All you can hear are screams of the wounded and the deafening roars of those never-ending cannon blasts. All you can smell is death and blood. I was not a good person when I signed up to fight. Oh, I had a sense of duty to my country, but that is all the good that could be said of me."

She was afraid to utter a word, but she knew he was not as bad as he made himself out to be. He had a strong love of family, had always been good to his brother and now his brother's daughters. He was also a dutiful marquess and took his responsibilities to those who lived and worked on his estates quite seriously.

"I look at Seline and see her for what I used to be back then. Arrogant. Selfish."

"I cannot believe you were ever that mean-spirited. You were never so cruel as to purposely harm anyone."

He shook his head. "I hurt *everyone*. I might have even been capable of hurting you, had I met you earlier. I like to think I would have kept away from you, for even as vile as I was, I did have somewhat of a code of honor. No virgins. No entanglements. Honesty about my intentions—but those intentions were rarely honorable. I gave no thought whatsoever to who might be hurt by my casual dalliances. What if I destroyed marriages?"

"Seems to me it is the spouses who do the destroying. It is one thing if those marriages were happy before you came along."

"No, they weren't. Even at my most despicable, I would not have…" He sighed. "Perhaps I was not the worst man alive. But neither was I a good man. Despite having a prosperous estate and a loving family, I never reached out to help those in need. I gave no thought to anyone other than myself."

He turned toward her and gave her cheek a soft caress. "I was in a bad way after losing my arm. I did not need Seline's cruelty to sink me lower, for I had already struck bottom. Hating myself and hating the world. Then Cain and Hen came to visit me. They mentioned you. *Phoebe*. That's all I needed to hear, and I somehow knew my heart was yours."

She gave him a smile. "Took you three years to get here."

He grinned back. "You would not have liked me if I had come any sooner. I was no prize even a few weeks ago, when you first set eyes on me. But I was ready to reform, ready to pledge my heart to you, since I was already in love with you."

"You were in love with the *idea* of me."

"No, with you. You are in my blood and in my soul, in every breath I take. *Phoebe*. You are the soft breeze against my cheek and the lavender-scented air surrounding us. You brought me here, no one else. I am surrounded by beauty because you are beside me. You have no idea how special you are to me. Cain knows it. He saw the look in my eyes. He feels the same about your sister."

Her heart melted as he spoke. She had never imagined anyone could feel this way about her, especially this man she loved so deeply.

"I hope you will grow to trust me, Phoebe. I just wanted to explain to you why I know our marriage will always be unbreakable. You've given me this." He motioned toward the village and sea. "You've given me love. Happiness. I was in such a deep, dark hole. You lifted me out of it. And don't say I did it myself. I didn't. I needed the hope of you. I needed you."

He was unburdening a decade of torment and unhappiness.

She did not know what to say.

She had done nothing but be herself.

Perhaps this was all he needed her to be. Just herself. Phoebe Killigrew, who loved him.

She thought she understood what was going through his mind at this moment, this new road he was about to take, one that would lead to happiness and fulfillment instead of emptiness and misery.

"It seems ironic that the rakehell marquess should find his freedom by committing himself in marriage, especially to me," she teased affectionately.

"Only to you, my Moonstone temptress. I would not find this happiness with anyone else." He kissed her with sweet urgency, pressing his lips to hers as he allowed hunger and craving to overtake him.

He drew her up against him, lifting her slightly off the ground, so that their bodies fit together like the final pieces to complete the puzzle of their lives. Their hearts beat together, hers ridiculously rapid but his steadier and matching every second beat of hers. "I love you, Cormac."

"I am insanely in love with you, my lioness."

A warm summer breeze enveloped them as they stood under the bright sun thinking of their future and all the hopes and dreams that lay ahead of them.

CORMAC'S GRIN WAS ear to ear when they arrived at the dressmaker's shop. His nieces were having their gowns pinned to their measurements, and they looked like faerie princesses.

They hopped up and down with delight when he strode in, ignoring the pins and simply ebullient in their pleasure as they showed off their gowns of palest pink silk.

"Ducklings, you look amazing," he said, his eyes alight with joy.

"Phoebe needs to choose something nice for herself," Ella said, and Imogen nodded in agreement. "Chloe's gown is the color of lilacs. It's so pretty."

Cormac gave each girl a kiss on the forehead. "Phoebe will have the best there is. She'll be the prettiest bride ever."

He turned to the dressmaker. "Madame de Clare, your best for Lady Phoebe."

Chloe took her sister's hand and drew her over to a display of fabrics. "Come look at these silks. What do you think of these laces?"

Phoebe, Chloe, and the dressmaker discussed the various choices while Cormac remained with his nieces. In the background, Phoebe could hear Cormac chatting with them, teasing them gently as he always did, and leaving them in giggles. She loved how good he was with them and how much they adored him.

"Phoebe," Chloe said, cutting into her straying thoughts, "you need a gown to rival the finest London has to offer. Is that not right, Lord Burness?"

"Yes, yes!" the girls responded before he could get in a word. They were so excited, and Phoebe quickly caught their enthusiasm.

She held up her hands and laughed. "All right. Let's show those stuffy Londoners how it is done here in Moonstone Landing. Right, Madame de Clare?"

"Indeed!" the woman agreed with a jovial smile.

Phoebe knew this was not merely going to be her day, but Cormac's as well. She wanted this for him more than anything, for he had not merely lost his arm but pieces of his heart. Those were healing, and this was what counted most.

He was all rakish grins as the dressmaker took her measurements. When she put the tape around Phoebe's bust, he remarked, "Need help with that?"

Chloe and the woman giggled inanely while he followed it up with a naughty wink. Phoebe stood there shaking her head, her cheeks flaming. "You are incorrigible."

Cormac kissed her on the nose. "And you are beautiful."

He took the girls down to the docks to watch the boats sailing in and out of the harbor while the dressmaker finished taking her measurements and began putting what would be her wedding gown together. "You'll need to come back tomorrow for a proper pinning."

Phoebe smiled. "Gladly. What time would you like me here?"

They made their appointment, then she and Chloe went in search of Cormac and the girls. It was not hard to find them even amid the crowd of vendors and shoppers by the harbor. Cormac was talking to Lieutenant Brennan, the young man they had met at the church fair. He waved to them as she and Chloe approached.

"What brings you back to town?" Chloe asked, her smile particularly bright.

"I finished scouting the nearby harbors and towns."

Phoebe nodded. "And what have you decided?"

"Well, my recommendation will remain to build the new

hospital in Moonstone Landing. The ultimate choice is not mine to make. I'm sure there'll be quite a bit of political wrangling once I file my report. But you have a good, deep harbor and plenty of room to build on the north side of town. An army barracks is already situated here, although that might need to be expanded. The town's transportation routes and amenities are well developed, so those should not be an issue beyond adding an access road to the hospital and a few modifications to the harbor."

"I'll be interested in seeing your plans and discussing your report," Cormac said. "So will the Duke of Malvern. I believe he is the largest land owner in the area. Will you be available to meet with us tomorrow morning?"

"Yes, my lord. With pleasure."

"Good. Join us at the Kestrel Inn at eleven o'clock. The duke and I should be done with our business by then."

"They're obtaining a wedding license," Chloe said with a squeal. "Lord Burness is to marry my sister."

The lieutenant seemed genuinely delighted. "My heartiest congratulations."

"The wedding will be next week," Chloe went on, for she was almost as excited as Phoebe was about the momentous event. "As soon as Lord Burness's brother arrives to pick up his girls. You must attend as well, for it is to be a grand affair and all the villagers are invited. Will you remain in town until next week?"

"Yes, but..." He glanced at Phoebe and Cormac. "I would not want to intrude."

"Nonsense," Cormac said. "You are most welcome. The duke and duchess have already taken this wedding completely out of our hands. The wedding breakfast will take place at Malvern House. The duke is not going to let my wedding day pass without turning it into a spectacle."

"And Hen will be planning it right along with him," Phoebe said with a laugh. "She always did like a good party. Do join us now for cakes at Mrs. Halsey's tearoom. We'd love to hear more about your plans."

The lieutenant fell into step with Cormac while she and Chloe led the way up the high street with the girls.

Mr. Bedwell waved to her as they walked past his mercantile establishment. "Good day to you, Lady Phoebe. Any adventures for you today?"

She laughed. "No, all quiet. Lovely day, isn't it, Mr. Bedwell?"

The aroma of freshly baked cakes tickled her nostrils. "Girls, just breathe deeply. Can you smell cinnamon and apples? Doesn't it make your mouth water?"

"I want a strawberry tart," Imogen said, wrinkling her pert nose.

"I'm going to have a ginger cake," Ella insisted.

Thaddius Angel was standing in front of the Kestrel Inn and waved to her. "My uncle wants to make you an honorary constable," he teased.

The lieutenant eyed her speculatively once they were seated. "I think I must have missed something while I was out of town."

Chloe quickly filled him in. "My sister was as brave as any soldier on the battlefield."

"Indeed, Lady Phoebe. What you did is to be commended."

"Chloe exaggerates," Phoebe replied. "Lord Burness did most of the work."

Cormac shook his head. "I threw a few punches, that's all. She saved my life."

Phoebe's eyes widened. "Oh, ho! Now you do admit I saved you."

His gorgeous eyes shimmered with mirth. "Yes, you impertinent baggage. But don't get too confident." He turned serious a moment later and covered her hand with his. "What you did was dangerous, and I would never forgive myself if you ever got hurt on my account."

She felt the ache in his words and did not have the heart to respond with a glib answer.

Imogen stared at them. "Can I have my strawberry tart now?"

Phoebe and Cormac chuckled.

"Yes, duckling," he said. "You may have as many as will fill your stomach."

They bade Lieutenant Brennan farewell a short while later and returned to Moonstone Cottage. Chloe took the girls up for a nap.

Phoebe and Cormac took a walk down to the beach.

He wrapped her hand in his, the feeling quite nice as they strolled along the shore together. But they hadn't gone far before he stopped and settled on the sand. He nudged her down so that she sank down in front of him, seated between his legs with her back resting against his chest.

He placed his arm around her as she nestled against the solid breadth of him. "It's this, Phoebe. Little moments like this that give me the most pain, knowing I can never wrap my arms around you or hold you with the embracing love you deserve. I don't even know on which side of the bed I should have you sleep. On my right, so you can sleep cuddled against my good arm? Or on my left, so I can more easily reach out to you? But that would leave you sleeping beside half an arm."

"Which feels worse to you?"

He gave a snorting laugh. "I hate the thought of either one. I think I would rather you sleep on my right. At least that way you'll see me whole."

"Hen always thinks things to death, and I see you are just like her. I'm glad you want me in your bed. I wouldn't like us to sleep apart. Beyond this, I don't think I'll care."

"You will, Phoebe."

She shrugged. "We'll see."

He planted a heated kiss on her neck, followed by a string of soft kisses along its curve to her shoulder. Then he turned her to face him and kissed her along the swell of her bosom. "You have the prettiest body. I'm going to enjoy our nights together, but especially waking up to you each morning."

"We'll see how much you enjoy it when I snore in your ear all night."

He laughed. "Love, I think mine will drown yours out."

They sat quietly after that, listening to the cawing of the gulls hovering over the water in search of fish, and the *whooshing* of the waves lapping the shore. The wind softly whistled around them and the sun darted in and out of white, tufted clouds.

The moment felt idyllic, and she treasured it.

But she was also eager to lie beside Cormac and know his touch. He said she had a pretty body, but his was museum-worthy. Big. Muscled. Broad and hard.

A man's body.

She wanted to talk to Hen about what would be expected of her on their wedding night. She thought it would be wonderful, but she couldn't be sure what would happen, especially if Cormac allowed his happiness to be diminished by the lost arm that still haunted him.

Was there something she could do to make him forget it once they were in bed?

Or was this something too intimate to ever ask her sister?

# Chapter Eighteen

CORMAC HAD WANTED a small wedding at first, but he was glad Cain and Hen ignored his wishes and turned it into a splash of a party. Had there been less bustle and activity swirling around him, he would have been thinking too much about everything.

Mostly of his wedding night with Phoebe.

Logically, he knew it would be fine because he knew his way around a woman's body and had no doubt Phoebe would respond to his touch.

But he hated the thought of baring his body, no matter that Phoebe had seen him without his shirt on and never flinched.

He cared about it.

She didn't.

So why was he fretting over something that was inconsequential to her?

He was also feeling nostalgic because today's nuptials would also mean the end of his month with his little ducklings.

The girls would return to London with his brother and Charlotte, who had arrived two days ago to reclaim them. For once, he did not mind Charlotte fluttering about like a peahen. It served as a distraction.

"John, you had better not cry at the wedding," Cormac said as he and his brother stood together in his bedchamber at Westgate

Hall while his valet assisted him in dressing.

"I cannot help it." His brother was usually the staid, even-tempered one, but he could not stop sniffling or tearing up. "They are joyful tears."

"Gad, you sound like an old woman. Why don't you go see if your daughters and Charlotte are ready?"

"Don't tell me what to do, you arse. I never thought this day would come or that you would make such a fine choice for yourself. You owe me. I'll have you know I lived through a month of hell because Charlotte was sure you would lose the girls or forget you had them."

Cormac sighed. "I never would."

"I know. I never would have sent them off to you had I a single doubt about your diligence. But Charlotte is their mother and missed them terribly. She was sure they would be miserable without us." John laughed as he wiped aside a tear. "I think they'll now be feeling miserable *with* us. You are clearly their favorite. They cry at the mention of our going home and will miss you so much."

"It is mutual. I enjoyed having them with me, although Phoebe and Chloe deserve all the credit. The girls spent most of the month residing with them. Of course, I was with them every day. It wasn't possible for me to take them in right away because of the deathbed promise I had made to James Crawford. That pressing responsibility got in the way. But it all worked out beautifully. You have raised two angels, and everyone adores them. Send them to us every summer. Phoebe and I would love it."

"Perhaps we'll come along with the girls next time. You obviously feel this place is special. And I see a miraculous transformation in you."

"I was ready to move out of that dark pit I'd created for myself." Cormac stood still as his valet adjusted his cravat. "Thank you, Gunyon. There, I believe I am now presentable. What do you say, John? Time to get to church. Phoebe might marry someone else if I show up late."

His brother laughed. "I still don't understand how she could love you, but who am I to look a gift horse in the mouth? You will be her problem now."

THE CHURCH WAS already surrounded by villagers eager to see the nuptials take place. Phoebe's sisters were there, and hurried over to take Cormac's nieces with them for the wedding procession. Their cousin, Prudence, who had married Cain's estate manager, was also fussing about and making certain the family was properly seated in the front pews.

Everyone had on their Sunday best.

Flowers and silk ribbons were draped everywhere.

The curate was beaming as he pounded out a tune on the organ.

Gad, this would be quite a formal ceremony.

Well, Phoebe was worth every effort, and Cormac felt good to have the wedding done right.

He and John stood at the altar to await the appearance of the bride.

The curate continued to play the organ as the church filled, and then the music stopped and everyone turned silent while the church doors groaned open to reveal Cain standing there with Phoebe on his arm. Gasps rose through the crowd, for she was stunning in her white silk and lace.

Cormac's heart leaped into his throat.

He gave silent thanks that someone above liked him enough to give him this angel. He surely did not deserve her.

Ella and Imogen walked down the aisle ahead of Phoebe. They looked so adorable, taking their roles seriously as they spread rose petals from the dainty baskets they held. He wasn't certain who was smiling broadest, him or John. The girls were two faerie princesses with their hair in ringlets and circlets of flowers atop their heads. All they lacked were faerie wings.

Then Phoebe stood before him, her lace veil framing her heart-shaped face, and her beautiful aquamarine eyes shimmering.

"Do you take this woman…" the vicar began, reciting the vows Cormac was to make to her, those vows to honor and protect her, and always be true.

"I do," he said, feeling the meaning of his oath of fealty to the depths of his soul.

Phoebe was beaming as she recited her vows. "I do."

He winked at her and kissed her on the cheek. "You're stuck with me now, love."

She reached up and placed a light kiss on his cheek. "As you are stuck with me. I really do snore quite loudly."

The vicar cleared his throat to remind them the ceremony was not quite over. They dutifully gave him their attention until he uttered the last words of the ceremony. "I now pronounce you man and wife."

As the vicar ended his recitation and congratulated them, Cormac slipped his arm around Phoebe's waist and lifted her up against him with a whoop of joy. "I love you," he whispered, and kissed her on the mouth with what the vicar would likely consider unseemly passion.

Well, Cormac was still no saint.

But there would be no woman for him other than Phoebe. Her mouth was honey sweet, and her lips were soft and delicious.

He heard his nieces giggling. Everyone stood and cheered.

As they marched down the aisle, Cormac realized how much the village and its inhabitants had become a part of their lives. He saw young Thaddius Angel and his uncle, the constable. Mrs. Halsey was there with her husband and daughter. They must have closed the tearoom and bake shop for the morning, although he knew they had been baking madly these past two days to provide a supply of their cakes, tarts, and pies for the wedding breakfast.

Lieutenant Brennan was there and helping Chloe avoid the crush of guests as she tried to make her way toward them.

Cormac's valet, Gunyon, had a wide grin on his usually stoic face.

Melrose and his staff were also here, smiling and nodding their approval of Phoebe, who would now keep his household in shape.

He recognized so many faces—the tavern keeper, the schoolmistress and her husband, the boat owner who'd taken them for a ride around the harbor.

Mr. and Mrs. Hawke wore the biggest grins. "Your Auntie Hen must be so proud of her nieces," Mrs. Hawke called out. "You girls made it such a happy place after she passed."

Even though Chloe would no longer be living at Moonstone Cottage, she had agreed to keep the Hawkes on as caretakers so the house would never be empty. In any event, Chloe was going to move back in as soon as Cain would allow it. She was already counting the days until her return. That house was in the Killigrew blood and would never pass to anyone but a Killigrew.

Everyone now climbed into their carriages to ride to Malvern House for the wedding breakfast. The tables groaned under the weight of the food piled atop them, and there was an orchestra hired to play for those who wished to dance.

Cormac and Phoebe led off the dancing with a country reel, for this was not a London ballroom and everyone simply wanted to have fun. No formal quadrille. Just stomping and twirling. Any qualms he might have had about sharing a dance with Phoebe quickly disappeared. Whenever she could not hold his arm—since he did not have one to hold—she merely twirled on her own and held out her veil so that it billowed becomingly around her.

Perhaps it was also the freely flowing ale, port wines and clarets, ratafia punch, and orgeat that made for such a pleasant celebration. No one seemed to notice or care about his missing limb. They were all too busy having a good time and admiring

Phoebe, who looked more radiant than a moon goddess, for she was all shimmer and silky starlight.

Well, they were presently enjoying a spectacular day in brightest sunlight...he must have downed too much of Cain's excellent brandy to be thinking of Phoebe as a goddess of the moon. Not that it mattered. He could hold his drink, and Phoebe was beautiful whether under the light of the sun, moon, or stars.

The party finally ended late in the day, and it was now time for Cormac to take Phoebe back to Westgate Hall. Her clothes had been brought over yesterday, and he'd assigned a maid to attend to her personal care.

While he would have enjoyed undressing Phoebe, he knew her wedding gown had too many buttons and lacings for him to manage on his own—especially those delicate pearl buttons, which he would have destroyed in the trying.

It also pained him that he could not sweep his luscious bride into his arms and carry her upstairs. But she did not seem to care a whit about this as she climbed the stairs beside him, the two of them hand in hand. "Cormac, I am going to kick you out of bed if you don't stop thinking about every little thing you cannot do."

He tossed her a seductive grin. "If you kick me out of bed, I'll just have to make love to you on the floor."

She arched an eyebrow. "I expect you will try it anyway, because you are still a naughty boy at heart."

"Any objection? It would only ever be with you, love." He kissed her on the mouth, a sweet, lingering kiss, before allowing Phoebe's maid to escort her into her dressing room. He heard laughter and the soft hum of chatter as the maid began helping her out of her garments.

He entered his bedchamber and strode to his own dressing room, where Gunyon awaited to assist him out of his clothes. There was an adjoining door between Phoebe's dressing area and his. Her door was closed for the moment. Even so, he and Gunyon could hear Phoebe still chattering away and her maid laughing.

Gunyon smiled as he helped Cormac undress. "My lord, a miracle has happened."

"Do you mean the ladies? They do seem to be having an awfully good time in there. I wonder what they are talking about."

"You, I'm sure. But I was not referring to them. The miracle is about you. For once, you are not snarling at me as I assist you in undressing."

Cormac chuckled. "Don't get used to it, Gunyon. I'm still an insufferable arse."

"I'll try not to get my hopes up, my lord," the valet said in jest, but they both knew Cormac's life would not be the same now that Phoebe was his wife.

She filled the house with warmth and light, and everyone felt it—Cormac most of all. He could not quite take it all in or believe that none of his limitations mattered to her.

Yet they never had. Not even the first day they met.

He silently berated himself, knowing he had to stop getting inside his own head and enjoy the evening. Phoebe was an innocent and had no idea what could happen between a man and a woman. He knew how to pleasure her. Even if he wasn't perfect, she had nothing to compare him to. He also knew they would enjoy their night together no matter what happened because of how strongly they felt about each other.

Once they were alone in his bedchamber—one they would now share—he made no move to rid her of her robe or his own that he had donned for the sake of her modesty. Even though Phoebe was a lioness, she was a shy one at the moment.

He meant to put her at ease. She needed to get comfortable with her own body as well as his.

The sun was still on the horizon and would remain so for another hour, casting the room in a soft amber glow. Phoebe looked so lovely with her hair unbound and her curves quite shapely beneath the thin nightgown and silk robe she wore.

The windows were open, the sheer drapes billowing in the

breeze wafting off the water. His chamber was large and befitting a marquess, the bed big and solid, with the footboard and headboard carved of finest mahogany.

The views from his windows were quite splendid. When Phoebe moved away to look out of one of them, he did not stop her, and instead joined her. Like most of the finer houses in the area, Westgate Hall had been built with views to the garden and the shimmering waters of the cove beyond. "It is quite a change from your cozier bedchamber at Moonstone Cottage, but the scenery is much the same. I hope you will be comfortable here."

She nodded. "I know I will be."

He kissed her when she turned to smile up at him, one deep kiss and then another. He slipped the robe off her shoulders, hardly noticing its soft *whoosh* as it slid to the floor. Then her nightgown came off, and she stood before him looking so lovely that he could hardly believe she was real.

He moved her away from the windows and their billowing drapes. Tonight, his gaze would be on Phoebe's beautiful body, the cream of her skin and the dusky-pink tips of her breasts. They puckered and then hardened at his touch when he gave them a light stroke with the pad of his thumb. He took one between his lips and suckled the exquisite pink pearl.

She gasped and took hold of his head, winding her fingers through his hair and clutching him as her body began to respond to his touch. He moved to the other breast and stroked his tongue across it in a light, flicking stroke, pleased when he felt her shudder.

"Cormac," she said in a shattered whisper. "My body..."

"I know, love." He removed his robe so they were now as nature had made them.

Her hair was down and curling about her hips in waves of dark silk. She had big, beautiful eyes the color of the ocean. Her breasts were firm and round, big enough to fill the cup of his hand.

This girl stole his breath.

He was glad they stood in the light of sundown, because it was particularly soft and bright, and he wanted her to see all of him as much as he drank in all of her. It was important to have nothing between them, to hide nothing and share everything of who they were.

He wanted to see her response when he entered her and made them truly man and wife. As they fell onto the bed, both of them quickly aroused and craving satisfaction, he forgot to think about his arm, or worry about propping his weight on one elbow so as not to rest too heavily atop her.

He sometimes crushed her and fumbled to position himself, but she only seemed more aroused by it, not minding that their lovemaking was not pretty. She was hungry for him and responded however and wherever he touched her, kissed her. Suckled her.

His heart soared as they coupled for the first time, her body so perfectly fitted to his, and both of them hungry and grasping, unable to get enough of each other. When she opened her arms to him, he realized she was not even aware of his missing limb. How could she overlook it? But she did, and her eyes held so much love for him.

Perhaps this was the answer.

He did not need to be perfect.

He just needed to be his imperfect self.

"I love you, Phoebe," he whispered as they shattered together, her tightly clinging to his neck and kissing his face as they spun out of control after reaching the stars.

"I love you too. I had no idea it could be like this. Did it feel wonderful for you, too?"

"Yes, love. Spectacular." How could she not tell? He was a grunting, panting, sweaty lump atop her. He shifted their positions so that she now lay atop him. He ran his hand through her silken mane, loving the feel of it through his fingers. It tumbled over his arm in a soft, dark wave.

Her breasts were pillowed against his chest, and he could feel their hearts still pounding wildly for each other.

For all the imperfection of their lovemaking, the one perfect thing was how they felt about each other. Everything she did made him love her more. Was it possible for a heart to feel so full without bursting?

He made love to her twice more in the night. Despite his best intentions to take his time and pleasure her slowly, their coupling both times turned quick and fiery. They ignited each other, each sparking fireworks in the other and going off explosively.

This was what they were—fireworks, brilliant and beautiful.

He laughed as he rolled onto his back and caught his breath, drawing her to nestle against his side after their third time. "You make me burn, Phoebe. I think it will be months before I'll be able to properly take the time to pleasure you as you deserve."

"Have we not been doing it right?"

"We have. There is no right or wrong way to go about it so long as we both enjoy it. But…" He shook his head and groaned. "I cannot…prolong myself. I spill myself into you as soon as I know you are pleasured."

"Oh, but it sounds to me as though I am the one who ought to slow down."

"No, you are perfect." She responded to him like a little fire-cracker, going off as soon as she was lit. Of course, her response immediately set him off too.

She hugged him. "Then what are you complaining about?"

He kissed her on the forehead and chuckled. "Nothing, love. It is just my wanting so much of you."

They drifted off to sleep, Phoebe nestled against his body.

HE AWOKE AT sunrise, that early-morning light warming his face and the soft breeze carrying in the scent of the sea. They had never closed the windows or drawn the drapes, which were sheer anyway and would not have kept out the sun.

He looked down at Phoebe, who was fast asleep and still clinging to him.

Her skin felt warm to the touch, and her lips were a rosy pink from being thoroughly kissed. He stared at her soft, round shoulders and the light swell of her breasts peeking out from under the sheet. She had fallen asleep to the left of him, to the side of his missing arm. Yet she seemed so untroubled by it.

"Thank you," he whispered, looking upward, and still having no idea what he'd ever done right to deserve her.

"You are overthinking things again," she muttered, apparently not asleep either.

"I wasn't thinking. I was rejoicing. There's a difference."

She cast him a sleepy smile. "What were you rejoicing about? As if I didn't know."

He rolled her under him and began to kiss his way down her body. "I love you for reasons other than just your body."

"Which I might believe if you were not telling me that while swallowing a mouthful of my breast."

"Shall I stop, love?" He kissed his way lower.

"No, you naughty man. And why do you have such a deliciously evil grin on your face?"

He nudged her legs apart. "Because I am about to do something quite wicked to you."

"What are you going to do?"

"Be patient and you'll see," he said, slowly and torridly kissing his way down her body.

# Chapter Nineteen

P HOEBE GASPED AND almost tumbled off the bed as Cormac...
Was such a thing allowed by law? Not that it mattered, since
no one was going to spy on them in their bedchamber.

But... *Mother of Mercy!*

She clutched the sheets to keep herself grounded as he
touched her in a way that shot her to the stars and beyond. How
could he have such power over her body? Not that she minded,
for his every touch, every kiss and intimate stroke, was done with
love.

He may have power over her body, but she had power over
his heart.

Perhaps this was why she responded to him with a mindless
abandon, for she felt safe with him and knew he would never hurt
her in any way. Quite the opposite—she was his treasure and his
salvation. Whether she had earned this respect was irrelevant, for
he had taken her into his heart and meant to keep her there
forever.

He knew how to arouse her body, and she was helpless to
resist his touch, especially the soft lick of his tongue...or the
rough pads of his fingers...or the possessive fire of his mouth. Nor
did it help that his muscled body made her ache just looking at
him.

He held her as waves of pleasure swept through her in a flood tide. "Cormac," she said in a breathless whisper.

"I know, love. And you are my love. My sweet, precious wife."

Once she had calmed, he slipped his arm out from under her and rose to stride to the windows overlooking the sea. He was a big man, but his body was a sleek line of taut, lean muscle. "I have another idea," he said, turning to her with a wicked smile she found irresistible.

"I am hardly recovered from your first bright idea."

He laughed. "The sky is clear and the mist has already burned off the water. Would you care to take a swim with me? It is early enough that only the scullery maids will be up at this hour. We can sneak down in our robes and be back before Gunyon or your maid knock on our door. If you prefer, we can don clothes. But we'd only need to take them off before we dive into the water, so there really isn't much point to the effort."

"We are going to swim without our clothes?"

"That is the gist of it. Do you ever see dolphins or whales don clothes when swimming?"

"No, but to compare us to those creatures is ridiculous."

"Why? They swim naked. We'll swim naked. I could compare you to a lovely mermaid, but that would still leave you clothes-less."

It did sound delicious. "Point taken. All right. But we wear robes and bring towels."

She also took a moment to pin her hair up, but he stopped her with a light touch of his hand. "Don't bother. I like the idea of you as a mermaid. I'll have those pins out as soon as we're down on the beach, and you'll only lose them."

"I'll have to wash the salt water out of my hair when we return."

He grinned. "Is that a problem? Do you have any other pressing plans for today?"

She shook her head. "No, I suppose not. And since this is the first full day of our marriage, I don't expect we'll have any callers until tomorrow at the earliest. However, my lord, I would like it read into the record that you are a very bad influence on me."

"Thank you, my lady. And may I also have it read into the record that you are a very *good* influence on me? It is all a matter of perspective. I've loosened you up a bit, but you've neatly tied me around your little finger. I am utterly lost to you, Phoebe. I am madly, wildly, crazily in love with you."

"Has it escaped your notice that I feel much the same way about you? Come on, let's get this done before we shock your staff. Well, I suppose this is mild compared to what they've already seen. But I am not one of those ladies, and they'll need to respect me."

"They will. Melrose has been walking on air ever since we announced our betrothal. I think he was plotting to have me drowned if I did not shape up and marry you." He grinned as he helped her into her robe and then allowed her to help him into his.

They grabbed towels but did not bother to put on slippers.

Their feet smacked lightly upon the polished wood floor as they walked down the hall. The floor in the elegant front entry was fashioned of finest marble and felt cool beneath the soles of her feet. The courtyard stone also felt cool, but a little rough.

The sand was just beginning to warm as they reached the beach. Phoebe sank her toes into it, and thought it odd how she took note of all these textures. She blamed it on her heightened awareness of Cormac and of her own body after the unforgettable night they had shared.

He had yet to shave, and there was a dark shadow of a beard now outlined on his jaw. His hair was casually brushed back, as though he'd hastily run fingers through his hair to tame it. He'd failed. He ought to look wild and unkempt, but he looked simply wonderful. His eyes were sharp as crystals and trained on her as she slipped out of her robe.

"Your turn," she said, attempting to frown at him until he took off his. But his grin was boyish and appealing, and she could feel his happiness in the soft breeze that surrounded them.

After a moment, he shrugged out of it and then took her hand to lead her to the water.

She squealed as they waded in. "It's cold!"

"Not that cold," he said, staring at her breasts. "Not that I mind, since it seems to be perking you up nicely."

She smacked him on the shoulder. "Cormac!"

"What? It is no sin for a man to admire his wife." He laughed and led her deeper into the water. "But it has the opposite effect on me."

"What do you mean?"

"Cold water shrivels a man's...organ." The water was calm, so he eased away and floated on his back, allowing the gentle current to carry him aimlessly. "It isn't really all that cold. At worst, one could say the water is cool. But it is about the same as the air temperature, and that is quite comfortable."

"Well, it's a little better now that I am immersed," she said, swimming lazily around him. "It helps that the sun is out and there aren't a lot of clouds to obscure it."

"See, not so bad," he said after a few minutes of relaxing in the water. "Your hot little body just had to get used to it."

"And what about your body?"

"Oh, it is fully recovered from the cold. Shall I prove it to you?"

She rolled her eyes. "Seriously?"

"Of course. The wonderful thing about that naughty deed is we can do it almost anywhere."

"As I suppose you have done."

"Not with you, and you are the only one I am going to do it with from now on. But we can also just swim, if that is really what you prefer. Your body might be sore from last night."

He stood up in the water that reached to the middle of his chest.

She swam over and held on to his shoulders.

He wrapped his arm around her and drew her up against his

wet skin. Hers was wet too, and so was her hair, which he seemed to enjoy. "You are the prettiest mermaid I've ever encountered."

She grinned. "I'm not sure what to make of you yet."

"Do you trust me?"

"Yes, on land. I'm not sure about you in the water," she said with a laugh.

He kissed her softly on the mouth. "You can always trust me. Anywhere. Anytime. Ready to try that naughty thing amid the waves? They're quite gentle."

"Will you hold on to me?"

"Yes, love. Keep hold of my shoulders and wrap your legs around my hips."

She was glad she did not deny him, for this was yet another way they sealed their bond of marriage. He easily held her up in the water with only one arm, something he seemed to manage with little strain. There was also something to be said in favor of wet bodies rubbing and sliding together.

Especially *their* bodies.

She held on to him as she felt her passion build and then erupt. She clung to him, her breaths shattered and quick. She loved him beyond reason for the way he held her and tenderly told her that he loved her.

As the tide began to roll in, they waded out of the water and hurried to dry themselves off. She put on her robe and helped him tie his. Yes, tying a belt was such a little thing for someone with two hands to do, and an impossible task for him.

She felt his ache as she assisted him.

But they'd had a nice time in the water, and she was not going to allow a moment's obstacle to diminish the fun they were having.

She stretched up on her toes and kissed him. "Love you, my lord."

He emitted a laugh, one that sounded rather mirthless. "You don't need to console me, Phoebe. I'll be all right in a moment."

He took her hand, and they returned to their bedchamber moments before her maid, Gwendolyn, and his valet, Gunyon, knocked at their door.

She allowed Gwenny to take her to her dressing chamber, where she washed Phoebe's hair, and then properly bathed and groomed her for the day.

Phoebe left her hair down to allow it to dry faster.

Cormac rejoined her shaved and groomed, but had not bothered to don a waistcoat, jacket, or cravat. "My brother won't care, and his girls certainly won't. Shall we join them for breakfast?"

She liked the idea. "Yes, let's steal as much time as we can with them. They'll be leaving tomorrow, so we must make the most of today."

When they heard little footsteps running down the hallway and pattering down the stairs, they stepped out of their bedchamber and joined everyone in the dining room. The girls leaped out of their seats and ran to their uncle. "Did you enjoy yesterday's party, ducklings?" he asked, kneeling to hug each of them.

"Oh, yes," Ella said. "It was the nicest ever."

Imogen nodded enthusiastically. "But I'm sad."

He sat her on his bended knee. "Why, duckling?"

"Because we're going to leave tomorrow, and we won't see you and Auntie Phoebe for a long, long time."

"We shall come to London soon. I have business affairs and parliamentary duties that will bring me there. Then maybe your mama and papa will allow you to come here for all of next summer. Would you like that?"

She nodded.

They spent the day with Cormac's nieces and their parents, going into town to show them the harbor—and then a stop at Mrs. Halsey's tearoom, where Imogen got her fill of strawberry tarts. They went down to the beach again in the afternoon, and Ella showed off her swimming abilities to cheers.

Cormac had put on an old shirt and pair of worn breeches, and went into the water with his nieces. He carried Imogen in with him, going no deeper than waist-high. He was the only one she would allow to bring her into the water. "Show your mama and papa how well you kick your feet," he said, ever so gradually easing her in beyond her ankles. "That's my girl! Look at you! You're swimming faster than a fish."

She was so proud of herself.

Phoebe cheered them on from the shore.

Cormac's brother joined him in the water, stripping off all but his trousers after asking Phoebe for permission to do so. "Please do. This is our private strip of beach. And anyway, I am married to your brother. Nothing is going to shock me."

Even Charlotte laughed at that remark. "Phoebe, would you mind if I kicked off my shoes and stockings? It looks awfully good fun."

"The water is lovely. Be daring, Charlotte. Wade in up to your knees." The two of them stood with their feet in the water and watched their husbands frolic with the nieces. When Ella and Imogen came out of the water to build sandcastles, Cormac and his brother turned into little boys themselves, splashing each other and trying to dunk each other. If Cormac felt the loss of his arm, he wasn't showing it.

The two men finally slogged out of the water with inane grins on their faces and wet everyone while shaking the moisture off them like dogs coming out of the rain. "Uncle Cormac!" Imogen squeaked. "You're getting me wet!"

"I'm sorry, little duckling. But don't ducks like water?" He scooped her up into his arm.

She wrapped hers around his neck. "No, they don't always want to be in the water."

"All right. It's nearing suppertime anyway, and we ought to get cleaned up."

With everyone in agreement, they packed up their belongings and made their way to the wooden stairs leading up to the house. Ella ran alongside Cormac. "I want you to carry me, too."

He couldn't, of course.

Phoebe wasn't certain what he would do.

John was about to step forward and offer to carry his daughter, but stopped as Cormac spoke to Ella. "I only have the one arm, duckling. How about you hold on to my sleeve?"

She nodded and skipped up the steps beside him.

Charlotte sniffled. "Phoebe, you've worked a miracle on that man. We spent three years walking on eggshells, daring not to breathe a word about his missing arm. He hated himself and hated all of us... Well, not John or the girls." She sighed. "I suppose he just hated me."

John put his arm around his wife. "No, love. He only hated himself, desperately wanted what you and I had, but did not think anyone could ever love him as I love you. How could he dare to dream of this when he loathed himself? But Phoebe came along and he's smiling again. He's my brother and I love him, but he was such an arse for a very long time. Not anymore, though. He is almost, dare I say it...chirpy?"

Phoebe burst out laughing. "He will toss you back in the water if you dare call him that." She looked up at the stairs and her husband's retreating form, Imogen in his arms and Ella holding on to his empty sleeve. "He's going to be a wonderful father, don't you think?"

"The best," John said. "This is how he was when we were younger, the older brother always looking after me. We hardly ever fought. He was always protecting me. This is how my girls feel around him. Safe, protected. Loved. I'm going to miss him. I liked having him with us...although he's the marquess and it is actually his London townhouse we all occupied. So we actually live with him. He'll spend most of his time in Moonstone Landing now. But I do look forward to having you join us as often as you can."

"So do we. He won't want to miss his little ducklings growing up. He'll be a bear when your girls are ready for their debuts."

John laughed. "Gad, I feel sorry for any young man hoping to win their favor. They'll have to go through Cormac, and I doubt any of them will survive."

They hurried after him and returned to their rooms to prepare for supper. Chloe, Hen, and Cain were to join them, as were Prudence and her husband. They would be a small, but genial, party.

"So much for having you to myself," Cormac teased as they readied themselves before their guests arrived.

"Oh, I think you had plenty of me today."

"No, love. Not nearly enough. I doubt I'll ever have enough of you. But you must be sore after all our couplings. I'll just hold you tonight, if that is what you wish."

"How very noble of you, but no need for us to decide now, is there? Let's see how we feel by the time we retire to bed."

"We?" He arched an eyebrow and smiled. "I should think my desires are clear. But I mean it, Phoebe. We don't have to do anything if you are too sore." He kissed her on the forehead. "Come on, let's go downstairs and see to our guests."

Her heart melted as she watched him stride to the door and open it. He paused when she did not immediately join him. "Phoebe?"

She cast him a tender smile. "You know I am going to say yes to you later. You are irresistible."

He chuckled. "Come on, love. Let's eat fast and be rid of these damnable guests."

It was not proper *ton* etiquette to have children dine with them, but no one was keeping Cormac from a last night with his nieces. Imogen did not quite make it to the dessert course before falling asleep in her chair. Charlotte excused herself and carried her up to bed. She had yet to return before Ella's eyes drifted closed. John carried her up to bed.

When they returned, Cormac motioned them all to the parlor, where port wine was served for the men and tea for the ladies. Usually the men gave over the parlor to the ladies while they remained behind with their smokes and port. But Cormac saw no point to it, and neither did anyone else.

Cain and Hen did not remain long after, since they had their own wee ones at Malvern House. Even though their children were still babies and had nannies to look after them, Hen was obviously not used to being apart from them. They took Chloe back with them. Prudence and Charles Weston also left with them. As Cain's estate manager, he was always kept busy and would likely be up at the crack of dawn to start his work.

Phoebe and Charlotte retired next, and walked upstairs arm in arm.

"I do hope you and Cormac will join us in London soon." Charlotte laughed and shook her head. "Goodness, it feels odd to call him that after all these years. He has always been Burness to me. And I have always been terrified of him. Not that he ever threatened me or raised a hand to me, but he was always in foul spirits. All it would take was a frown from him and I would turn into a fluttering goose. The more I fluttered, the more he frowned."

"That was not well done of him. He should have been more understanding of you."

"I suppose I could have been a little braver, too. I don't have anywhere near your courage. But I think you are exactly the sort of wife he needs. Someone strong enough to stand up to him and also love him with equal strength."

They reached the top of the stairs and stood beside each other on the landing. "Well, it was lovely to spend time with you, Phoebe. Let's save our tearful farewells for the morning. Goodness, I think we shall all be in tears. I don't know who will cry more, John or the girls. Perhaps it will be me, for I am very much about family. This is the first time in three years I've felt we truly *are* a family."

She gave Phoebe a quick hug and hurried to her bedchamber.

Phoebe went to hers, easily managing to undress herself and return her pearls to her jewelry box. She donned her nightgown and stood by the open window to brush out her hair. The air was laden with moisture, and she could hear the waves breaking to shore with more ferocity than usual. A full moon was on the rise, and this accounted for stronger tides than usual.

She was still standing by the window when she heard the door open and Cormac walk in. He shut the door softly, smiling as he walked toward her. "I should be used to the beautiful vision of you, but seems I'm not. You take my breath away every time."

Phoebe nestled against his broad chest as he reached her side and put his arm around her. "You do the same for me. Good thing we like each other, since we are sharing quarters."

He laughed. "I'd say we more than like each other. Lord, you make me ache."

She turned to face him. "The feeling is mutual, my lord."

"Does this mean I am going to be lucky tonight?"

She reached up to unknot his cravat. "Lucky? Depends on your definition of the word."

He shrugged out of his jacket and set it aside on a nearby chair. "The definition encompasses a lot of meanings. First and foremost, that you consented to be my wife. Then there's also my good fortune in finding you to be as much in love with me as I am with you. As for my luck tonight? That is the baser meaning, for all I can think about is being inside of you and holding you close. By the way you are looking at me, I'd say I am about to get my wish."

She undid the buttons of his waistcoat and laughed. "You men wear too many layers."

He tossed the waistcoat and cravat onto the chair, and smiled as she worked on removing his shirt. "Gunyon has no reason to fear I will displace him in his role as valet," she muttered, fumbling over the links at his cuffs. "I'm sorry I am so slow about it."

He kissed her lightly on the lips. "We have all night, love. I am enjoying your hands on my body."

The shirt soon went onto the pile on the chair.

He sat on the bed while she helped him off with his boots, and smothered his laughter when she landed on her backside from the effort of tugging them off. "Are you all right, love?"

"Yes, I'll survive. But I must say, Gunyon goes up in my estimation with every task I botch."

He took her onto his lap and kissed her again. "You are a dream come true for me."

"Keep saying those nice things about me and you are going to be very, very lucky indeed."

His smile was broad and appealingly wicked as he rolled her under him, his big body warm and deliciously male as he proceeded to show her just how much he loved her.

His love was not merely in the act of their joining, but in the way he held her afterward and the soft words he spoke in the quiet of the night.

COME MORNING, THEY did not linger in bed and quickly readied themselves for the day ahead. Phoebe dismissed her maid and left her dressing area to return to their bedchamber in time to watch Gunyon finish assisting Cormac.

"Ah, you are smiling again, my lord," Gunyon teased. "I had no idea I gave you so much pleasure."

Cormac laughed. "That smile is for my wife, I assure you. Doesn't she look beautiful?"

"Stunning, my lord." Gunyon bowed toward Phoebe and quietly left the room.

She went to Cormac and put her arms around his neck to kiss him. He was freshly shaven and his hair was still damp from its washing. She caught the scent of lather on his cheek and a hint of musk on his body that had her immediately responding to him.

"If you keep looking at me that way," he said, a broad grin on his face, "I'm going to undress us both, and we'll be right back where we started."

She sighed. "You are right. We cannot tarry this morning. I'm sure your nieces are eagerly awaiting us downstairs."

He wrapped his hand around hers, and they walked down together. Chloe had stopped by with presents for the girls, so their farewell was not as sad as it might have been. "Open them once you are on your way home," she told Cormac's nieces as they all sat around the breakfast table.

Afterward, Cormac spent ten minutes hugging his nieces, for neither girl wanted to let go of him.

"Come along, girls. We have a long ride home and need to get an early start," John said, coaxing his daughters away from Cormac. Then John, Charlotte, and the girls climbed into their carriage for the trip back to London.

Chloe waited for her horse to be brought around so she could return to Malvern House. "By the way, Cain and Hen would love you to join us for supper tomorrow night. Cain has invited Lieutenant Brennan and several of his superiors up for more discussions on the hospital plans."

"We'll be there," Cormac said after exchanging a glance with Phoebe and seeing her nod.

A few minutes later, they were finally on their own.

The sky was overcast, so they returned indoors. While Cormac retired to his study to review the work piled on his desk, Phoebe met with Melrose and their cook, a local woman by the name of Bessie Angel, to plan out the week's chores and menus. This task did not take very long, since the pair had all well in hand. She was soon knocking on Cormac's study door. "Come in."

She stepped in and shut the door behind her. "Would you mind if I hired a housekeeper? It needn't happen right away. There's no rush. But I will be resuming my charitable activities with Hen and Chloe, and I'm sure I will be asked to host several functions. In any event, if we have children—"

"Whatever you think best, love. This house is as much yours as it is mine." He came around to the front of his desk and wrapped his arm around her. "As for children, perhaps we had better work on those right now."

"Here? In your study?" Her eyes widened in panic. "Don't you dare unlace me here! I'll never get my corset tied once you undo it. I—" She inhaled sharply. "I'm sorry. I... But I can't run about the house with my gown falling off me. I'm so sorry..."

"Phoebe, just breathe. I am not angry or frustrated. I would have summoned your maid to assist you. But I suppose that is just as bad. She'll know you've been taken by your husband in the middle of the day in his very study. Why, it is quite shocking. You'll be forever considered a wanton."

"Now you are mocking me."

"No, love. Just some gentle teasing. We'll save our escapades for the bedroom. Melrose will never forgive me if I corrupt your morals. Besides, it will be a refreshing change for me to be considered respectable. I have no problem with it." He kissed her with a hungry ardor. "I still have a little work to do. Care to stay with me? It's starting to rain anyway."

"I'll choose a book from your library."

She selected one about Italian gardens and settled in one of the big leather chairs by the hearth to read it.

The thud as it slipped from her fingers startled her awake. She realized she'd fallen asleep while reading.

She blinked her eyes open and saw Cormac settled in the chair beside hers. He was thoughtful as he watched her. "Oh, my snores must have disturbed you."

"No, love. You weren't snoring. You just looked so beautiful, I couldn't resist watching you." He rested an elbow on his knee as he continued to regard her. "I love you, Phoebe. I love us together. I never thought I could feel this way. We've been married little more than a day, and already I cannot remember a time without you. Is that not ridiculous? But it's true."

She picked up her book and set it aside. "Do you know what moonstones represent?"

"They have a meaning?"

"Yes, most gemstones do. The moonstone represents marriage and fertility. Flourishing. I think I am going to dub you my moonstone marquess, because this is what this place seems to have done for you—made you flourish."

"And also had me marrying the prettiest girl in existence."

"Thank you. But you did that all by yourself."

"No, I'm sure it was those moonstones guiding me."

"I'm sure it was all you. I shall never forget your drunken words to me on the day we first met. *Marry me.* My first thought was, what idiot says that to a woman he's only just met? Then you cleaned yourself up a few hours later and I knew I would marry you. There could never be anyone else for me." She rose and held out her hand for him. "What do you say we go upstairs and watch the moonstones on the water? You can see them shimmer beneath the surface on rainy days when the tide is low."

He took her hand. "You thought I was an idiot?"

She giggled. "Yes, my love. You thought even worse of yourself."

"That is true. Turns out I was a lot smarter than either of us gave me credit for. I married you, didn't I?"

She laughed. "Indeed."

"See, your moonstone marquess is no fool." He led her upstairs, both of them glancing up as thunder rumbled overhead. "That's quite a storm coming on. Are we just going to look at moonstones? We could spend the rest of the day in bed, you know. I'll have supper brought up to us. We needn't leave our bedchamber until tomorrow. In fact, this is what we must do or we'll anger the moonstone gods."

"I don't think there is such a thing."

"But why take chances?" He led her into their bedchamber and kicked the door closed behind them.

They sent their apologies to Cain and Hen.

They did not come out for the next three days.

# Epilogue

*Moonstone Landing*
*July, 1819*

C ORMAC'S NIECES HAD their faces pasted to the carriage
window and huge smiles on their faces as it drew up in front
of Westgate Hall. The carriage had hardly stopped before Ella
threw open the door and would have leaped out if her father had
not stopped her. "Dear heaven, they still like you and Phoebe
better than they like us," John jested, also smiling from ear to ear.
"Wait a moment, girls."

Cormac laughed as both little ones ignored him and held out
their arms for Cormac's embrace. "One at a time," he reminded
them, for they never could remember he had one arm.

"We missed you, Uncle Cormac," Ella said, giving him several dainty pecks on the cheek.

He hugged her and then handed her over to Phoebe just as
Imogen was about to hurl herself at him. "My littlest duckling,"
he said, so happy to see her smiling face. "Look how you've
grown."

"I'm seven now."

"Already? Your Papa had better start preparing for your
come-out," he teased as John hopped down after the girls and
assisted his wife out of their carriage. "Come onto the terrace

with us while Melrose arranges to have your bags brought upstairs. There's a lovely breeze off the water."

"We have lemonade and strawberry tarts for you on the terrace," Phoebe said, still holding on to Ella's hand while Cormac remained with Imogen on his arm. "Chloe and the others will join us for an early supper tonight. They cannot wait to see you girls again. Of course, they are also eager to see you, John, and Charlotte."

Charlotte laughed. "As we are to see them again. The girls could speak of nothing else all year. I must say, John and I are intrigued and cannot wait to spend the month with you."

"Well, we have lots planned for you," Phoebe said, now pouring lemonades for everyone. "Even a little exploring around Moonstone Landing. Lord Crawford has been maintaining a correspondence with Cormac about his own explorations. He will be leading an expedition to Mesopotamia next month and is quite excited about it. In the meanwhile, he has kindly been sending us interesting bits about ancient Cornwall. We thought we might make a few day trips to these places."

"Sounds fun," Charlotte said. "What do you think, girls? Shall we all become explorers?"

The girls nodded enthusiastically.

"But first we must have our strawberry tarts," Imogen said.

Cormac set her in a chair and winked at his brother as Imogen and Ella both began to dig into their tarts. "Phoebe and I have something more to tell you."

Charlotte gasped. "I knew it. Oh, I did not mean...but I took one look at Phoebe and... Do tell us."

"I am five months along, so it is hardly a surprise." Phoebe patted her stomach.

John clapped his brother on the back. "I should have realized immediately by that banshee grin on your face when we arrived. I thought you were happy to see us. But I see you are happy for completely other reasons."

Cormac held up his lemonade in a toast. "We are overjoyed

to have you with us and hope to have three of us to greet you when you return next year."

"Four," Imogen said, licking a bit of strawberry off the corner of her little bow lips.

"Yes, four," Ella confirmed.

Cormac and Phoebe exchanged glances.

Cormac knelt beside the girls' chairs. "What makes you say that?"

"Brioc and Hen told us," Ella replied.

Phoebe looked around. "When? Just now?"

Imogen nodded.

John took his wife's hand as her face paled. "It's all right, Charlotte. Girls, are the ghosts here?"

"They were," Ella explained. "But they've gone back to Moonstone Cottage. They are very happy for Aunt Phoebe and Uncle Cormac."

"Two boys," Imogen said.

Phoebe's eyes rounded in alarm. "But my sister, Hen, has twins. A boy and a girl. How is it possible for me to have twins, too? And two boys?"

Imogen shrugged. "Yes, two boys."

"It's those moonstones," Cormac teased.

Ella scrambled to her feet and gave Phoebe a kiss. "That is from your Aunt Hen."

Imogen also pattered to Phoebe and gave her a kiss. "This is from me."

Cormac leaned over and tipped Phoebe's chin up so that their gazes met. "And this one's from me," he said, leaning down to kiss her beautiful lips. "I love you, Phoebe. So very much. I think we had better hire four nannies."

"Why four?" she asked, unable to suppress a smile.

"We are having two boys, my love. *Two.* Lord help us if they are anything like me. They will be holy terrors. We may require the services of an entire regiment to contain them."

Imogen shook her head furiously.

"What is it now, duckling?" Cormac asked.

"Aunt Phoebe is a lioness. She can easily handle two little boys like you."

Phoebe grinned. "Do you hear that, Cormac?"

He kissed her again. "I surely did. I am not afraid of battle. Nor afraid of ghosts. But I shall always tread carefully around you, Phoebe."

"No, that is awful. You can never be afraid of me."

"No, love. Not afraid of you...just of ever losing you."

Phoebe leaned her head against his shoulder. "You never will. True love is forever. This is what Brioc and my aunt have shown us. This is what we have."

John smiled over at his wife. "Can Charlotte and I get in on this, too? I love you, Charlotte. You and our girls fill my heart with joy."

Everyone raised their lemonade glasses in toast and shouted all at once, "Happy summer!"

"The happiest, my love," Cormac whispered, and kissed Phoebe again.

Ella and Imogen watched them and giggled.

## *The End*

## Also by Meara Platt

## About the Author

Meara Platt is a *USA Today* bestselling author and an award winning, Amazon UK All-star. Her favorite place in all the world is England's Lake District, which may not come as a surprise, since many of her stories are set in that idyllic landscape, including her award-winning fantasy-romance Dark Gardens series. If you'd like to learn more about the ancient Fae prophecy that is about to unfold in the Dark Gardens series, as well as Meara's lighthearted, international bestselling Regency romances in the Farthingale series and Book of Love series, or her more emotional Braydens series, please visit her website at www.mearaplatt.com.

Printed in the USA
CPSIA information can be obtained
at www.ICGtesting.com
LVHW011311140324
774486LV00022B/427